<u>AFFINITIES</u>
LIFECYCLE 1

by Chris Hollis
Sometimes, you can't even trust yourself.

Affinities: (noun)(pl)
1. Close connections
2. Close resemblances
3. Chemical attractions

PROLOGUE

Agony.

It started in his head, buried deep beneath his temples. A feeling of expansion, like his brain swelling up and trying to squeeze out of his skull. The kind of feeling a balloon must have in the second before it bursts.

Faster than he could raise his arms, it spread across his face, forcing his eyes shut for fear they might pop out of their sockets. He had never known a pain like it – jaw clamped closed, teeth barred. He tried to scream, but the sound couldn't make it through the tightness in his throat.

His legs gave way, bringing him crashing down hard on the thin carpet. Though his head cracked, he couldn't feel it. All he knew was this intolerable strain that had him blind to everything else, this violent pressure in his scalp.

This agony.

He would have given anything to make it stop, torn his hair out just to ease the pressure. Fingers were frozen rigid, ready to claw through skin and bone.

Then as abruptly as it started, the pain just went away.

In a wash of pale numbness, it was gone. Suddenly, he was back to his senses, face down on the floor, a cold sweat creeping over his body. He didn't dare move an inch for fear that he couldn't, lying petrified and silent.

Andrew's life had taken a turn from which it would never recover, a series of events that didn't make sense if they weren't somehow related. He couldn't begin to explain it, but one thing was for certain – the pain in his head was a stark warning.

A show of control.

A sign he had taken a step too close to a truth he wasn't meant to uncover.

The reason he died every night.

PART ONE: NIGHT
1|NSOMNIA

The noises drove him mad, never too loud, but always there. They woke him in the small hours of the morning and made sure he couldn't get back to sleep.

Every night, over and over...

Standing in the hallway, Andrew Goodwin dearly wanted to put a stop to it. His bare toes sank into the carpet, warm summer air grazing the hairs on his chest. The lounge ahead was in pitch darkness, but he knew something was lurking inside. He could hear it moving.

With trepidation, he reached through the doorway, feeling for the light switch. The dark played tricks on him, and the goading image of the bedside clock was plastered everywhere he looked.

3:14am.

Strange sounds had been haunting him since the day he moved into that flat – scratches and scrapes, akin to rats, but a good deal louder. The weight they implied suggested whatever made them couldn't fit behind the walls, yet he had never once laid eyes upon them.

Meaning they were fast as well as large.

The neighbours claimed they couldn't hear a thing, but tonight, one sound was so loud that there wasn't a chance of sleeping through it: A deafening slam, almost like a gunshot.

When it happened, Andrew had hit the ground running, awake before he knew it. He didn't hesitate until he reached the doorway, pausing for courage, reaching his arm into the black.

They were close now. He could hear muffled voices that hissed like radio static, cars rushing past in the still night outside. Tense and alert, he stiffened.

Enough messing around.

Andrew swung the door open and hammered the light switch. Instantly, the lounge was bathed in sheer white, making him shield his eyes to catch a first real glimpse of his antagonist.

Or perhaps not.

Without his contact lenses, the room was a mixture of blurs, but even then, he could tell there was nothing in there. He owned a sparse collection of furniture – leather sofa, matching chair, glass coffee table. There were blinds on the windows, rather than curtains. Nothing to hide behind.

Andrew stepped inside, feeling the cool kiss of tiling underfoot. The whispering had ceased, gagged by the light switch, and in a stark silence, he once again called off the search. Once again, they had vanished before he could catch them.

He knew the routine. Andrew rubbed his eyes, wishing he was still in bed. They wouldn't make another sound until the next morning, then once he stirred, the process would start all over again.

Every night, over and over...

It was relentless, and with less than five hours before he had to leave for work, Andrew felt the strain. It brought to light a dull throbbing from beneath his temples, a headache which he seemed to have battled for days. Fatigue.

With a sigh, he walked over to the counter. There was no separate kitchen in Andrew's flat, just a row of units along one wall of the lounge. With his back to the sofa, he took a glass and filled it from the tap, taking huge gulps of refreshing water that spilled out of the corners of his mouth.

Sharp relief from the summer heat.

Drained and disheartened, he leaned against the side, wide awake in the darkest hour. He should have moved out a long time ago, but noises were only part of the problem. For weeks now – months even – he had found himself trapped in a cycle of recurrent dreams.

And there was nowhere to run from his dreams.

It didn't matter where he put his head down – in the car, in the office – he always dreamt of a prison cell. He had never been to jail, but he imagined this was nothing like it. The room was brightly lit in spite of bars across a tiny window, and he lay in a bed, under burgundy blankets, pinned by their unexpected weight.

It seemed harmless, innocuous, but the cell was just a springboard to other places, and wherever it sent him, Andrew was always met by harrowing, bloody violence. The circumstances differed wildly, but the result was always the same.

Every night, Andrew died.

Drowning, burning, falling. The violence was always aimed towards him, rarely self-inflicted, and almost always resulted in his death. At which point – mercifully – he would wake up again to hear the noises.

As time went by, however, the deaths were becoming more graphic, to the point where he was starting to feel the effects long after he was awake. Andrew was being traumatised, and as his strength was gradually sapped through lack of rest, the toll it took grew steadily worse.

Leaning against the counter in the stuffy lounge, he could feel bags under his eyes. Andrew stood and walked to the window, parting the blinds with his fingers. Blurry vision looked down towards the silent car park, surrounded by tall office blocks and flats. Other than streetlamps, there wasn't a single light on anywhere, the city sound asleep, despite the hot weather.

He tried to open the windows and let fresh air in, but they were locked, and he had long since lost the key. So instead, Andrew pattered over to the refrigerator and used a carton of milk to cool himself down, holding it to his chest. Much more satisfying than drinking it.

He popped off the light and went back down the hallway, determined to salvage the night before sunrise stole it away. The clock on the bedside table now read 3:26am, and as he lay back down with his head on the pillow, Andrew's body seemed to realise what time it was.

A sweeping fatigue washed over him. Almost without trying, he plunged right back into his dream world.

For the time being, at least, Andrew was almost glad of it.

***

Scratching, clattering.

He couldn't say for how long he was unconscious, but when Andrew came to, it was still dark. Perhaps only an hour had passed, but his wracked body had succumbed to such a deep slumber that it felt like much, much more.

The noises were back, the same muffled sounds. He turned over and put the light on, well aware of what would happen. Once he could see, they would retreat to the lounge and continue to taunt until he followed them in there.

The air felt heavy, the bedroom claustrophobic. Andrew's lips were dry and cracked, a sensation he likened to the early throes of a hangover. With a frustrated groan, he felt little chance of drifting off again without prising himself out of bed for another glass of water.

At least he could shut those sounds up in the process.

He swayed across the bedroom and back to the lounge, listening to a distant, excited scuffle as he approached the door. It was impossible to tell how many things were in there or what they were doing. There could have easily been a dozen or just a few.

Trying to ignore them, Andrew turned the lounge light back on, and they fell silent. He went to the counter and filled the same glass he had used before, pausing only when it finally registered what he had just read on the bedside clock.

3:14am.

"That's strange," he thought out loud with a croaky voice, and went back to the bedroom to check. It was a full twelve minutes before he had gone to bed, the exact same time as when he had first woken up.

Andrew rummaged through his work trousers, hanging off the back of a chair, and amidst loose change, he produced his wristwatch. Luminous hands confirmed his worry.

Time was definitely running backwards.

Unable to believe it, he returned to the lounge and switched on the television, finding a news channel. Definitely no mistake, and to make things worse, below the time was the date.

Thursday the fifteenth of July.

Two days after he had gone to sleep.

Andrew froze. That would have meant he had slept right through Wednesday, that he had slept for twenty-four hours instead of next to none. It couldn't be possible.

He stood and walked to the window. The car park below was full, indistinguishable from the last time he had looked. There was a crispness to the atmosphere, bright lights bouncing off car bonnets, the shallowest puddles on the pavement.

When he realised he could see it all clearly.

His contact lenses were in.

Shocked, Andrew backed away and lost his balance, collapsing onto the couch. They hadn't been when he went to bed, he was sure of it. So unless he had put them in while he slept, one fact seemed disturbingly likely: It was a completely different night.

Andrew Goodwin had lost an entire day of his life.

Cool leather rubbed against his bare legs. He could remember Tuesday evening – A steak dinner with his girlfriend, Cheryl – but he had no recollection of anything beyond it. Scratching his face, Andrew felt fresh stubble, and needed to see what he looked like. He walked to the bathroom and splashed cold water on his cheeks, trying to suppress a mounting concern that there might be something wrong.

What could have happened to make him lose such a long space of time with absolutely no memory?

His reflection looked tired, eyes bloodshot, skin pale. He leaned in close and used his fingers to examine for lumps and bumps, gripping the sides of the sink. He wanted to run straight to a hospital, but it didn't feel like any of it was real. People don't lose entire days of their lives. They just don't.

He took a long, deep breath, exhaling as slowly as he could. *Stay calm,* he told himself. *It might all come flooding back with a little rest. At least give it another four hours until morning.*

He took his contact lenses back out and felt his way back into the bedroom, trying to fight the panic down. With slow and delicate movements, he sat on the mattress and lay still, willing the sun to come up.

The clock hummed in the darkness and he imagined the minutes ticking over. If he still felt this way in the morning, he would skip work and head straight for the emergency room.

Andrew took his clock and set the alarm to wake him at seven. Then, as a final gesture, he reached for the curtains and tugged them a few inches apart. Morning sunlight would enter the room and make all but the deepest sleep impossible, and he could try to make sense of it after he had been checked by a doctor.

Who knows, he thought. *Hopefully this will turn out to be a dream after all.*

He left the covers off to compensate for the muggy air and lay down, willing the time to pass. It was the strangest thing, but after that, it was only a few seconds before he drifted right off.

***

Andrew opened his eyes to find he was in bed. Bright yellow sunlight cut a swathe across the room and particles of dust floated in still air. But he could instantly tell things were not as they appeared.

He was still asleep.

It was the prison cell from his dreams, a room with four white, featureless walls. The floor was a deep shade of burgundy, as were the covers on the bed as he lay beneath them.

He felt wide awake, pinned to the mattress. In an odd way, he was glad of the chance to relax, relieved of his headache and able to suspend free thought. There were no details to anything – no shadows, threads or creases – as though it was all merely an image of a stolen glance that had somehow become his warped reality.

He had been in that room dozens of times before and had little doubt he would be there again, staring blankly at the ceiling and feeling somehow safe. Nothing ever seemed to happen in that room, but this time, something was different.

Slam!

Clouds of dust flew into the air, the walls shaking on their foundations. It was the same sound that had woken him before. A gunshot, so loud that it hurt his ears. The bed leapt off the floor and his eyes moved towards the door.

Someone was coming.

Slam!

Plaster rained from the ceiling. He heard a scratch, like nails running along the walls, and a scuffle from behind the door. Andrew felt an overbearing urge to get up, but the taut bedding held him firmly in place.

Slam!

The room shook again, rattling his jaw. Andrew tried to wriggle out from under the covers, but the weight pressing down grew stronger, more determined. It crushed the air out of his lungs with an agonising wheeze, and all he could do was lie there, a prisoner, watching in horror as the handle on the door turned slowly and the first of his ribs began to crack.

Wake up, he told himself. *For God's sake, wake up.*

And then he was awake – not violently or suddenly, but calm and gentle. The weight on his chest eased off and his muscles relaxed. The dream world peeled back and he opened his eyes to find himself back in his own bedroom, loosely under the covers.

And it was still the dead of night.

Andrew's skin was caked in sweat and his ribs felt bruised, his chest hollow. He immediately turned to the clock, finding his eyesight once again worked perfectly without the need for glasses.

3:14am.

Anxious and petrified, he threw off the covers and jumped out of bed. Another day of his life had gone, and now all he wanted was to get out of the flat. Back to a normal life, back to the daytime.

He hurried to the bathroom, calf muscles aching and stiff, barely even noticing the noises in the lounge as he slammed on the light.

Standing in front of the mirror, he looked himself over. Short, brown hair was greasy and plastered to his scalp, like it hadn't been washed in days. Thick stubble made his face appear dirty. He looked like a man who had barely moved from his bed all week, and it terrified him to think why that might be.

Wasting no time, Andrew hurriedly dressed in the shirt and trousers he had worn to work that Monday, still draped over the chair in the bedroom. Then he turned out his pockets, but his wallet was no longer in them, and neither were his keys.

With mounting anxiety, he picked up the laundry hamper and tipped the contents all over the sheets, searching frantically, rummaging through t-shirts and vests, looking for anything with pockets that could hold his valuables.

Andrew got down on all fours and looked under the bed to see if they had fallen on the floor, when something caught his eye – a white object under the mattress. He slid his arm across the laminate and brought it out to look closer.

A shoebox.

He never kept things under the bed, or even cleaned down there. Months of dust clung to his arm from the floorboards, but the box itself was spotless.

It was made of shiny, white cardboard. Andrew curled his fingers around the lid and lifted it off. Inside, he found a small pile of opened envelopes and some pieces of notepaper, and on top of those was his first physical evidence that things were beyond his control.

His keys and wallet.

There was no way he would have put them there without recalling, no way at all. There were other items in the box too, letters he had received in the days he had lost. Among them, he found a folded piece of notepaper, chewed at the edges where it had been in somebody's pocket. He unfolded it to find a hastily drawn layout of the roads nearby.

A map to his flat.

The handwriting was too rough to identify, almost illegible. Andrew stood and snatched his keys, needing more than ever to be outside. He left the room in its disarray, laundry all over the floor and the opened box by the side of the bed. He pulled on a coat, intending to go straight to the hospital, but something happened in the hallway.

Something at the door.

The moment his hand made contact with the latch, there was a tingling in the middle of his forehead. *Something pressing out from within.* Before Andrew knew what was happening, his headache erupted into a sudden, intense shriek of pain from behind his temples, a funnel of searing heat that shot down his spine like a crack of lightning.

His head felt like it was expanding, pushing outwards in all directions. Before he could react, his jaw shut tightly and his arms became rigid. He fell backwards, legs refusing to help him, sending him careering to the hallway floor.

Blind and senseless, Andrew crawled away with flailing arms, clawing back towards the bedroom. He clutched his head and screamed through barred teeth.

When it stopped.

Just as suddenly as it started, the pain disappeared. He was left shaking on the floor in a state of disbelief, a cold shudder as he struggled to comprehend what had happened. His brain throbbed behind his eyes and he felt sweat on his palms and feet, terrified to make even the slightest movement in case it came rushing back.

He felt his forehead. It had looked fine in the mirror only minutes before. Anything that could have done that had to be beneath his skin. *Inside his head.*

He stared at objects in the hallway, trying to focus, to recover from the outward pressure. *Hairs on the back of his hand, thin fibres of the carpet.* As he glanced along the skirting board, he noticed it seemed to be swaying, and something new took over him.

Andrew's sense of balance distorted, as though he were teetering on the balls of his feet instead of lying in the middle of the floor. It scared him into action and he sat bolt upright.

The room was spinning.

Steadying himself on the wall, he felt his head take on weight, pushing down on his neck. A horrifying wash of tiredness replaced the pain, creeping down his spine, pushing him to the verge of collapse, as though he could faint at any moment.

Andrew rose to his knees, but instantly crumpled back down as they denied his weight. Heartbeat galloping, he clawed back up and stumbled off the carpet, catapulting his heavy bulk into the bedroom.

The second he made it through the doorway, he lost all sensation. The momentum carried him to the ground and he landed awkwardly on his elbows. It should have hurt like hell, but there was so much adrenaline flowing through his body that he felt nothing.

Surely a rush of adrenaline would make him more awake?

Andrew made it to the bed, but couldn't find the strength to get up onto the mattress. His arms and legs were like dead weights and he lay on the floor with hollow limbs, exhausted. His mind, however, was racing. *Stay awake,* he told himself. *Don't let it win. Stay awake.*

He was convinced he would die if he fell asleep, but for no reason he could fathom, fear of sleep put him under even faster. His vision faded and a black, deep slumber crept upon him. It couldn't have been natural, it was too fast and frightening.

Andrew's senses shut down until he was alone in his mind, floating in darkness, a single question left ringing in the silence.

What in God's name was happening to him?

2|RICTION

Andrew's wife was called Katie, though her surname caused debate. He hadn't set eyes on her in months, and it no longer felt appropriate to refer to her as Mrs Goodwin.

Ex-wife suited her better.

Even on their last encounter, hateful eyes had warned him to approach at his own risk. It was a look he hadn't noticed before, but friends assured him it had always been there. So maybe they were right about other things, as well.

Maybe a year hadn't been enough time to get to know her.

The marriage lasted twenty months, and for half of that, it was coated with a glaze of novelty. Having a wife brought a smile to Andrew's face, still learning her bad habits, but with a glossy coat that made them somehow more forgivable.

It's my wife *leaving clothes all over the bed,* he thought. *It's* my wife *parking her car too close to mine.*

The notion didn't last, however, and the second year saw those things degenerate into what they really were – annoyances. Though Andrew made no attempt to excuse his own behaviour, it would have taken skills beyond him to hide how much it came to grate when he couldn't drive anywhere without having to move her car out of the way first.

For every single trip.

He tried to accept it. There was no point complaining. It would have been an argument that stretched on for days and weeks until he eventually conceded. Not defeat, but more of a strategic withdrawal. Katie was a woman who took pleasure in winning arguments. Andrew took pleasure in avoiding them.

Bad habits weren't to blame for the collapse of Andrew's marriage. Instead, the cause could be pinned to a single afternoon, and the consequence of a split-second decision that went horribly wrong.

The day that Andrew died.

***

Andrew drove a three-door hatchback in rusted silver. The years had been unkind to it, and he struggled to keep it roadworthy, especially in the heat of late spring.

There wasn't the money to look after it, not for over a year since the wedding. He and Katie hadn't been able to afford much of anything in that time, and they certainly hadn't been away since the honeymoon.

Eventually, it fell on kindness to get them out of the house. Two nights in Brighton, a gift from her parents.

They drove down on a Friday after work, taking turns behind the wheel and arriving on the cusp of a record-breaking heatwave. A forecast without clouds.

Excited, the two rose early and headed straight for the seafront, where beneath a clear blue sky, they set towels on the sand and lay down, a stone's throw from the sloshing waves.

Katie relished the chance to wear a bikini, and Andrew wore an unbuttoned shirt, modesty keeping him from taking it off completely.

As they sat down, he revealed a second surprise. While clearing a friend's house, he had discovered an old video camera. Though low tech and worn – and the battery didn't last for very long – at least it worked.

And memories, in those days, seemed worth preserving.

Katie, however, was unimpressed. It took ten minutes of wasted footage to convince her not to hide her face, and longer still to show a smile. But eventually, Andrew won her over, and once she had learned how to delete the footage they recorded, she even began to flirt with it a little.

The morning sun quickly gained intensity. Within an hour, they were already sweating. Andrew fell asleep with a bucket hat on his face and Katie took over the camera, filming the sea as he quietly snored. She trained the lens on the other sunbathers – of which there were hundreds – and once that ceased to be entertaining, she woke Andrew with a sandy toe in his side.

The camera caught his convulsion.

"What was that for?" he yelled, peering through the lens instead of looking at his wife.

"Welcome back to the world of the living," she spoke formally as she stared at the viewfinder. "Tell me how you slept."

"Just fine until you woke me up," he said. "How long were you filming me for?"

"You can watch it back later, if you like. There's snoring."

"Thanks, but no." He sighed and rubbed sleep from his eyes, inadvertently filling them with sand. She giggled as they watered, zooming in for a close up.

"Do you mind?" he said, feeling blindly for a clean towel.

"You're the one who wanted me to use this thing," said Katie. "I think bringing you to tears is a memory we can both savour."

In those days, it was merely a joke, and Andrew laughed it off without a thought. Once he could see again, he grew restless. The sand was becoming hotter and the beach brighter, unbridled sunshine from a clear and endless sky.

If anything, it was too hot, and getting worse. They decided to abandon the beach entirely and packed up their things, yearning for shade. Katie filmed every second as they trudged up the beach, sand sifting between bare toes, almost scalding hot.

They padded up stone steps and paused at the top to sweep their feet clean. The promenade was busy in the mid-morning, and as Andrew pulled on his socks, he grew impatient at Katie, meticulously cleaning between each toe.

"Do you really need to be so thorough?" he said, impatiently. "I can already feel my skin burning."

She put the camera on the ground. "That's what you get for not wearing enough sun cream."

"I didn't know it would be this hot," he said.

"Yes, you did."

The car was parked right beside them, literally yards from the steps. Katie had managed to squeeze into a narrow parking space, and – fuelled by jealousy – the next car along had drawn so close that the bumpers were touching. No chance of backing out.

As soon as she noticed, Katie reached a conclusion he saw coming a mile off.

"By the way, it's your turn to drive."

Andrew and Katie weren't alone in their thinking. People were leaving the beach en masse, an earlier inrush turning into an exodus. Traffic thickened, weaving past cars that were parked sloppily, hastily, many at an angle.

Bonnets and boots jutted into the road, and passing vehicles came within inches of Andrew's wing mirror. He couldn't get to the door to climb in, and instead stood beside it, impatiently waiting for a break in the traffic, feeling his sunburn worsen along with his mood.

When the chance finally came, Andrew took a deep breath. Katie could sniff out impatience and had no tolerance for it. He slid into the driver's seat with a plastic smile on his face, finding it drawn right up against the steering wheel to fit Katie's short legs.

Sadly for him, the camera saw everything.

"Are you okay?" she inquired with him in center frame.

"Fine," he replied curtly.

"Good." She chose to take him at face value. "If you want my advice, I say head straight on until we find a way off the seafront."

He wrestled with the seatbelt as it pulled on his shoulder. "No problem."

The engine started lazily, irate at being woken up. Andrew rolled the car forwards six inches, then reversed, trying to worry out of the space.

Katie soon realised how tight it actually was. "On second thought," she said. "There's no point messing if we can't even get out. We'll just look for shelter on foot. Put a note on their windscreen and try again later."

There was a clunk as they made contact with the car behind, and Andrew hoped it would leave a mark. He noisily changed gears and rolled forwards again, making a smidgeon of progress, then repeated his actions, only this time more forcefully.

When they touched bumpers for the second time, however, any last trace of his good mood was shattered to pieces.

As he set the alarm off.

Arrrrrgh! Arrrrrgh! Arrrrrgh!

A deafening whine summed things up for him. Andrew hung on the verge of losing control, waiting impatiently for a break in the traffic, both hands on the steering wheel and glaring at his wing mirror.

Katie grew uncomfortable. "Come on, Andrew. Let's just leave it. We can get a drink somewhere around here."

She lowered the camera, trying to calm him down, but Andrew was past the point of no return. He nudged the edge of the car out into the road, and the traffic swerved around him.

"This isn't going to achieve anything," she said. He kept edging out, determined to force a bottleneck. There was a bitter taste in his mouth.

"Either wait for a break or just give up," said Katie.

All of a sudden, Andrew saw a tiny gap and rammed his foot down on the accelerator, determined not to miss it. The car lurched forwards, pushing them into their seats as they catapulted into the road. With one eye firmly fixed on the car behind, Andrew tore away, up to speed in less than fifty meters.

Katie gasped. Andrew smiled inwardly, but he had paid all his attention to the car behind, and nothing to the ones in front. He raised his eyes to see red braking lights, a slew of slowing traffic.

His elation turned to horror, foot stuck rigidly to the pedal and their speed still increasing. By the time he realised what was going to happen, it was too late. The split second in which to react passed with Andrew's hands frozen to the wheel. There was nothing he could do about it now.

They were going to crash.

***

The alarm clock hummed quietly in the night and he watched the minutes pass by, driven ever so softly out of sleep, but petrified of leaving the bed.

3:14am.

Andrew's face was half-buried in the pillow, one eye wedged closed and the other wide open. His contact lenses were still in and he could read the clock face clearly – earlier than it had been when he went to sleep, which could only mean one thing.

It was a entirely new night.

The fourth since he had been confined to his home.

His crippling headache had grown dull and distant, though it threatened to return with the slightest misstep. He wanted to be checked over by a doctor, but was reluctant to move. *What if it came rushing back?*

Muffled scratches jeered from behind the walls. In the darkness, he could see echoes of his latest dreams, new images mixing in with the familiar. Between the prison cell and his violent end, Andrew had started to experience forgotten snapshots of bygone times. Striking landscapes, faces in crowds.

His life, flashing before his eyes.

Something about it made him petrified, out of control both in sleep and out of it. He took a deep breath, trying to get his head straight, and rolled gently out of bed, landing on his knees with his back to the wall. Then he turned on the light to look around.

It was tidy.

The dirty clothes he had thrown out of the hamper had all gone, returned to their rightful place. Looking down at himself, Andrew realised he was wearing a t-shirt when he had previously worn a jacket. *And he woke up under the covers when he had passed out on the floor.*

He reached under the bed, searching for the shoebox. Something was there, but his outstretched fingers found metal, cold and hard. He drew the object to his knees – a small, red tin casket with smooth, polished faces and rusted corners.

It didn't look familiar, and it certainly hadn't been there before. What was more, it was locked. Andrew lifted it up to feel its weight, tilting it from side to side. He could hear papers sliding about and his heart sank when he heard the jangle of keys. That settled one argument.

Someone was going to increasing lengths to keep them from him.

It was a cooler night than before, telling him before he looked out of the window that the weather had deteriorated. He stood and peered through the bedroom curtains, seeing intermittent clouds, wondering what it felt like to be outside.

The front door, however, wouldn't let him leave. Andrew went into the hallway – slowly – and looked at the exit, shut tight and foreboding. He could still feel the embers of last night's pain beneath his temples, unlike anything he had felt before.

He stepped forwards and reached for the latch. The door looked no different to how it had always been, smooth gloss frame and wooden grooves. Andrew extended a finger and gently touched the keyhole. Nothing, so he moved towards the handle.

Rising pain behind his temple.

Smaller this time – just a threat, hovering behind his eyes. Andrew's nerve collapsed. He couldn't face the full force of it again, not when there was another way. He would bring others to the door instead of trying to pass through himself.

Let the police worry about it.

He backed away and returned to the bedroom. What Andrew needed was to know who was doing this to him, and why. He searched through the wardrobe and cabinets, looking under the furniture. Someone must have been in that room at some point. With unsteady hands, he slid open the bedside drawer as he sat on the mattress.

And almost fell right off it.

His mobile phone was inside, along with its charger. He had expected them to be in the locked box.

And as he opened the drawer, something else slid out with them. A couple of things.

Syringes.

There were two transparent needles rolling loosely around, no labels and with plungers sunk all the way down. Empty.

Andrew immediately straightened his naked arms and ran his fingers over the skin, looking for puncture marks. *Was he being drugged? Was that why he was missing so much time?*

He stood and started pacing up and down the room, trying to control his breathing. There it was, beyond a shadow of a doubt, evidence he couldn't possibly explain away.

He took his phone from the drawer and held the power button, checking the walls for trip switches, electrodes, or hidden cameras. *Could someone be spying on him, gaining sick pleasure from watching him unravel?*

When the phone came on he found nine missed calls, five of which were from work, clearly concerned at his absence. Two other calls were from Cheryl, the woman he was dating, along with a text message that read simply *'Where are you?'*.

His head thumped, chronic fatigue trying to draw him back to bed. Four days of confinement and still, he felt an urge to rest. The remaining calls were from an unknown number – *blocked* – who hadn't left a message. He locked his phone and caught the date. Saturday the seventeenth, and still no clue what his captor looked like.

It gave him an idea. Andrew put the metal tin back under the bed and rummaged through his chest of drawers until he found another box, one of his own. Inside was a collection of old photographs and letters, what little he had managed to salvage from the house before Katie threw him out.

There was a defaced wedding picture, and scraps of holiday photos, torn to shreds by heartless hands. Underneath all that, he found what he was looking for.

His video camera.

The same one they had used on the beach all those lifetimes ago. He had never used it since, not once, but hadn't been able to part with it. And of all the things they owned, it was the one item Katie had shown absolutely no interest in. It could rot in hell for all she cared.

Andrew plugged the camera in by the phone and fiddled with the buttons. It took a while to get it working, but then Katie's face appeared on the tiny screen, sat on a beach towel in her bikini, showing reluctance while his voice goaded her on.

Play along, sweetheart. Pretend we're the only ones here.

He forwarded through the footage – climbing the steps, wiping their feet. She really hadn't turned it off for one second of that day, filming every detail until he started the car, at which point she had lowered the lens to save his bad mood.

Which, of course, hadn't worked.

It left four hours of empty space on the camera. If Andrew set it recording right then, it would run until half past seven, long enough to provide some clues. A touch of insight into what the hell was going on.

He swept back the curtains and placed it on the floor behind them, trying to hide it so only the lens was sticking out. He propped up the front end to point directly at the bed, then painstakingly fed a power cable around the back of the furniture. To him, it was obvious, but a stranger might not notice.

Excitedly, Andrew reached down to press record, but as his finger neared the button, something stopped him in his tracks – a throbbing sensation, building up in waves. Tiredness, the same as the night before.

He had only been awake for a few minutes. Andrew shook his head, trying to fight it off, but that only made it worse. His limbs took on weight, trying to drag him to the ground.

And a pain rose behind his forehead.

Someone knew what he was doing, and they were trying to put an end to it. One by one, Andrew's muscles started to shut down. *Turning numb, limp and heavy.* Andrew dragged himself towards the camera, managing to push the little button before he failed completely. Even if they came right in and turned it off again, he still had to try.

With useless legs, Andrew heaved himself up onto the bed, growing weaker by the second. The walls seemed to twist and compress, closing in all around as he collapsed on the mattress, back to the headboard, half-sitting, half-slumped.

His fingers found the mobile phone and he blindly, hopelessly tried to dial.

Nine.

There was barely enough charge for it to ring, but he had no strength to try anything else. *How was this happening so suddenly?*

Nine.

The feeling of death crept up his neck and spread behind his eyes, dark and horrible. Andrew's heartbeat slowed and his consciousness faded.

Nine.

He lost all feeling. Paralysed. Eyelids grew heavy and pulled his gaze down with them, staring at the phone. The number was right there, ready to dial. His thumb rested on the keypad, but Andrew was too weak to press it.

His captors had reduced him to nothing in a matter of seconds, completely helpless. All the willpower in the world couldn't keep him from falling into a deep, disturbing sleep. Eyes drifted closed, and in darkness, something happened which hadn't for years.

Something Andrew had vowed never to do again.

He prayed.

3|ARM

The dreams that night were the most intense yet, almost flawlessly vivid. It wasn't the physical detail that made them so believable, but the feel of surfaces, the sense of familiarity.

If anything, in those first few nights since losing his freedom, Andrew lived more through his sleep than at any other time.

He went right back to his prison cell, the stark white room he had seen so many times before. Metal bars ran across the window and taut, burgundy covers pinned him to the mattress.

Trapping him in place.

Andrew stared helplessly at the ceiling, listening to the unnatural silence and trying to understand why he felt so completely aware of himself. He could even remember falling asleep, paralysed on the bed with the phone in his hand, poised to dial for help.

That night, however, there wasn't time to ponder. The surroundings changed, walls and windows distorting, and Andrew found himself somewhere new, a place he didn't recognise.

It looked like a hotel room, but in a state of disrepair. The woodchip ceiling was a jaded brown, almost orange in places. A musty smell lingered in the air, damp from water that had seeped through the rooftop and dried in crusted rings on a thin, blue carpet.

He was in another bed, on an aging mattress with the covers peeled back over him. He could feel weight on his chest, and realised he wasn't alone.

There was a girl in his arms.

She lay draped across him, holding him tightly, that same pressure he had felt from the blankets. *Pinning him down.* He couldn't see her face, only long curls of thick, mousey blonde hair that tickled his bare skin.

The anonymity made the scene somehow empty, a tension in the air that he couldn't put his finger on, as stale as the damp wallpaper. Andrew drew breath to speak.

Slam!

He was cut short by a thud from the ceiling, making him look up. Suddenly, the room was gone and he was elsewhere, thrown off the bed into a strong gust of wind. A flicker of white light peeled back to a palette of blues, greens and greys. The outdoors.

He was on a cliff top, looking out into a billowing, undulating sea. The wind ploughed inland, pushing him back from the crashing waves far below that broke endlessly over jagged rocks.

A howling gale kept constant pressure on his chest, but the dream was so intense – so exhilarating – that he scarcely even noticed. The sense of space was overwhelming, breathtaking.

Stealing his breath.

Andrew saw an object hovering in the air beside him, just off the edge of the cliff. A bird of prey – a kestrel, stark against the blank horizon. It flew against the current of the air, as though trying to head out to sea and thwarted by the powerful gusts.

Wings were flapping furiously, yet the bird stayed in one place, meters from where Andrew stood. He could see its feathers ruffle, close enough to almost reach out and touch it. But there wasn't time.

Crashing of the waves became the murmur of a crowd and he was suddenly in a restaurant, a place he had been to before. Instead of standing in the open, he was sitting on a short wicker chair, pushed tightly against a table.

Right up against his chest.

Spread before him was an endless banquet of fatty foods, fried eggs and hash browns. It almost turned his stomach, but the knife and fork were already in his hands, compelling him to stuff his face.

His arms took on a life of their own, stabbing through strips of bacon and shovelling them into his mouth. His throat constricted as it tried to retch, but he couldn't stop. It wasn't him in control.

The food kept coming, and his fork rammed it deeper into his mouth, compacting the mush like rubbish in a skip. His mouth could hold no more, so it pushed past his tonsils, right down his throat.

Andrew's stomach lurched and his airways blocked. Panicking, fighting against his own arms. He started to choke, feeling blood rushing to his head. The other people in the restaurant just sat there and ignored him as he tried to mouth the words. *Somebody help me.*

With a tightened fist, he thumped at his chest, trying to combat the pain and force the food out. Huge chunks dripped from between his jaws, but it did no good.

He was choking to death.

***

Andrew jerked painfully out of sleep to find he was in his bed. Back in his flat, arms and legs back under his control. He clutched at his throat, gasping for breath. The air felt stale – thick and muggy – but just to breathe at all was immeasurable relief.

Once again, it was the small hours of the morning. He gripped the side of the mattress and pulled himself up, a sickening feeling in the pit of his stomach. The pain had been so real this time that he was in a state of shock, unsure whether it had actually happened while he was unconscious.

He turned on the lamp and looked apprehensively around the room, willing something to have changed. Before him, the furniture – wardrobe, chest of drawers – was exactly as he had left it, tidy and looking like his flat hadn't been lived in for almost a week.

The bedside drawer hung open just a crack and he grabbed the handle, searching inside to find his phone. Once again, there were used syringes rolling around. Three of them now.

Once again, he had been drugged.

Andrew shut his eyes tightly, then remembered what he had been doing the night before. He saw the trail of a power flex along the skirting board and bent down to look behind the curtain.

His camera, undisturbed, exactly how he had left it.

Excited, Andrew threw off the duvet and took the camera through to the lounge, turning on the light to banish the scratching noises. He sat down on the couch and immediately started to play back the footage, ignoring all else. It showed the top half of the bed, looking up from floor level, and – crucially – the bedside clock, so he knew when things were happening.

One hour of sleeping, then another. Despite how he felt, Andrew appeared to be resting after all. Having passed out above the covers, his sleeping form rolled flat and curled towards the window, limbs apparently free from paralysis.

He stayed there for hours, eyes twitching as he dreamt almost constantly. *Perhaps that explained why they were so lifelike.* The picture grew brighter as the blue hue of morning seeped through the curtains and doused the room. The clock on the table turned past six, sunlight working its way over the horizon, when all of a sudden, there was a flicker of movement.

Sat on the edge of the couch, Andrew stared in disbelief as the person on the screen stirred, threw the covers back...

And got up.

Awestruck, Andrew watched himself crawl ably out of bed and walk towards the bathroom, using more dexterity than he had possessed all week. *Clearly aware of what he was doing, and yet Andrew couldn't remember.*

A shocking pulse thundered down his back. He rewound the footage and played it again. *Eyes were open, barely a slit, like someone moments from sleep.*

The recording continued as he disappeared from view, and a moment later, Andrew saw a shadow on the wall walking down the hallway. The clock read half past six in the morning. Three hours after he had gone to sleep.

He slumped back on the couch and stared coldly at the window. Nobody had injected him with anything and he clearly wasn't sedated. He had just woken up as he always did and got on with the day.

How could he do that and not remember?

Suddenly, Andrew caught more movement on the screen, as from nowhere, a face appeared. He saw the mouth and chin of a man, right in front of the lens – so close that it filled the picture, too near to be in focus.

A knowing smile creased across their lips, and the camera went off.

Someone had been in the bedroom with him, right there inside his flat. A chiselled jaw and a faint cloud of stubble. Andrew had walked right passed them and couldn't remember, just like he couldn't remember a thing he had done on Thursday, or Tuesday. Even Monday was starting to feel hazy, back before it all began.

He needed to look himself in the eye and hurried to the bathroom. The cool tiles of the lounge turned to soft threads of the hallway carpet, then warm linoleum. He clicked on the light and leaned into the mirror, shocked by what he saw. Andrew was almost unrecognisable. One eye was swollen, painted in browns and yellows. Tender, fresh.

He saw blood. Tiny crimson flecks were all over the mirror. Andrew looked down at his hands and saw red crusts under his fingernails, scratches on his forearms. He pressed down and felt pain, very real and irrefutable.

It couldn't be a dream.

He ran his arms under the cold tap, freezing water pouring into open wounds. The footage on the camera hadn't shown any bruises, so something must have happened during that day. This had to stop.

Andrew went to the bedroom and took the mobile phone, surprised to discover it was switched on and fully charged. There were several missed calls, only one of which was from work. Most were from a blocked number, which he couldn't return.

It didn't matter, anyway. Right then, he only needed to talk to Cheryl. Andrew dialled her number, and after five rings, she answered.

"Do you know what time it is?" Her whispering voice hissed down the line.

"I'm sorry," said Andrew. "I wouldn't call you if it wasn't important. I need your help."

"What is it? Be quick."

"I'm trapped in my flat."

There was a pause on the line. "How do you mean?"

"I mean I tried to get out, but something stopped me. I think I'm being held prisoner."

"You think? Surely you either are or you aren't."

"Just come over and have a look, will you?"

"I can't leave now. It's half past three in the morning!"

"Cheryl, *please...*"

"This isn't just an excuse to get me to stay the night, is it? We've talked about this before and I'm not going over it again."

"Of course it isn't. I don't normally call you like this, do I? I'm worried someone is keeping me here."

"I don't see how you could be so unsure of it. Open the window and shout for help."

"I can't do that," he said. "It's locked and I've lost the key."

"For Christ's sake. If it's that bad, then break it." There was silence on the line and she sighed. "No, don't start doing that. Listen, I'll try my best, but I can't promise I'll get there tonight. If you still feel this way in the morning, I'll come over on the way to work, okay?"

"It has to be tonight, Cheryl. In the morning I won't be able to-..."

Eeeeeeeeeeee!

The line crackled and an ear-splitting screech blasted Andrew's ear. He leapt clean out of his skin and the handset slipped from his fingers, shattering to pieces on the ground.

It sounded like a scream, like something had happened to Cheryl. He dropped to one knee and scrabbled on the floor to find the fallen parts, hurriedly putting them back together. The screen was cracked and it wouldn't work, so he smacked it with the heel of his hand.

"Come on, damn it!"

She needed him, just as he needed to know she was alright. Without hesitation, he picked himself up and grabbed a long serrated knife from the rack on the counter. He threw on some trousers and a grey t-shirt, threading the blade through his belt for protection. Then he dared to approach the door.

He didn't see that he had a choice. Andrew couldn't abandon her to the mercy of his kidnappers.

He had to get out.

With a deep breath, Andrew sprinted down the hall and grasped the door handle. Instantly, he shuddered, arm seizing like an electric shock. A horrific pain began to emanate from the front of his skull, but this time, he was determined.

He knew that he couldn't stop now, or he would never find the courage to try again. His vision distorted, pressure mounting from within, but he wouldn't let go.

A voice screamed inside his head, but he held it back, blinded and trembling. The room was spinning, walls pulsing in and out.

With shivering, taut muscles and churning innards, Andrew twisted the handle, and with every fibre in his body, pulled it slowly open.

And he left the flat.

4|NJUSTICE

Andrew stood in the corridor outside his front door, alone, quivering in disbelief.

Closer to freedom than he had been in days.

The moment he left the flat, every trace of the pain in his head evaporated, leaving him alert and quivering in disbelief, bathed in cold sweat, but unspeakably relieved. Whatever it had been, now that he was outside, it didn't seem to work.

He realised his keys were still under the bed, but he didn't care. Going back inside was the last thing he wanted to do. The stairwell at the end of the corridor was well lit, unimposing, and he descended to the ground floor to embrace his release, unsteady on his aching legs.

No one came for him, nor tried to intervene. Andrew walked unopposed out of the building into a cool evening breeze. Fresh air filled his lungs and almost brought him to tears, looking to a sky of intermittent stars, twinkling lights breathing life to the sleeping city. He saw his window, with a light on in the lounge.

Would they know he had escaped?

Quickly, he set off, heading down the pavement between tall, empty office buildings. Progress was sluggish as he struggled to walk, fuelled by a desperate need to get to Cheryl before something happened to her.

If he wasn't already too late.

Surrounding buildings looked run down and abandoned, covered in dense shadows where anything could be lurking. He tried to quicken his pace, glancing constantly over his shoulder. If his captors got to Cheryl so quickly, there was no telling how broad their reach was.

He took the mobile phone out of his pocket and held it tightly in his hand, trying to crush the pieces back into a workable form. He attempted to run, but just then, a car appeared over the hill.

Andrew was drenched in a punishing white light and he froze like a startled rabbit. The vehicle slowed as it came towards him, and drew to a halt.

He was less than four hundred yards from his flat. The doors opened and two dark silhouettes climbed out. Andrew took a step away. "Just stay back."

Without speaking, one of them walked between him and the headlight beam. The other slammed their door shut with a clunk. "I'm warning you now," said Andrew. "Keep your distance."

He caught the glint of reflective strips on a brightly coloured jacket, heard the crackle of a radio. The man in the beam approached and Andrew realised they hadn't come to drag him back to the flat at all.

They were police.

"Oh, thank God." Andrew spoke with a heavy sigh. "You startled the life out of me."

The officer nearest to him was tall and pale, with crew cut hair and broad shoulders. His partner was a woman, almost as tall, also with a stern expression. She took her hands out of her pockets and spoke directly.

"What's your name, sir?" she said.

"Andrew," he replied. "I'm sorry I sounded aggressive. I couldn't see you for the light and I thought you could be anybody."

"What are you doing out at this time?" she asked. "Don't you think you should be at home?"

"I'm trying to get to a house about a mile from here. It's important."

The man drew breath. "So important that it can't wait until morning?"

"It would take a long time to explain, officer. It's not far though. I can make it easily enough on my own."

The male officer took his hands out of his pockets, and Andrew noticed he was closing in. The policewoman saw he was distracted.

"Look at me," she said. It made him nervous. "Where have you come from tonight?"

Andrew edged away. "I live in a flat just up the road."

"And what compelled you to leave it so late?"

His eyes darted from left to right as he struggled to keep an eye on them both. Instinctively, his hands lifted from his sides, expecting to be jumped at any moment.

"I'm not doing anything wrong," he said. "There really is somewhere I need to be, and I don't have much time. Come with me if you want and you'll see I'm not lying."

The man took another step, almost within reach. "Tell us what you're doing with that knife," he said.

Andrew glanced down, the twelve inch kitchen knife protruding from under his belt. He had completely forgotten about it. "Now, let's not be hasty here. I only brought that with me for protection."

"Can we have it?" said the policewoman. The headlamp played off the side of her face and he could see her eyes were cold and unwavering. Whether Andrew gave her the knife or not, she would clearly get it from him.

"I'm not trying to create a situation," he said.

"Just give us the knife please, sir."

Andrew slowly reached down and put his fingers around the handle. His other arm stayed raised, palm outstretched. "I'm not going to do anything rash, so please don't come at me. I'm just going to put it down on the ground and step away from it, okay?"

He did as he said and backed away from the knife. They left it sitting on the pavement.

"Do you have any other weapons?" the policeman asked.

"No, nothing." His legs grew increasingly restless, aware Cheryl needed him.

"Are you sure?"

"Yes of course I'm sure," said Andrew. "Are we done here? Can I go?"

The officer recoiled from his breath, screwing up his nose. "Sir, how much have you had to drink?"

"I don't think I've had anything," said Andrew. *Or had he?*

The woman reached into her pocket and sighed. "That's enough. I'm going to have to ask you to come with us."

"Are you arresting me?" he asked.

"Well, I could do that," said the woman. "Or you could just come voluntarily. You're under the influence and carrying a weapon. I think it would be best if you slept it off in a cell, don't you?"

"Have you taken anything else that you'd like to tell us about?" asked the man.

"I don't think so. I mean, nothing. Look, I won't be any trouble. I just want to get on my way."

Andrew wanted to know just as badly as they did what was running through his veins. *Would a blood test find traces of sedatives? Perhaps narcotics or something worse?*

The policeman reached for his handcuffs. Andrew was either going to the station or they were going to escort him home, but either way, if he wanted to help both Cheryl and himself, he had no choice but to run.

Andrew shut his eyes and drew breath. Before the policeman could react, he lunged forwards and kicked the knife towards the woman. She instinctively recoiled, and he used that split second to turn on his heels and run away down the pavement.

In a heartbeat, the man was after him, long legs giving him an advantage on the flat pavement. Andrew, however, had urgency inside him and an advantage of his own: He knew where he was going.

He turned on his toes and suddenly changed direction, sprinting down a narrow pathway between tall houses. The policeman faltered in his step, giving Andrew a few valuable second's lead as he tore down the unlit path, blindly hoping there was nothing on the ground to trip him over.

The echo of footsteps were mirrored from behind as he broke into the open and rushed across the road without a thought for his safety, passing terraced houses, able to hear the scraping sleeves of the other man's coat as he closed the gap.

Andrew took a sharp breath and held it, pushing for an extra bolt of energy. Cheryl's house couldn't have been more than a handful of streets away and he was coming for her, police in tow.

The officer slowed as they reached another corner, waiting to see which way Andrew would turn. "Stop," he shouted. "Come back here!"

Andrew's arms pummelled like pistons, cutting through the cool night air, but with no more bends on his journey, Andrew was outclassed. He felt a hand grip his shoulder, and before he could react, he was jerked violently backwards.

Andrew lost his balance.

He came crashing down on the tarmac. The full weight of the policeman landed on top of him, pinning him to the flagstones. Andrew fought wildly, kicking and flailing, but the policeman clamped his legs tightly around Andrew's chest and tried to grab hold of his arms.

Andrew heard the click of handcuffs and knew he had run out of time. Lashing out, his foot landing a lucky blow to the back of the policeman's head, but all he received for his efforts was a well placed fist that caught him square in the eye socket.

He couldn't give up, not with Cheryl in danger. He put his body into spasm, bucking like a mule, and managed to catch the officer again. With agility that neither of them thought he had, Andrew slid out from beneath him and transferred all of his weight to his legs, kicking with the heel of his shoe.

It caught the policeman squarely in the face, and there was an agonising crunch as his jaw gave way.

Andrew felt the impact.

The officer crumpled to the ground with a bloodcurdling shriek that was muffled by broken bone. Andrew didn't hesitate. He scrambled to his feet and ran, faster than he had ever moved before. He ran from the police, ran for his life.

Blood thundered past his ears, making him deaf to the world, and he didn't slow down for quarter of a mile, until the officer was nowhere in sight. His chest hurt, desperately short of breath. Andrew came to a halt and put his hands on his knees, lungs burning, caked in sweat. But he had made it.

Cheryl's door came into sight. She lived in a semi-detached house with three bedrooms, and seeing it made him hesitate. She was a strong woman, pretty and flirtatious, kind and giving. The only flaw in an otherwise perfect package was sadly fundamental.

She was married.

The house was still and lifeless, drawn curtains and open windows. Two empty cars were queued up the driveway and a garden lawn was protected from the road by a four-foot border hedgerow.

Andrew gasped for air, consciously lowering his heart rate before he approached the gate at the end of her driveway. He had never been there before – because of her husband – and he was nervous. Exhausted legs grew stiff, each step feeling cumbersome and he crept onto concrete paving.

He tried to swing the gate closed behind him, but it somehow put up fierce resistance. A warm sensation came with a horrific realisation.

His body was trying to send him to sleep.

Calming down from the exertion, lethargy spiralled out of control. Tired limbs grew heavy, and he took a laboured step forward that felt like wading through wet cement. Andrew stumbled – half fell – through the gate and onto the paved driveway, collapsing to his knees in full view of the front door.

They had let him get in sight of her house before they put him right back out of consciousness. His bones shook as they connected with the hard surface. "Cheryl," he cried, but his lungs were empty, words muted on a tight wheeze. The house looked dead, hollow.

Could he be too late?

The weight of his arms tried to bring him horizontal and there was nothing he could do. Sleep was going to take him. Fatigue welled up from the base of his skull, just like it had done the past two nights.

With precious seconds left before he blacked out, Andrew fell onto his side, landing in the loose soil of a flowerbed. With every ounce of his fading strength, he dragged himself into a narrow gap between the hedge and a row of stout, prickly bushes.

Clothes snagged on the blunt thorns as he clawed at the undergrowth, pulling himself out of view. A last, desperate attempt to hide. Numb feet dragged over the soil and he collapsed, facedown in the dirt, mortified by failure. Sickened at all he had done for nothing.

Darkness swept over him and the ground seemed to swallow him whole. In his mind's eye, seconds passed, then – in a flash of lightening – he was awake again. Andrew felt the soft invitation of the ground beneath him, tried to dig his fingers into soil, but what he felt was fabric.

He was back in the flat.

Andrew sat up, eyes open wide. He was in bed, just as he had woken up for the last five nights. The room was in darkness, but he could see the clock, taunting him from its place on the table by the bed.

3.14am.

There was a voice in his head that made it to his lips. No, no, no...

He rose on pounding limbs and staggered across the room, unable to believe it. *How had they found him? What had they done with Cheryl?*

Someone had gone to great lengths to bring him back there, undress him and put him to bed. He was right back where he had started from, a whole night later and no better for it. He cleared his throat and shouted out loud.

"What do you want from me?"

His eyes sank downwards, unable to lift for the sense of defeat. His rescue attempt had failed drastically, and instead they had shown him that, wherever he went – with that thing inside his head that hurt so wildly – they could still somehow control him.

With eyes downcast, he noticed something in the middle of the floor. An object that stood out. Andrew suddenly forgot his self-pity and limped cautiously over the floorboards, stiffly bending down and scooping it into his hand. He looked it over, not a clue how it got there.

A letter.

And it was addressed to him.

5|UBTERFUGE

Black.

Katie made a sudden yelp as she braced for impact, a frightened whimper that sneaked out on a tight breath. Andrew had never heard such a sound from her before.

Their rusted silver hatchback skimmed past the car in front, missing it by inches, and the steering wheel was swept out of his hands, as though he hadn't been gripping it with all his strength.

They bounced onto the curb and careered helplessly into a lamp post on the promenade. Andrew was flung forwards, catching a glimpse of Katie's black hair whipping through the air before her seatbelt snapped her back from the windscreen.

Andrew, however, hadn't put his on.

A lacerating pain thrashed down his spine. He could almost hear the bones break. He caught a last fleeting image of blue sky and shattering glass, and then black was all there was.

Andrew would never forget what happened next. He was floating, adrift in a great expanse of sheer, unpolluted darkness. He felt outside of his body, stripped of his very existence. And he loved it.

There was a numb, dreamlike warmth to the air, mind emptied of burdening thoughts. Total sensory deprivation – no pain, no fear or discomfort. It was scarcely existence at all, but he didn't mind. In fact, he wanted it to continue, only it wasn't set to last.

Just as quickly as he had gone under, the darkness peeled away, shapes and shadows looming in the corners of his eyes. The weight returned to his body and emotions came hurtling back.

He was lying on his front, but couldn't feel the ground, only a dull pain in his lower back. Andrew opened his eyes, fully expecting to see that same blue sky above him, but they were stung by the glow of a light bulb on the ceiling.

He was in bed, his head twisted awkwardly into a hard pillow. There were green curtains in the shape of a cubicle. It didn't look like he made it to Heaven after all.

He was in a hospital.

There was an ache down one side of his body, and the more he thought about it, the worse it felt. He tried to move, but couldn't. The only thing that seemed to work was his hand, and he weakly flexed his fingers, relieved that something did what he told it to.

The movement brought a bustle of excitement as people hurried over. In the corner of his eye, Andrew saw a man in a white coat, and beside him, someone else. Something about the way they carried themselves that was instantly familiar. He sighed through a constricted throat, inexpressibly relieved.

Katie was alright.

"Thank God you're awake," she said, moving close.

A smile cracked on his lips and it hurt like a raging fire. He drew a breath delicately. "Hi there."

The doctor – a tall, thin Indian man – leaned over and looked into his eyes. A thick brow sat atop chestnut eyes that stared without blinking. There was something hypnotic about it.

"Please don't try to move, Andrew. You've hurt your back quite badly and we need to be careful you don't strain it. How do you feel?"

"I can't." Andrew closed his eyes and embraced darkness, trying to hang onto the feeling of floating. "Sorry, doctor. I mean, I feel faint, but I think I'm in one piece. Only I can't move my back."

"Don't even try. Just relax if you can and give yourself a chance to rest. Are you in any pain?"

"Not really. What does it look like down there? Is it serious?"

"One step at a time," said the doctor. "We'll do some tests once you're feeling a bit better and discuss it then."

The doctor smiled, broad and comforting, but Katie shot him a worried glance, and Andrew caught it. She stepped in and rested a hand on top of Andrew's, not that he could feel it.

"They weren't expecting you to come around just yet," she said. "I think you took them by surprise."

"What's going on? I feel worse by the second."

"You just need to get some rest, like they told you. The anaesthetic hasn't quite worn off, that's all. They'll find out more once the dust has settled."

With a nod, the doctor left the cubicle, leaving Andrew and Katie alone together. As the drugs slowly drained from Andrew's system, he was coming to realise just how much he wanted them back.

"I feel like crap," he said.

"Your back took a lot of the impact," said Katie. "You were too close to the airbag for it to do you any good."

She seemed distant, something he put down to shock from the accident. "Are you alright?" he asked.

"A few bruises here and there, but otherwise I was lucky."

"Are we still in Brighton?"

"Yes, only a few miles from the accident. They cleared most of it up yesterday, but you can still see where it happened."

"How long have I been unconscious?"

"A day," she said. "They kept you under while they operated. You've been out ever since they found you, in one form or another."

He frowned. "What do you mean by that?" She sealed her lips tightly, too many words spoken already. "It's alright, Katie. You can tell me."

"Well, when they cut you out of the car, you were in and out of consciousness, but... well... for a moment, they lost you completely."

Her words triggered a memory, a glimpse of the paramedics. "I died," he said.

She nodded. "Only then, you came right back. They said it couldn't have been for a minute, if that, but I was there when it happened."

Andrew knew it was true. He closed his eyes and the comforting darkness was replaced with flashes of blue sky and splintered glass.

"Do you remember any of it?" she asked.

He couldn't shake his head. "The last solid memory I had was breakfast, and from then on, it's a mess."

She gave him a condescending look. "But we didn't have breakfast."

"Of course we did. I remember it clearly. Bacon, sausage, beans... I can almost still taste it."

Katie straightened a stray lock of hair on her forehead, composing herself. "All they had in the hotel was cereal and toast, so we decided to leave it until later, which never happened."

"I swear I'm not making it up, Katie."

"Neither of us has eaten for a long time, believe me. I've been too sick with worry."

With his face jammed into the pillow, Andrew couldn't see her properly, but he could tell by her voice how exhausted she was.

"Well, I suppose it doesn't bear thinking about it now, anyway," he said. "You can get some rest now I'm awake, if you like."

Katie smiled, grateful for the dismissal. "I wasn't dropping hints, you know, but thanks." She slung her bag over her shoulder. "You should rest, anyway. I'll let everyone at home know you're awake, then maybe find a change of clothes."

He smiled. In spite of the sedation, the expression was painful. Katie squeezed his hand then left the cubicle, heels clicking as she strolled out of the ward. Andrew was left alone with his thoughts and a cloud descended over him, struggling to come to terms with the accident.

That he had died.

It put his life in a new perspective. Lying trapped on his front with his face half buried in the pillow, Andrew made a new resolve. He would take her away again as soon as he could, making up for this ruined holiday. Forget about the savings. They needed to enjoy life while they still could.

He closed his eyes and felt himself drift effortlessly away. The dull pain down the side of his body didn't stop him. Dreamless sleep came upon him and he felt eager to get home to his wife.

Had he known what his home would turn into, he might have felt differently.

***

Andrew,

By now I'm sure you know things aren't how they should be. You can't change that so stop fighting. Stop wasting time. Stop trying to run. Just stay put. It will all be different soon.

Andrew cradled the note in trembling hands, standing frozen in the middle of his bedroom. It was written on a scrunched up piece of paper, in handwriting that was almost illegible. Childlike and messy, but it told him everything he needed to know.

Someone really did have him captive, and there was nothing he could do about it.

Andrew pored over the words. He could scarcely believe they had found him where he collapsed, hidden away in the flower bed outside Cheryl's house. They must have seen him crawl into the bushes, watching from the windows.

Things aren't how they should be. He recited the words over and over in his head, trying to decipher them. *It will all be different soon.* They were right about that much. When the police caught up with him, they would lock him away for breaking the officer's jaw. He was a fugitive now, and on borrowed time.

The drawer at the bedside had been emptied during the day, the phone and syringes removed. Confiscated. He walked into the hallway, finding all the lights still on in the flat, just as he had left them the previous night.

Before he reached the lounge, however, he noticed one thing untoward. In the bathroom – brightly lit in crisp clarity – he could see a smudge on the mirror, a narrow streak where a dirty hand had wiped away the condensation.

It stood out by a mile. Andrew went in and looked closer, following the trail to a similar mark on the side of the medicine cabinet. He reached up and ran his hand across the top, where – over a thin layer of dust – something moved beneath his fingers.

A key.

Andrew knew instantly what it was for and took it to the bedroom, putting an arm under the bed to retrieve the small, metallic chest he had found on the previous night. He slid the key in the lock and twisted it with nervous hands.

With a click, it came open.

Inside was a deepening pile of letters, days of unopened mail. His mobile phone was there, along with his wallet, keys and a small box of syringes. *Full ones.*

He picked one out, holding it to the light. There was a clear liquid inside with just a hint of yellow, which he worked out had come from a small, glass bottle with a screw top. The label on its side, however, made no sense.

Adrenaline.

That couldn't possibly make him fall asleep – the opposite. Adrenaline must have been the means to wake him from his deep slumber. It would explain why he always woke up at the same time, minutes after three in the morning. How they mocked his lack of control.

Andrew!

From the lounge, he heard the wind pick up and howl against the window, making the wooden frame creak. He thought he heard a voice.

Someone calling his name.

Andrew rushed into the room and parted the blinds to look down at the car park. In the deathly calm, his eyes were instantly drawn to a shadowy figure at the far end. A woman, dressed in a green coat that sank down to her knees.

Even from a hundred yards, he could tell that she was quivering. He tried to force the window open, but the lock resisted.

"Hey!" he yelled through the glass.

Her long, blonde hair looked sodden, clinging to her scalp. She stood stiffly on the spot, facing right towards his window like she was being shown to him.

Cheryl.

He waved his arms up and down. *"Cheryl? Can you see me?"*

Andrew yanked the blind cord open and closed like a signal lamp, but she didn't respond. He ran to the dimmer switch on the wall – making the room as bright as possible – but by the time he made it back, she had gone, vanished into any of a hundred shadowy corners.

Taken away.

Something thumped inside his skull, fingers curling into fists. He ran to the bedroom and threw on some clothes, getting ready to leave. *This is all your fault,* his conscience derided. *She would have been safe if you just hadn't called her.*

He took the metal box and, without hesitating, ran down the hallway to the front door, preparing to face the pain when he touched the handle.

Nothing happened.

He pulled the door all the way open and realised the lock had been broken off the door, as though someone had smashed their way in from outside. The mechanism was ruined, and in its ruin, it no longer had the power to harm him.

Who had done that?

He ran downstairs and into the cool night air, raising goosebumps on his bare forearms. Rushing across the car park, Andrew went straight to the place where he had seen Cheryl standing. He tried every door around him, rattling hinges. All locked.

"Cheryl?" he shouted. Distant traffic was the only reply. Andrew turned and looked up at his flat – the only one around with a light on. She wouldn't have been able to miss him standing up there.

Stop trying to run. He thought of the note. It could even have been written by Cheryl, forced to scrawl it for them.

He saw his car, a red Honda Civic. Someone had parked it almost diagonally across one of the spaces. He opened the door and slid into the seat, placing the red box beside him. Andrew's own face looked back in the dipped rear-view mirror, pale and unravelled.

To find out where they were keeping Cheryl, he had to start where he knew she had been. He turned the key in the ignition and felt the engine growl to life, swinging back out of the parking space and speeding onto the main road.

He ploughed down white lines of the same streets he had travelled just hours ago. *A policeman with a broken jaw.* A mile passed in a minute, and before he knew it, Andrew was pulling up outside her house. It was empty again, quiet, deserted.

He got out and crept over the concrete. The clear summer night sky carried a blue hue that almost silhouetted the property, though streetlights showed him open windows in the bedroom – *still open* – and curtains drawn, almost closed.

Down in the front garden, he could see the bushes he had crawled behind before he passed out, stout and bushy. Sandwiched between them and the thick slats of the squat picket fence, he would have been well hidden. They must have seen him fall or they would never have found him.

Andrew approached the door, and almost as soon as he did, heard a creaking noise behind it. He hugged the wall, slowly edging into shadows, when without warning, it was wrenched open.

A figure in white stood in the hallway. A woman, bare arms hanging by her sides.

Cheryl.

"What the fuck are you doing here?" she hissed. Clean, golden hair hugged the curve of her face, and a thin nightgown was draped over her shoulders. The moonlight revealed a stern expression – judgmental eyes, thin lips parted in anger.

"I-... I needed to check you were safe," said Andrew, stunned.

"Keep your voice down, for God's sakes!" She stepped onto the porch and pulled the door closed behind her, looking down her nose at him. "Well, I see you're not trapped in your flat, after all."

"Are you alright?" he asked, though she looked absolutely fine. "I tried to get here last night. Didn't you see me?"

"Why the hell are you here at all? You know what would happen if my husband found out."

The slightest dip in the corner of her mouth portrayed hurt.

"I'm sorry, Cheryl," he said. "I saw you from my window and I thought they had you."

"What on earth are you talking about?"

"You were there, not ten minutes ago. Standing in the car park. You looked terrified."

"What's going on, Andrew? You look worse by the second."

He took a deep breath, suddenly filled with self-doubt. "Listen, Cheryl. Something is happening and I can't control it. Here, look at this."

He took the crumpled note out of his pocket and showed it to her. She took an idle glance at the messy handwriting. "What's this supposed to be?"

"I don't know. I thought you might have written it."

She read the first line, brow furrowing as she struggled with the scrawl. "This is all the evidence you have?" she said. "This looks like a child wrote it. I wouldn't show it to the police or they'll lock you up in a heartbeat."

Cheryl looked at him with disdain, almost pity, but the gaze he returned softened her resolve. "What on Earth have you dragged yourself into?" she said.

Andrew shrugged. "Honestly, Cheryl. I swear on my life I don't know."

"Well, either way, you can't stay out here, and you know I'm not going to invite you in." She backed inside and stood behind the door, poised to close it.

"What am I supposed to do now?" he asked.

"How should I know? Just go home and sort yourself out, Andrew."

His mouth formed words he couldn't speak. She was clearly in no danger, and made him feel a fool for thinking otherwise. All he could do was watch as she pushed the door closed and disappeared from his life.

Alone in the porch, Andrew shut his eyes and welcomed darkness. He felt unhinged. *How could he have seen her standing outside in such fear and then find her at home and oblivious?* Maybe she was right. Maybe he was going insane after all.

He retreated to his car and buckled the seatbelt, feeling lost and bewildered. The clock on the dashboard read three, fifty-eight and the approaching sunrise ushered in the morning. He cradled the crumpled note in his hands. *Just stay put,* it read. *It will all be different soon.*

To him, it sounded threatening – like something bad was about to happen – but as he read it back in the dim streetlight, his resolve was shattered. It was, after all, just a letter.

He opened the box and rifled through it. There were over a dozen banknotes floating loosely inside. Unused syringes rolled around, next to the adrenaline vial. He couldn't make sense of it, why someone would have been keeping it under his bed.

There was just one more place he could think of to look for answers, one more piece in the puzzle that didn't seem to fit. Andrew twisted the key and gunned the engine, a loud noise to remind the world that he was losing patience.

He was going to Katie's house.

Andrew released the clutch and the car shot off the pavement, squealing tyres leaving a trail of rubber on the concrete. Behind him, Cheryl would be sliding into bed alongside her husband, scarcely a care in the world. It only served to anger him further.

He felt the need to drive fast, to create some more adrenaline before the drugs in his system wore off. He gripped the wheel with white knuckles as the car spun around a corner, clipping the curb as he barely made it.

Katie only lived a few miles away, in a right-sided semi-detached, hidden from the main road by a six foot tall hedgerow which was thick and untended. Andrew knew the house all too well, because he had lived there himself.

He was even still paying for it.

Carelessly, Andrew pulled onto the gravelled driveway and parked down the side of the house, exactly the way he used to before they separated. He got out and marched to the front door, singling out the one key he thought he would never use again.

It slid perfectly into the front door. At least she hadn't changed the locks. The hallway was pitch black, cold, and the door jammed as he pushed it open, a pile of newspapers wedged underneath it. He entered to a stranger's house, dark and hollow. There was tension in the air, a strong feeling that something was wrong.

"Katie?" he called. "Are you there?"

They had lived in that house for years, even before they were married. It was hard to believe he was back again. There were so many memories he had locked away in the depths of his mind.

"Hello?" His voice echoed down the hall. He opened the lounge door to see a big empty space, cavernous in the moonlight. He check the kitchen to find all the appliances had been stripped out. The house was deserted.

Katie appeared to have long since vanished, leaving their marital home abandoned. Andrew walked through the echoing shells of his former life, checking upstairs, expecting in each doorway to find it was just another trick.

The wallpaper on the landing bore gashes where furniture had caught it on the way past. Every last item had been taken, from the toilet roll in the bathroom to the shades on every light bulb.

It didn't feel like it could ever be the same. Katie was gone, and any answers she could have given had vanished with her. Andrew snapped, anger boiling over. Gathering the syringes in hand, he took them to the bathroom and placed them in the sink, crushing them to pieces with the metal box. Liquid spilled out and gargled down the plughole.

Things were going to have to change. Let them see he wouldn't cooperate. *Andrew Goodwin wouldn't be controlled.*

Almost immediately, he felt the first well of tiredness, the inevitable comedown starting to spiral out of control. Andrew had been awake for the best part of an hour, and it was apparently all his kidnappers deemed fit to grant him.

There was no point trying to fight it – he knew much that by now – but the house was a good place to hide. Andrew made sure the door was locked and bolted shut, then checked all the windows.

As his legs grew heavy, he climbed up to the master bedroom and sat on the carpet, behind the door. He knew his car would be secluded behind the hedgerow, and he didn't think he had been followed. The room would do until morning, or the next night, or however long it took for the drugs to completely drain out of his system.

It felt strangely sad to be back in back there. A long time ago, he and Katie had shared real love, and it was depressing to see it so cold. Though perhaps, it was strangely appropriate. As Andrew's eyes glazed over, he felt almost as hollow as that house.

For all his effort, he was starting to wonder if there was a life worth stealing back.

6|OSTILITY

Andrew Goodwin drifted in sleep, once more haunted by the same twisted dreams – the stark white room with the deep red sheets, the restaurant with unending heaps of fatty foods.

Only at the end were things any different. Somewhere between the sleep and waking worlds, time seemed to freeze. There was no bloody violence, no horrible death as he had come to expect. The dream faded, but he didn't exactly wake up.

Instead, Andrew found himself shrouded in unnatural darkness, a limbo between two realms. *Somewhere he had been before.* The sense of space was overwhelming, a vast expanse with him floating inside it, paralysed, listening to a suffocating silence.

Until he heard a voice.

"Andrew... are you there?"

It was a man, clear and distinct, speaking faintly into his ear, but heard with crystal clarity. So close that Andrew could feel the urgency on his breath.

"Andrew?" he said. *"There are things you need to know."*

Andrew tried to breathe as fast as stifled lungs would allow, but the air just poured back out, barely even forming a word.

"I realise you're scared right now," said the man, *"but you're making everything much harder on yourself. Running around in the night isn't helping anyone."*

Andrew saw a glimpse of something distant, hundreds of feet away, standing out against the darkness. There was no haze, no mist to cloud the detail.

A person.

"I'm not asking for you to cooperate," the man said. *"I'm telling you to consider the consequences of your actions."*

Andrew could almost feel the cold tingle of chemicals shuffling through his bloodstream. A raise in blood pressure slowly heightened his awareness.

"You're the last man on Earth who deserves my sympathy, so stop interfering and make your peace. This will end soon, one way or the other."

Andrew managed to prise his eyes open. He was indoors, a naked bulb on the ceiling. The floor beneath him felt hard and unwelcoming, his head twisted to one side. He fought pins and needles as he parted his lips.

"Who are you?" he asked. Andrew shut his eyes tightly – aware of rustling trees through a windowpane – and when he opened them again, things were back to normal.

And he was still in Katie's house.

Andrew raised his head to find he was lying on the floor with his head against a wall. The kidnappers hadn't taken him back to the flat. Instead, he was in his old lounge, sat with his back to drawn curtains.

And there was someone in the room with him.

Andrew's blood froze on sight of a stocky man with short, fair hair and the broad shoulders of a rugby player. He was seated on a plastic chair with both arms behind his back and his head slumped forwards.

Andrew wasn't alone.

The man looked poised to lunge off his seat, and it was only as Andrew looked closer that he realised he was tied to it.

"Hello?" said Andrew. The man showed no sign of movement, eyes closed. A black smear of a bruise ran across his temple, streaked with dried blood.

Andrew tried to climb to his feet, but something tugged him back down. The kidnappers had bound his wrist to the inlet pipe of a radiator using a dozen loops of twine, pulled tightly.

Helpless, Andrew looked around the room, finding it easy to spot what had changed. On the carpet in the corner, he discovered his mobile phone – smashed, crushed to pieces. *Retribution for the broken syringes.*

Using his free hand, Andrew pulled the curtains open to see darkness behind them, and it gave him an idea. There were still a few things Katie hadn't taken when she emptied the house, things he could use. On each side of the window, he saw metal holdbacks, silver half-circles for bunching the curtains.

Andrew could recall fitting them himself, years ago. No one else would have known how the plaster around them was too thin.

They were loose.

Arching his back, Andrew reached up and grabbed hold of the nearest one. The metal wobbled in his hand, and with a swift few yanks, he managed to dislodge it from the wall.

Plaster rained down as it came free, and Andrew examined what had held it in place for so long – inch-long screws, two of them, each with a sharp point.

Andrew started to hack away at the twine, picking the threads loose while he kept an eye on the man in the chair. It didn't seem real that there could be another like him, and he refused to believe his eyes.

Snapping through the strands, he managed to slide his hand out and crawl to his feet. The holdback became a weapon, held with the screws facing out. Andrew walked over to the unconscious man and pulled his head back, getting a good look at his face.

"Are you awake?" said Andrew. "Can you hear me?"

Disturbed by the light, the man groggily opened an eye. It took a few seconds to register what he was looking at, then he stiffened in the chair. "Get away from me," he said.

"I'm not a threat," said Andrew. "Can you tell me your name?"

"R-Ryan."

The man shivered as though he was freezing, but Andrew was still cautious. He circled around the back of the chair to find another length of twine had been used to secure Ryan's wrists through the slats, digging into his skin. There was no way he could have done that to himself.

"A moment before I woke up, someone spoke to me," said Andrew. "Did you hear it?"

You're the last man on Earth who deserves my sympathy, the voice has said.

"I don't know what you're talking about," said Ryan.

The pitch dark outside made the window work like a mirror. Andrew stood behind Ryan's chair and used the reflection to observe his face.

"Have you been drugged?" ask Andrew. "Is it giving you headaches?"

Ryan frowned. "What?" He tried to look back over his shoulder, but Andrew stayed out of sight, afraid there might be more at stake than caution would cost.

"I need to know some things before I can let you go," said Andrew. "Are we alone in the house?"

"I don't know," said Ryan. "Please, I've lost the feeling in my fingers."

Andrew left the room and checked the hallway, turning on the light. The front door was drifting off the latch and he peered outside at a narrow garden lawn, glistening silver in the moonlight.

He pushed it shut and returned to find Ryan trying to pull his way free.

"What are you planning to do with me?" said Ryan.

"I just want to know who you are and what you're doing here," said Andrew. "Then you can go, for all I care."

"You know why I'm here."

"No, I don't. What happened to your face?" said Andrew.

Again, Ryan frowned, but then he realised something. "Your name wouldn't be Andrew, would it?"

Andrew shuddered. "What do you know about me?"

"Not much, but I'm starting to get a better picture." Ryan studied his expression, eyes darting left and right. *Analysing.* His fear seemed to be replaced with a childlike curiosity. "You're carrying yourself differently..."

Andrew raised his fist. "If you know something, you'd better say."

"You mentioned headaches?" Ryan cleared his throat, shuffling on the seat. "Are you losing whole days of your life? There's a very good reason for that, and believe me, you've got worse problems than I have."

"Tell me what you know," said Andrew.

"Gladly. Get these knots off and we'll talk properly."

"How about you tell me now, and I'll take the knots off when I know you're not lying?"

Ryan grit his teeth, a dimple in his square jaw. "Not good enough."

"I could walk out of the door and turn myself into the police at any time," said Andrew. "My story won't sound any stranger for you being here. They can come and ask you the very same questions, but one way or another, you'll end up having to answer them."

Ryan took a drawn out breath. "Andrew, you seem to have forgotten just a little too much of what we spoke about this afternoon. Protest your innocence all you want, but understand what I'm about to say because

I don't say it lightly: If you don't stop this soon, I will kill you."

"Stop what?"

"Trying to steal my wife!"

Andrew stumbled back against the wall. *So that's who he was.*

Cheryl's husband.

Suddenly, Andrew was afraid to set him loose. Veins bulged out of Ryan's neck, the muscles in his arms so tight that he could have ripped the twine clean apart. He caught Andrew's shocked expression and nodded. "You remember that part just fine, don't you?"

Andrew's feet drew him across the floor, making a beeline for the door. "You'll just make it worse if you leave me tied up here," said Ryan. "Stay for a minute and we'll talk about it."

Andrew paused in the doorway, taking the weight off his sore leg. *Consider the consequences of your actions,* the voice had told him.

"Alright then," he said. "A minute is all you have."

Ryan talked fast. "You don't come across as a person who would kidnap or threaten violence without good reason, and for your part in all of this, I don't hold it against you. But you've made it clear you don't know what you're involved in and that's dangerous, so let me go and I'll try to fill you in."

"Why on Earth should I trust you?" said Andrew. "Especially when I can leave you here and handle this problem with the police."

Ryan closed his eyes, speaking with reluctance.

"Because I know the man who's doing this to you."

***

There were no utensils in the kitchen cupboards, stripped bare when the house was abandoned. As well as Andrew knew his ex-wife, he couldn't understand what had possessed her to take everything and disappear.

Especially when he owned so much of it.

He ducked around the side of the house to a little shed by the side of the garage. It had always been his domain, so he doubted Katie would have remembered to clear it. And he was right.

Feet crunched over gravel as he opened the lock and, from memory, retrieved a retractable knife and a wheel brace, taking them back indoors. The latter was for protection. He wasn't going to loosen Ryan's restraints unless he was armed.

In the lounge, he found Ryan in a position of increasing confidence, realising how much Andrew relied upon him for answers. What Ryan didn't realise was that the kidnappers might think differently.

For that night, at least, Andrew considered them to be in a similar amount of trouble.

"How long do you think it'll be before you lose control again?" Ryan asked.

Andrew knelt behind the chair and used the knife to cut through the twine, discovering the blade was blunt. "There doesn't seem to be a hard and fast rule," he replied. "Half an hour, if I'm lucky."

"What happens to you, then?"

"I wake up the following night with no idea what happened or why. It's been like this for a week."

The twine had been pulled tight and wound thick around Ryan's wrists, literally dozens of times. Andrew sat down, making slow progress.

"That must feel pretty strange," Ryan continued.

"I've had six hours of conscious thought in as many nights," said Andrew. "Of course it feels strange. In case you didn't notice, I'm taking a huge leap of faith cutting you loose here, and I'd appreciate some help instead of blunt observation."

Andrew could see the colour slowly returning to Ryan's hands, and heard him sigh with relief.

"Okay," said Ryan. "I'm sorry. Listen, I need to get something off my chest. I don't know all you've done behind my back, but for what it's worth, you've convinced me that you probably don't either."

"There isn't much I can remember at all. You made a comment before that I was carrying myself differently..."

"Yes, I can't put my finger on it, but you looked heavier this afternoon, like you were finding it harder to walk. You look lighter on your feet now."

"I don't feel it, but if you say so."

"His name is Daniel," said Ryan.

Andrew stopped picking the binds. "Do you know what he wants?"

"I don't think it's personal, not that you'll take any comfort in that."

"He put something in my head," said Andrew. "Something I think he's controlling." Three lengths of twine gave way at once. A few more and Ryan would be free.

"I don't want to get involved," said Ryan. "Daniel's a desperate man, and God knows how far he might take it."

"Surely the police will be able to stop him?"

"What evidence do you have to make them believe you?"

"Just a note he left for me two nights ago, but I'll get something better. He has to slip up sometime."

"I highly doubt that, but then what do I know?"

With a snap, the binds came loose. Ryan wriggled free and stood up, rubbing red marks on his wrists. There was a real complacency in his expression, and Andrew didn't like it.

"I'm just a bystander," said Ryan. "And I'll happily stay that way. But for what it's worth, he always loved to talk about himself. If he wrote you a note, have you tried writing one back? He might just fill you in."

Ryan backed through the door and into the hall. "Hold on a second," said Andrew, scrambling to his feet. "Where are you going?"

"You've had your answers, and I'd say that makes us even."

"You hardly told me anything."

"Why do you act like I owe you something? Any way you try to dress it up, you've done some bad things, Andrew. *You.* I'm not going to the police anymore, and that's more than you can ask for."

Andrew tried to get between him and the door, but Ryan puffed out his chest and made it clear he wouldn't make it. Andrew spoke fast.

"Ryan, I've had seven days of my life stolen from me, and it's going to keep on like this until I either collapse or find a way to stop him. A name just isn't enough. Who is Daniel? Where can I find him?"

"You don't have to find him, you know that. Just sit right here and wait. He'll show up eventually."

"But he makes sure I'm unconscious before that happens. He's got too much control over me to resist him on my own. You have to confront him. You can name your bloody price!"

"You think money would change my mind?"

"What about everything he's done to you? Don't you want to get some payback for the bruises on your face?"

"Well, I suppose there is that..."

"Wait here." Andrew ran to the kitchen, scrabbling down onto all fours. He ran his arm underneath the cupboards, picking up layers of dust and crusted foods. Amongst it, he felt something he remembered losing down there years before – a pencil.

He tore off a piece of the peeling wallpaper and scribbled his address. "The other morning, I woke up at half past six, only I wasn't aware of my surroundings. Daniel was there in the room with me." He walked over and stuffed the note into Ryan's shirt pocket. "All I'm asking you to do is talk to him."

Ryan's eyebrows sank into a frown, then without provocation, he stepped forwards and smashed his fist onto the bridge of Andrew's nose. The shock sent Andrew flailing backwards, and he crashed to the floor.

"Just so the two of us are clear," said Ryan, "I meant what I told you before. Whether you have any control over it or not, if I catch you near my woman again, I swear I'll kill you." He tapped the paper in his pocket. "And thanks for giving me your address."

Ryan turned and marched out through the front door, slamming it behind him. Andrew lay on the floor, dumbstruck, tasting blood on his upper lip. Realising his mistake.

He had just told a complete stranger everything he knew about the kidnapping, including where he lived and when he would be most vulnerable. Andrew pulled himself off the floor and ran to the door.

"Ryan?" He called out as he turned the latch. "Ryan? Come back for a second!"

There was no reply. Andrew stepped outside, but there was only silence.

And tiredness.

Now the game was over, Daniel was putting him under again. In a blind panic, Andrew stole back to the kitchen and tore another piece of paper off the wall, hastily writing a second note, an attempt to use reason.

Daniel,
I found the man you left for me and let him go. You can't hope to control me all the time, so if there's something you want then just tell me what it is. We need to talk.

Before he had a chance to finish, a swell of dark erupted from the base of his neck and flung him to the floor, without warning or remorse. He was out cold before his head struck the ground, pencil still in hand.

Abruptly, that was the end of the night. There were no dreams that followed, no state of suspended awareness. Nothing but black.

Like the flicker of a light switch, the sounds around him changed. The temperature of the air on his face was suddenly cooler. Andrew stirred, disorientated, and felt his muscles sigh as he tried to breathe life back into them.

Thin crusts of sleep fused his eyelids together, locking him in denial of the world outside, adrift on an ocean of empty thought. He came to realise he wasn't lying down, instead sat upright, head lolled to one side.

Even before he opened his eyes, he realised something else was profoundly different.

It was daytime.

7|PPRESSION

For the first time in a week, the kiss of sunshine fell across Andrew's sleeping face. He allowed his eyes to slowly drift open and saw vivid colours, smelled freshly cut grass.

He was in his car, unbuckled in the passenger seat. Andrew raised his head and looked through the window to see a playground, greens and browns against a sky marred only by a thin layer of clouds.

Birds and insects teemed in the good weather. He could see a gentle wind blow across a vast lawn, and adults sat on benches while their children played on climbing frames.

He drew in crisp, clean air and let it drain slowly from his lungs. After his imprisonment, it felt like paradise. A complete change of setting.

But why?

The rear-view mirror was twisted upwards, as though knocked aside in a hurry. Through the sunroof, he could see the branches of a weeping willow arch down and drape themselves over the car, keeping him in cool shadow.

Something brushed against his hand, and Andrew looked down to see the sharp corners of a photograph, caught between his legs where it had apparently slipped from his fingers.

He could only see the back – an inscription, written in tight, uniform handwriting.

Me, Dad and Isabel, March 4th

Andrew reached for it, but in doing so, his arm touched something cold. A sharp jolt ran through his leg and he looked down with horror.

There was a needle sticking out of his thigh.

Yellow-tinted liquid shimmered inside. Adrenaline. He glanced across the park. Someone must have been trying to inject him with the drug, someone brave enough to do it broad daylight.

Daniel, the man Ryan had told him about.

However, less than half of its contents were in his system, and it wasn't enough to bring him back around. Andrew tried to pull the needle out of his leg, but his arm refused to lift.

Abruptly, the drugs started to wear off. His head bobbed as he fought weariness, eyelids gaining weight. He tried to push down the plunger – to inject the rest himself – but instead, his hand just slumped lifelessly across his lap.

There was only one thing he had strength left for. Andrew caught the edge of the photograph with his fingertips and peeled it over, catching a brief but lasting glimpse of the inverted picture.

It was a family of three. An elderly man stood beside a couple in their mid-twenties. The girl was striking, with long, blonde hair and a smile with rows of perfect teeth.

The man she linked arms with was short, with a pale complexion. Although there was life in his blue eyes, it was somehow diminished. Like a man feigning happiness. *Green t-shirt, silver watch, blue jeans.*

Tiredness overpowered him. Colours dulled, and Andrew drifted off with the picture embedded in his mind. Barely a minute after coming around, he drifted right back out of consciousness.

***

When Andrew reawakened, it was sunset. This time, it happened more gradually, the listless feeling folding away and replaced by a debilitating headache.

He was in a different car – a Range Rover with dark leather upholstery, sat behind the steering wheel. A taut seatbelt dug into his neck and his legs were resting off the pedals.

As though he had been placed there like a puppet.

It was late, but not yet dark. The curvature of the sun was still visible on the horizon, the sky bathed in purples and reds. He could see the first stars emerging – nine o'clock at the latest. The world might still be awake, if only he was close enough to be a part of it.

Andrew was parked in the middle of the countryside. A patchy hedgerow gave way to a tree-covered valley that stretched into the distance. He could see for miles in all directions, empty fields and quiet houses.

Winding down the window, he put his head outside and listening to rustling vegetation, refusing to believe he was alone. Daniel would be out there, not too far away. Andrew doubted he would leave him alone.

He checked his thigh. The muscle felt like it had been used as a pincushion for days. He lifted his leg to find crusted mud around the hem of his trousers, and something rattled as his knee brushed against it – a key ring, still dangling from the ignition.

Hesitantly, Andrew reached down and turned it.

The engine sprang to life.

With trembling wonder, he put the car in gear and moved off, amazed when it responded without complaint. Andrew rolled away from the hedgerow and onto the road, unable to believe his luck. *Was this intended?*

Seizing the chance to gain distance from his problems, he pushed the pedal to the floor and accelerated down the hill. The lane felt narrow in the lowlight, growing darker by the second, but the sense of freedom was nonetheless exhilarating. The feeling of control.

He stretched his face muscles to soothe a growing discomfort, and felt new pains. Yet more wounds. He flipped on the inside light and examined himself in the mirror. Scratches across his cheek, deep and scarlet. Torn skin.

He leaned in for a closer look, when something caught his eye.

There was a body on the back seat.

Andrew slammed on the brakes and slid to a halt in the middle of the road. Immediately, he leaped out of the vehicle and wrenched open the back door. He could see a dark figure slumped across the seat, dark clothes absorbing the light that shone inside.

Without giving himself the time to think, he scrambled over the body to get a good look at their face, and by the time he saw who it was, he was right on top of them. Too late to prepare himself.

It was Ryan.

The man he had untied the night before, lying prone and lifeless in the back of the car. There were bruises on his jaw and neck, black and yellow in the light. Strangled.

Andrew tilted Ryan's head back to clear his airways, but it just flopped lifelessly back down again. His skin was cold and grey. There was no point looking for a pulse.

Andrew felt a wave of nausea and struggled back out of the car. In the darkness of the silent road, he staggered across the tarmac, trying to distance himself from the body. Cramps in his stomach forced him to double over and he gulped air, trying to hold down vomit.

In his mind's eye, it had only been minutes since he picked through the binds that held Ryan prisoner. Andrew's legs took on a life of their own, and before he knew what he was doing, he had started off down the road away from the vehicle.

Anywhere.

The tarmac seemed to shimmer as the moon rose in the sky. He could make it across the valley before morning. Perhaps he could find a better hiding place along the way, a house with people in it. Someone who could protect him.

Even in the open, Andrew couldn't shake the feeling of having no control, and his position in that dark scheme was becoming all too clear. If he didn't get rid of the corpse, he only had one role left to play out.

Andrew would be there to take the blame.

He stopped for a moment, standing still in the calm of the countryside. There could be evidence all over his flat linking him to Ryan by now, clear motivation for everyone to latch onto. *And Andrew was dating his wife. No one would care about anything else.*

The darkness played canvas to a cold barrage of grim logic. He couldn't leave the body in the car or it would be discovered. He had to buy himself more time.

For revenge.

Andrew turned back and started up the road, heartbeat growing louder with every step. Even if he just moved the car into a field, it might gain him a few more hours. He talked to himself as he set a fast pace.

It'll be fine. It'll be fine. It'll be fine.

The silence as he approached was deafening. The back door of the car hung open, the light inside like a beacon in the still night. Andrew crept towards it, afraid the body would be disturbed, terrified Ryan might suddenly spring back to life.

He laid his hand on the roof, touching cold metal. Shivering and petrified, Andrew eased himself into the driver's seat, trying not to look behind him. Whether it had been his hands around Ryan's neck or not, he was responsible for this.

As the voice in his sleep had told him last night, *everything he did had a consequence.*

He gripped the steering wheel. Andrew's fingerprints were all over that car, all over the corpse. Bloodshot eyes looked back in the mirror and held his gaze. There was only one thing for it.

With a powerful growl, the engine started. He turned on the headlights and moved slowly down the hillside, heading for the woods. It was going to take a miracle to dispose of the body without being seen, and time was against him.

At the bottom of the valley, the road narrowed and turned sharply as it followed the banks of a lake. Trees stood between him and the water's edge, three-deep, forming a wall through which he caught fleeting glances of the shimmering surface.

It beckoned him from the corner of his eye, offering a murky solution. The road veered away into dense woodland, soaking up the headlights – almost like driving through a cave – before it came right back to the waterside. Secluded from the outside world.

This was where it had to happen.

Andrew pulled over and stopped the engine, killing the lights. He sat in darkness and clasped his hands together, trying to summon the courage to move. *There was no other way.*

A rush of air came into the car as he opened the door. His terrified reflection in the window amplified the claustrophobia, the deafening crunch of gravel beneath his shoes. His galloping, stumbling heart.

Coaching himself through every second, Andrew felt his way to the rough plastic handle of the back door. This was his last chance to run. *Turn away,* screamed the voice in his head. *Don't give Daniel what he wants.*

Rustling branches applauded his staying power, giving him the strength to open his eyes. There in front of him, like an exhibit in a museum, was Ryan's corpse, laid passively across the upholstery. Cold and undeniable.

Murdered.

Andrew recognised the shirt he was wearing, his broad shoulders and fair hair. Ryan lay on his back, one arm trailing beneath the front seat. His skin was drained of colour and the flesh around his neck was badly bruised.

Andrew swallowed hard and tried to keep calm. He swung the door open and put a hand on Ryan's leg, seizing cold ankles and pulling them towards him. The body was astoundingly heavy, a relentless weight that refused to budge, but determination quelled Andrew's fatigue.

With a burst of effort, he slid Ryan towards him, clothes squeaking along the leather. Andrew wrapped his arms around the body's waist and tried not to look it in the eye, his bruised sockets wide open with trembling fear.

It'll be fine. It'll be fine. It'll be fine.

Though every inch of him resisted, Andrew leaned over the body and tried to lift it. Ryan came halfway to his shoulder, but was just too heavy, and he slumped out of the vehicle, thudding down hard onto the ground below.

There was nothing else for it. Andrew took Ryan's wrists instead, and fuelled by dread, pulled him backwards. *Dragging him across the undergrowth.*

With no stiffness in his joints, Ryan's body stretched unnaturally, scraping over branches and gravel. It made a loud shifting sound as he backed between the tree trunks, a noise that warned with each haul just how much mess Andrew was making.

Shhhhhhhhh! Shhhhhhhhh! Shhhhhhhhh!

He dreaded the thought of a car coming around the corner and felt the tree trunks close in around him, swallowing him up. *Had Ryan confronted Daniel like he asked, and was this his reward?*

Andrew emerged by the lake, hidden from the roadside. The surface gleamed like crude oil and the moon hovered high in the sky, shining unopposed on the forest and the murky waters.

He let the body slip through his fingers and come to rest. In the daytime, it would have been a beautiful setting, but the fallen night made it foreboding. Lonely.

He could make out Ryan's pale face, mouth hanging open. An effigy of terror. He saw black eyes cast judgement and a black mouth scream for help. Andrew's conscience was reflected from that vacant vessel, gnawing at the pit of his stomach.

His feet resisted as he looked down the bank. They knew what had to happen next. A gentle slope ran four meters to the water's edge, where it suddenly plummeted into reeds and lapping water. The ground was hardened by the hot spell and his shoes left no impression. He was thankful for at least a little luck.

Stopping down, Andrew grabbed the sleeve of Ryan's shirt and heaved with all the strength he had left. The body lurched forwards, sliding across the grass much easier than the forest bed. With a few strong pulls, he managed to get down to the water.

When he heard a sound from across the lake.

Andrew ducked as he scoured the shoreline. Flickers of light emerged from the darkness, reflections on glossy clothing. There were people on the far bank, perhaps a hundred meters away. He could hear them talking.

Andrew knelt beside the body. The distant ground flickered, a pair of flashlight beams pointing at the ground. He couldn't tell which way they were heading, but sounds were carrying far in the calm. The slightest noise could alert them.

And there was no time left to waste.

He reached down for Ryan's shoulders and unwittingly placed a hand on his neck. On contact with his skin, something happened. The icy temperature sent a shudder up his arm like a bolt of electricity, and it triggered something in his head.

A barrier broke down, bursting like a dam. Memories came flooding in from nowhere, things he had done during the day. Things that occurred when he hadn't been in control.

Andrew's feet went from under him, bringing him down onto the grass. He saw an image of Ryan, alive and well, his face smiling down as Andrew lay on a pavement in broad daylight. A memory of something he hadn't done.

Or didn't remember doing.

Then Andrew's hands were around Ryan's throat. He was kneeling on the passenger seat of the Range Rover, bearing down on Ryan as he sat behind the wheel. Andrew could see his own fingers choking the life out of him.

Daniel had turned Andrew into a murderer.

The shock was unbearable. Andrew scrambled away from the corpse, overcome with revulsion, denial, and horror. Cheryl's husband was dead and it was all his fault. There was no escaping what he had done.

Daniel had to pay, and for a chance at retribution, the body needed to be hidden. Andrew jumped up and dragged it down the slope with renewed vigour. In one furious strain, he rolled Ryan's corpse across the ground until it toppled over the edge.

Ryan slipped silently among the reeds.

And there he stayed.

The shallow water wasn't deep enough for the body to sink. Instead, it just stopped, half-submerged as the vegetation curled around it. Andrew knelt down and tried to push it in, but Ryan was too heavy to move, and much too obvious to leave.

Icy liquid poured into Andrew's shoe. He hovered at the edge of the lake, struggling to renew his grip, and reluctantly stepped in. His heel was sucked down into sticky mud, holding fast.

The cold sent his heart into frenzy. Taking hold of Ryan's sodden shoulders, Andrew tried to heave him into deeper waters. Ryan seemed to pivot on his submerged elbow and rolled onto his front, head bobbing under the surface.

Andrew crouched, feeling his foot sinking ever deeper. Around the lakeside, the people were still on the move, and he watched as both flashlight beams swayed to and fro, lighting up the ground before them. They were closing, inadvertently bearing down on that horrible scene.

Andrew took another step into the water, muscles tensing as they dipped into the frosty temperature. The body had to go further, right to the center where it would sink and never be discovered. He put his forearms under the oily surface and flipped it again, watching Ryan come upright with water pouring out of his mouth.

Long, thick, sun-dried reeds bent under his weight. Suddenly, one of them snapped, sending a whip crack into the dark.

Andrew froze.

He ducked against the surface in the nick of time as the two flashlight beams swung towards him. He closed his eyes and played dead, hiding his face, trying to pretend he wasn't there. Ryan's body bobbed on the surface and he tried to keep it steady, shivering uncontrollably.

From the lakeshore came brief chatter – discussion – then the lights moved away, retreating. Andrew breathed a short-lived sigh before he realised the people were heading towards him with renewed enthusiasm. *Coming over to investigate.*

There wasn't time to think. Andrew picked himself up and waded back to the water's edge, stumbling onto the bank. If he was going to see tomorrow then he needed to get the hell out of there.

Shivering and terrified, he staggered back into the woods, water pouring off his clothes. Ryan's body lingered on the surface, but Andrew had to leave right away or be caught with it.

He stumbled into the trees and strode awkwardly back to the car. The ground beneath his heavy feet kept tripping him up, and he grabbed hold of branches to keep from careering headlong to the ground.

The light from inside the Range Rover still shone like a beacon. Andrew hurried over and wrenched the door open, climbing inside as icy breath misted up the windows. He started the engine and swallowed hard, pushing back tears, praying silently not to be discovered.

With a sick feeling in his gut and a heavy heart, he eased off down the road. Trees closed in on all sides as he left the lake, moonlight swallowed by the canopy above. For an agonising mile, he crawled in isolation, desperate to know if the body would be found. *Or would it last until morning?*

He came across a muddy track by the side of the road and lost his nerve, turning down it. Potholes worried the suspension as he rocked from side to side, edging ever deeper into the claustrophobic woodland.

Andrew wanted to hide. *From everything.* After a hundred yards, the track opened out into a tight clearing, no more than a few cars wide. Secluded.

He pulled over and parked, turning off the engine and leaping out. He chose a direction – *any direction* – heading blindly into the woods. He didn't care where he was going, only that he was leaving it all behind. Sodden legs picked up dirt and leaves, rustling as he hurried stiffly between the tree trunks.

Andrew wanted never to be found, and the dark seemed to heighten his guilt. His mind was filled with images of Ryan's body tangled in the reeds, and of Andrew's hands around his neck.

Where would it end? Would he wake up tomorrow to find he had murdered Cheryl as well?

The forest was impenetrably black at its heart, no trace of light, not even from the stars. He decided to keep going for as long as he was awake. This was his last chance to disappear, and if he could lose himself in the forest, then maybe – just maybe – he could finally be released.

Andrew felt helpless, like he had failed to carry out Daniel's task, and failed to do right by a man who had done no wrong. He pressed further, deeper, somewhere he would never be found.

Because, if he didn't manage to escape this time, Andrew might as well be dead himself.

8|ERCEPTION

Summer used to be a happy time.

Long before Andrew first heard Daniel's name, his life was already in ruins. From the moment he pulled out of that parking space at the seafront, he condemned both his livelihood and his marriage.

His death at the scene was just the beginning of his hardships.

A string of operations on his lower back saw Andrew's dreams of a fresh start cruelly dashed. He spent weeks in hospital, lying helplessly on his front, watching summer contrive through the windows. Confined to the ward.

Katie had to return home for work, and she could only get to the hospital on weekends. By the time he was well enough to leave, a gulf had opened up between them which they would never bridge. Married strangers.

Andrew spent most of his time in a wheelchair, incapable of doing the most simple of things by himself. He needed help to reach into cupboards, or to make it down the short step at the front of the house.

Few people thought he would ever walk again, and he grew to hate his lack of independence. Andrew spent most of his time trapped indoors, too proud to ask for help to leave.

Katie cooked and cleaned for him, but she could never lift his spirits, and eventually, she stopped trying altogether. As he came to live in the lounge, she stayed upstairs where she knew he couldn't follow.

Andrew stopped sleeping, no exercise to tire him out. Two or three hours of broken rest were all he managed at a time, and whenever he drifted off, he woke soon after in a cold sweat from puzzling nightmares.

It slowly changed him as a person.

In the end, money was the final nail in the coffin. Andrew had been off sick for so long that his income had dried up. Katie struggled to make ends meet on her own, plunging bad debts into a worse state than ever. By the time he could stand – and by a miracle, walk again – there was nothing left.

There was no more talk of a holiday. Even when Andrew returned to work and things slowly improved, they were trapped in their new routine. A muted Christmas saw him rejoin her in the bedroom, but it didn't last for long. Within a few weeks, he moved into the spare room, and their fate was sealed.

Neither would forget the day they separated – February 14th, a Saturday.

Valentine's Day.

After a day avoiding the house, Andrew came back to find Katie in the kitchen by the microwave, waiting impatiently for her food to defrost. It was almost like catching her in the act, rushing to get it done before he arrived.

It was written all over her face, and he took offence to the frosty welcome. "Don't say hello if you don't want to," he said with sarcasm.

"I'm sorry," said Katie, amazed at having to speak. "I've got a lot on my mind today."

The microwave buzzed in the background as Andrew rooted through the fridge. "In that case," he said. "I'll try to be quick so I don't spoil your concentration."

"Maybe you should be asking me what the problem is, instead of taking everything so personally," said Katie. "I say something that's supposed to trigger a conversation and you just make stupid comments."

Andrew closed the fridge and looked right at her, something he wasn't used to doing. "Saying there's a lot on your mind isn't a conversation starter. What happened to just telling me we need to talk?"

"If that's what it takes to get out of this mess, then alright: We *do* need to talk."

The microwave pinged, but she ignored it. Andrew pulled a chair out from the table and sat down, waiting while she joined him. She went straight to the point. "You make me feel like a stranger in my own house."

"That's only because you isolate yourself in the bedroom," he said, ready to counter. "I'm only downstairs watching television, and you're welcome to join me any time you want."

"You're so passive," said Katie. "Every night you come in from work, sit down on the couch, and that's where you stay. When we accidentally cross paths, the first words out of your mouth are never simple things like *'Hello'* or *'How are you?'* They're jibes and putdowns. You don't seem to care whether I'm in the house or not."

"That's not fair," he said. "I'm the one who's been confined to it! You walked away from that crash with hardly a mark on you, but my life was turned inside out. Would it have been so hard to support me through that?"

"I did, Andrew, in more ways than you seem to realise. I've held myself together. I haven't complained once about the debt or the distance between us. Even sitting with you now, it's like you're a completely different person!"

"It's been hard, Katie. Something like this would change anyone."

"But that's not it. It's like something fundamental just isn't the same. I used to think you were bottling up your feelings, but it's gone beyond that. It's like you're dead inside."

"How could you say that when you've hardly seen me?"

"Look at everything that's happened to you, Andrew. You almost lost your life, you've almost lost your marriage, and here you are just sitting about like it's going to somehow wash right over you."

"They said it would take time-..."

"Yes, but you don't communicate anymore," said Katie. "It used to drive you insane if we stopped talking, even for a few hours, but now you don't seem bothered if I talk to you or not. It's like you don't even care."

Andrew sat numbly at the table, freely admitting he couldn't see her perspective. "I've been through a lot and my head is full of it," he said.

"No, there's something else. Even when I catch you in a good mood, you don't seem to have the same sense of humour. You hardly laugh. You haven't said anything nice to me in months. You don't even get angry anymore. *You don't do anything!*"

"I don't know what to say," said Andrew. "It isn't that I'm not still emotional. I just feel... less so."

She took a deep breath, laying her fingertips on the tablecloth. "I'm scared the crash has affected you in ways the doctors didn't pick up on."

"That's just silly," he said. "Look at me, I feel okay."

"Don't you see my point? You feel *'okay'*. Not happy, not sad, giddy or fantastic. Just *'okay'*. Doesn't that bother you? The nights you wake up screaming are the only times I see emotion from you, and even then you don't remember any of it."

"They said it might be tied into the trauma and we shouldn't be worried."

"But of course I'm worried," she said. "If you could only see your face when it happens. I've never seen you so scared."

Andrew couldn't think of anything more to say, so he sat there in silence. Katie could see him close off from the conversation and her eyes glazed over, exactly how she looked when he first entered the room. It reminded him why he was there, and he stood up.

"Where are you going?" she said.

"I'm going to see what we have in to eat. I'm not ignoring you, I'm just hungry."

He opened the fridge and put his head inside. She sighed heavily. "Are we going to make it through this, Andrew?"

"Everything is going to be fine," he said, fingering between vegetables and opened jars of sauce. "I'm more or less back to full strength, and eventually the dreams will settle down. Things like this take time to heal. That's all."

"Some things never heal."

She stood up and retrieved her food from the microwave, a plate of leftovers that he would have killed to have himself. He could feel her eyes on his back.

"You don't say you love me anymore," she said.

Andrew froze, head among the shelves. She didn't need a reply to know what he was thinking. For all the vulnerability she had just shown, he offered nothing but his logic.

Katie left the kitchen, and Andrew heard footsteps thudding up the staircase. *Of course he loved her.* He knew how he felt because he had always felt that way, since long before the car crash. It was engrained in him. Andrew loved his wife.

So why couldn't he bring himself to say it?

***

Andrew's head slumped into his chest and it woke him with a start, suddenly realising he had nodded off. It felt like hours since he sat on the forest floor and resolved to wait for morning.

And still, the sun hadn't come up.

Arms were wrapped around his knees and he held them close, trying in vain to retain some warmth. He could feel the cold forest bed bite through his trousers and shuddered, scrunching his eyes tightly closed.

All he could think of was Ryan – his hands closing around the poor man's throat as he squeezed the life out of him, the grey and lifeless body as he heaved it out of the black car and dragged it down to the lake.

Daniel would be out there in the valley, trying to track Andrew down. *His obliging slave, his unwilling instrument.* It was fear of Daniel that kept him rooted to the spot, the thought that his captor could be out there anywhere, searching for the car he abandoned down the narrow track.

Thick tree tops rustled overhead, the only sound in the quiet valley. The cold saturated both his fabric and his flesh, and eventually Andrew couldn't stand it.

He rocked onto his knees and pulled himself upright, searching for a bearing in the black. Something – *anything* – that stood out from the darkness. He reached out his arms and shuffled forwards until his fingertips met with a hard surface, too smooth to be bark. He ran his fingernails down it.

Plaster from a wall.

Andrew shuddered. He followed it upwards – searching for a way over – and found a ceiling. Something touched his leg and he looked down to a horrifying sight, glaring back at him out of the darkness.

The neon hands of his alarm clock.

It can't be true, he thought. *Please don't let this happen.* He bent down to find a mattress, bed sheets, and a pillow. He felt for the lamp and turned it on.

Andrew was back in the flat.

Soft orange light smothered everything, and he could see it wasn't a trick. Andrew stood in his bedroom, astounded, a prisoner again. Even in the most remote place – somewhere even Andrew couldn't pinpoint – Daniel had got to him.

And how had the setting changed so suddenly?

It really didn't matter where he tried to hide, Daniel found him every time. Andrew cursed his flat, his empty life. Living alone as he did those days, Andrew had no one looking out for him. Daniel couldn't have asked for a more expendable puppet.

He looked down at the damp outfit he had been wearing for days. The sleeves were encrusted with dirt and his trousers still held water. He saw a long, jagged scratch up his arm that kept twitching uncontrollably, and every time it did, he felt the pinch of cold metal on his wrist.

He appeared to be wearing a watch, and not one of his. It had a black face and a silver strap that held it loosely on his wrist. The gold hands didn't seem to be moving. It wasn't even ticking. He glanced at the time and felt a shiver as he read the face.

3:14am.

The same time that had tortured him for so long, frozen on inanimate hands. Deliberately set on his wrist. *A message, but what the hell did it mean?*

On the beside table, he noticed a picture and picked it up. The same photograph he had seen between his legs the day before. An elderly man standing with a young couple in a garden.

The inscription on the back identified them all:

Me, Dad and Isabel, March 4th

This time, he got a closer look. The woman in the center was unfamiliar. *Isabel*, he assumed. The elderly man must have been the father, leaving the man in the green t-shirt as the subject.

Andrew looked closer, noticing a silver watch on the man's wrist. It looked the same as the one he was wearing. *So was this Daniel?*

Just then, he heard a noise and slipped the photograph into his pocket. He circled the room, eyes fixed on the joining of the walls. As he moved towards the corner, the sound grew more distinct before it separated into whispers, faint and muffled.

Scratching, clattering.

A hiss like radio static. In past nights, it had retreated to the lounge when he put the light on, but not that time. Now it was closer, more specific.

He searched for something heavy to break through the wall. Tonight, he needed to know what it was, beyond a shadow of a doubt. But he didn't get far before another sound interrupted.

Knock-knock-knock!

He spun on his hips, frozen between the two sounds. Someone was at the front door. Three rapid, urgent knocks. He crept into the hallway and edged towards the door as a muffled call came from the other side.

"Andrew?" it said. "Andrew, are you there?"

He recognised the voice. "Cheryl? Who sent you?"

There was a pause. "Nobody sent me, Andrew. I just want to talk."

Andrew put his hands on the door and peered through the spyglass. It was Cheryl, alright. She wore a long, dark coat and a cream-coloured top with a plunging neckline. Her face was made up and her hair tied back, clearly trying to impress.

"Can I come in?" she said.

"Not tonight. I just need to be left alone."

"What's going on, Andrew? You've stopped answering when I try to call you. You're hardly ever in when I come over. The only time you make any attempt to contact me is in the middle of the night when you know I can't talk."

"I'm sorry," was all he could say. *How could he tell her what had happened to Ryan?*

"Can you please just let me in?" said Cheryl. "The other day you mentioned some things that really hit home. They've been on my mind ever since."

"I want to talk with you face-to-face," he said, "but I can't. Don't ask me to explain. You can't come into this flat."

"Is it me? Are you having second thoughts?"

"It's not that, Cheryl. I don't know what's happening. I honestly don't." He drew a deep breath. "Listen, I can't guarantee you'll be safe if you come through this door. Please, this isn't goodbye, but I need space until some things are sorted out."

He felt the photograph in his pocket and it gave him an idea. With as few movements as possible – in case he was being watched – he dropped it on the floor, then with the toe of his shoe, slid it under the door.

Cheryl saw it. "What's this?"

He leaned in and whispered through the wood. "Something I need you to look into."

She bent down to pick it up, and he saw her puzzled face through the spyglass. "I don't understand," she said.

"Neither do I, but it's everything I have to go on. I need your help."

"What am I supposed to do with it?"

"That's all I can say."

He backed away from the door, trying to put some distance between them. He wasn't going to put her in any more danger. He owed her that much.

She heard the creaking floorboards. "Andrew?"

The only person he cared about stood unloved in the hallway, her husband gone, and holding the only piece of evidence that Daniel even existed. But Andrew couldn't guarantee what price he might pay for being more specific.

"...Are you there?" she said.

He bit his lip, standing with eyes closed until she understood. If they were being watched, it was too dangerous to say more, and if she wasn't, then at least he had something to show for it. Footsteps echoed down the hallway, and the next time he dared to look, she was gone.

"Don't think for a second that I won't put a stop to this."

Andrew turned. A man's voice rang out of the bedroom, and someone had turned out the light.

"Is that Daniel?" said Andrew.

Garbled chatter crackled from the darkness, a hiss like radio static. One voice rose above it.

"Yes, it's me. I'm not sure what you're doing, but I hope you realise it won't make any difference to the outcome."

There was a whining every time he spoke, a high pitched whistle that undercut each word. It was literally unpleasant to hear him speak.

Andrew stepped up to the doorway and saw something in the corner of the room, a shapeless mass in the shadows. "All I'm trying to do is get my life back," he said. "I don't even think I know you. Why are you holding me here?"

Daniel laughed, and the whistling went straight to Andrew's temples. *"Don't pretend you're not guilty,"* he said. *"You're a murderer!"*

"Ryan's blood is on your hands, not mine."

"But it's all your fault, Andrew, whether you see it or not. Take my word for it – you've ruined too many lives to play innocent."

"Tell me what I'm supposed to have done, and give me a chance to fix it."

Andrew's legs quivered. He could hear upset in his own voice and it made him feel vulnerable. The mass in the shadows trembled with anger.

"It's too late for that," it said. *"Neither of us can go back and change it. We have to live with what you did."*

"And now Cheryl has to live without a husband, and a man is dead."

"You made you own bed when you started seeing a married woman," said Daniel. *"If something's happened to Cheryl's husband, then it's all on you."*

"Oh no, I may have dragged the body, but I wasn't the one who strangled him. I refuse to believe that." Andrew shouted. "You set me up."

There was a brief silence. *"Wait a second,"* said Daniel. *"Are you saying you think Ryan is married to Cheryl?"*

Andrew stopped dead in his tracks, frozen in the doorway. He had carried the body in his arms, felt the coldness and the weight.

"You mean he isn't?"

There was a calculating pause. *"You really haven't worked it out yet, have you?"*

Daniel seemed to revel in his anguish, watching him deteriorate ever closer to madness. But Andrew had taken all that he could stand. He made a dash for the light switch, and all at once, the room was flooded in stark, bare light. Instantly, it fell silent.

There was nothing there.

Andrew peered around an empty room. "Where have you gone?" he said.

"I haven't gone anywhere," came the reply. The voice was next to him, almost close enough to touch. Andrew almost fell over.

"Why won't you come out here and show me who I'm dealing with?" Once again, he scoured the walls for hidden devices. Cameras, speakers. Anything.

"Well, it wouldn't be half as easy as it sounds," said the voice.

"For Christ's sake," Andrew screamed at the walls. "Why won't you face me?"

"Because I can't, Andrew. I'm you."

And everything went black.

9|MASCULATION

Andrew floated in the void, no dreams or haunted memories. No thought or worry.

All he knew was pain.

Deep beneath his forehead lay an ache like tearing muscle, pressing against his eyes and squeezing them out of their sockets. He could feel pressure in his veins, bulging out of his skin and forcing his fingers apart.

He tried to speak. *"What are you doing to me?"*

The words never made it past his lips, but he heard them clearly. The reply was instant – hissing static, the mindless chatter of madness. He tried to turn his head, but taut veins wouldn't let it budge.

"Daniel, what's happening?"

Arteries swelled and blocked his windpipe. Limbs started to prise themselves apart. His head pounded like a fist on a door, hammering a harrowing thought into his skull.

I'm you, it said. *I am you.*

Daniel is you.

His heart beat a single, almost deafening thump, and a surge of pain catapulted him back out of consciousness. Arms sprang loose and he collapsed to the floor, landing heavily on hard tiles. A feverish panic swept him onto his feet and he stood, arms raised in self-defence.

He was in the flat.

Andrew stood alone in the lounge, lit only by the television screen. He was back once again in his prison, back in the dead of night. Daniel had put him under without so much as a wave of his hand, switching him off like a machine.

Andrew listened to the echo of the empty room, and in the flickering light, immediately started to notice things that were out of place. *A blanket on the settee, takeaway wrappers strewn across the coffee table.*

A handful of used syringes were scattered carelessly across the floor, no thought for who might find them. He saw a crusted stain soaked into his rug, clothes discarded in the corner.

After so many nights of pristine cleanliness, it looked like something had gone direly wrong. There were two wine glasses on the table, a red crust of lipstick dried around the edge of one of them. Looking down, Andrew's clothes were unfamiliar – a red-checked shirt covered in creases.

He crept over to the counter and drew a knife out of the rack, beside the empty slot where he had taken one over a week ago. On his wrist, he found that same silver watch with the black face. The time that taunted him at every turn.

3:14am.

If Daniel was a part of him, it explained how Daniel always knew what he was up to, and how to find him.

Flashes of colour danced off the walls as he found the remote and scrolled through the channels, searching for news. As soon as he saw the date, the last threads of Andrew's world were torn to shreds.

The morning of the twenty-third, eleven nights since that nightmare had begun, and two since he had last been awake.

Or had Andrew been wide awake the whole time? He backed away from the television, stumbling on stiff legs, mind racing overtime. Long ago, Katie had called him a changed man. *"The crash has affected you in ways the doctors didn't pick up,"* she said. He hadn't thought for a moment that she could have been right.

He leaned against the kitchen counter and felt like a scavenger, searching for scraps of life. Ryan had said he knew Daniel from years ago, but he could have been bluffing.

What if Daniel was a personality Andrew had come up with to take the blame for truths he couldn't face? Was that why Katie seemed to have disappeared?

Was she dead, too?

He looked down at the knife he clutched to his chest, to see his anguished face reflected in the blade. Anything could have happened in the time he had lost. *A stranger's clothes, a stranger's lifestyle. Everyone* and everything could have been taken away.

Daniel had to be stopped, or that mess would never end. The light from the lamp caught sharp, polished steel, and it gave him a sweeping sense of resolve.

Andrew only had one option remaining – to prevent more bloodshed by spilling his own.

Fingers tensed around the knife handle, and his thumb caught the edge of the blade. The pain was somehow satisfying. It confirmed his control. He turned his back on the room and let his eyes drift happily closed.

Andrew doubted everything that had happened between him and Katie. Had the breakdown really been their fault?

There was no tingling pain in his forehead, no lingering doubt. He revelled in his last act of defiant power, but then something stayed his hand.

He could feel a presence behind him.

An icy cold draught brushed against the hairs on his neck. Andrew turned towards the room, knife held tightly. The blinds on the far wall rippled, and he watched dumbfounded as a figure emerged from the shadows.

Cheryl, or at least it looked like her.

She wore the same green coat he had seen from across the car park a week ago, though it looked almost black in the light from the television. Long, sodden brown hair fell across the porcelain skin of her pretty face.

Now that he could see her close up, there was something different about the woman's appearance. She looked older than Cheryl and her eyes were darker. Despite an uncanny resemblance, it wasn't her.

The woman stopped in the middle of the room, staring transfixed at the knife. He felt suddenly self-conscious and put it down, raising his other hand.

"I won't hurt you," he said. "My name is Andrew. Can I ask who you are?"

She didn't respond. He took a step towards her and could feel the drop in temperature.

"Just take a seat, okay? I'm not going to harm you."

Her eyes flickered to the knife on the counter and back again, afraid he could lunge for it at any moment. Andrew tried to keep her calm by taking another step away.

"You're in my flat," he said. "I don't know how you got here, and I'm sorry if I had something to do with it. My actions aren't my own in the daylight. Tell me your name."

Her face was a meld of silent terror and a studious determination to hide it. "Please," said Andrew. "I want to help you, but I need you to talk to me first."

She shook her head without even attempting to talk. *What could have happened to make her so afraid?*

"Say something!" he yelled. "For God's sake, anything!"

Suddenly, she wasn't there. In less time than he had to blink, she was gone from the room like she had never been there. The temperature rose and he found himself alone.

Something inside him snapped, and before he could stop himself, Andrew heaved the chair right off the floor and hurled it at the window. The blinds shuddered. Behind them, he heard glass crumple and come raining down onto the floor, a cascade of tiny glass bullets that scattered over the laminate.

She was an apparition. There was no other explanation. He had seen her twice now, and both times she had disappeared, leaving no trace of her presence.

The way that she looked at him, as though she were terrified...

It made him wonder what part he may have played in her death.

Andrew looked down at his bare feet and saw tiny pieces of glass hover dangerously close to his toes. A gentle, soothing breeze fluttered the blinds as he backed slowly out of the room, working his way into the hallway. The front door loomed in its menace and he stared at it, intimidated by such a mundane object.

Something about it had provided a link, a means to communicate with his captor. He walked up to the handle and took hold, trying to concentrate, and a blockage burst somewhere in his mind.

There was a blinding white flash as new memories started to pour in. Suddenly, he could see what he had done during the daylight. Eleven lost days revealed themselves to him all at once.

He could see Ryan sipping coffee, then driving the Range Rover, then Andrew's hands around his throat. He could see Cheryl – *the real Cheryl* – sat on the edge of the sofa with a wine glass in hand.

Andrew saw the woman from the photograph, with blonde hair and intensely deep hazel eyes. He had talked to her.

Laughed with her.

Andrew's life no longer belonged to him. He forced himself down a spinning hallway, visions filling him with nausea. Walls writhing, he pulled himself into the bathroom and made a beeline for the toilet.

Everything he was, turned inside out right under his nose.

Unable to hold it back, he emptied a stomach-load of bile into the toilet, disgusted to see chunks of food flood into the bowl. Despite his distress, Andrew had somehow been eating fine for days.

Emptied and frail, he rose and ran the tap, splashing cascades of icy water over his face. He just wanted to feel, to know he was still alive.

He caught sight of his face in the mirror and leaned in, staring at bruises that didn't seem to be healing and a mess of uneven stubble. He barely recognised himself anymore. A stranger's clothes on a stranger's body.

He was ruined, at the end of his tether. Irrevocably changed. In fact, behind the dirt and the scabs, it looked as though it wasn't even Andrew staring back at him.

He could have sworn his very face was starting to change.

END OF NIGHT

PART TWO: DAY 10|ECESSITY

A beam of sunlight poured through the window, slicing the room neatly in half. Particles of dust sparkled as they floated through it, giving the place an almost dreamlike tranquillity.

Daniel Lawton, however, was awake.

He was pinned to the mattress by burgundy bed sheets, tucked in on both sides. It took great effort to fold them back and let his bare chest breathe, but even then, he kept his stomach hidden. Embarrassed by it, even in an empty room.

He tried to savour the unfamiliar surroundings – featureless, pallid walls. Lately, Daniel craved such distraction from his life, to be freed from constant struggle. Even his father – usually an affable man – had turned hostile, dealing stern advice which really hit home.

Stop lying to yourself. Some things can't be fixed.

It helped to be distant, if only for a night. But as the morning haze eroded, he became aware of his itching scalp – stubble coming through – and his problems all resurfaced.

Daniel drew back the covers and sat up. He must have shaved too closely for the job interview, and he would have looked thuggish, head shiny and red. Now, nervous doubts would haunt him every day until he knew if it had blown his chance of a fresh start.

Some weekend.

The watch on his wrist said nine o'clock. With a sigh, Daniel rose onto stiff legs and peered out through the curtains at a bright and sunny morning, daunting for a man who couldn't stand the heat.

Only a rousing hunger – unwelcome and insatiable – had the power to steer him outside, and it quickly seized control. Powerless to resist, he pulled on yesterday's clothes and hurried out of the hotel into hazing sunshine, an incessant glare from a cloudless sky.

Across the road, a concrete promenade yielded to ochre sands and the crashing sea. *As far from his crumbling life as he could get without leaving the country.*

The day was so bright, it almost hurt. A long pier stretched away from the shore, stark white, and crawling with tiny speckles of people. By contrast, every other building on the coastline looked lifeless, dull and weathered. Pale tans and faded terracotta.

Having been raised near the coast, Daniel identified with the scene, soothed by such an uncluttered expanse of undulating water. Blissfully uncomplicated.

Saturday was already in full swing. Road and pavement heaved with a constant stream of rushing traffic. Obeying his growling stomach, Daniel joined in, weaving between pedestrians, feeling the first tingles of sweat beneath his t-shirt. Drawn onwards by the smell of cooking grease.

It led him to a café, set back from the beach, with a chalkboard sign promising *All Day Breakfast.* Daniel ducked down a short flight of steps and through an open door to find a thin room with a dozen wooden tables.

All of them unoccupied.

"Hello?" he called out, clearing his throat. "I'm here for the breakfast."

Almost instantly, a head appeared in the kitchen doorway – a middle-aged woman with silvery hair. "We aren't serving at the minute," she said, with no hint of apology. "I'm afraid you'll have to try somewhere else."

A tiled floor absorbed the daylight and fans on the ceiling did a poor job of circulating the air. The restaurant was heating up fast, fighting a losing battle with the unusual weather.

"If you're not serving," said Daniel, "then why can I smell cooking?"

"Just bad timing. We ran out of food not ten minutes ago."

Daniel looked over his shoulder to see scores of cars streaming past, repulsed by the agitation. "Busier than you were expecting?" he said.

"We should be so lucky," replied the woman. "I'm afraid it's just the opposite. Something knocked off the power in the kitchen. We had to cook all the meat in the hopes of a sale. Such a waste."

She had a pear shaped body with wide hips, ill-befitting of her thin neck and narrow shoulders.

"So would I have been your first customer?" Daniel asked.

"It's not quite that bad," she laughed, "but a waste nonetheless. We could still do you an omelette, if you'd like?"

He shook his head. "Not my idea of a cooked breakfast."

"Well, wouldn't you be better off looking for lunch, anyway?"

"At ten past nine?"

"It's a lot later than that."

She wiped her hands on a cream-coloured apron and nodded to the clock on the wall. *Quarter past twelve.* Daniel checked his watch and realised the hands weren't moving. It had stopped working, letting him sleep right through the morning.

Had he really drunk that much last night?

"It appears you're losing track of time," said the waitress.

"I'm just hungry," said Daniel. "I can smell what you've cooked and it's driving me mad."

"Well, you look as though you've run a marathon, and I hate to disappoint you, but there's nothing like that left until my husband gets back. You'll either have to wait or try your luck somewhere else."

Daniel raised his hand and touched his forehead. She was right – he must have been glistening with sweat. He leaned against one of the wicker chairs. "Perhaps I ought to wait," he said. "Can I order a drink? I feel really thirsty."

"Of course you can. Sit down."

He slid onto the seat while his gut called for alcohol. Luckily, the waitress brought a glass full of shimmering tap water instead, which he emptied in seconds.

"This is supposed to be a change of pace," Daniel said between deep gulps, "and yet here I am, still feeling like a wreck."

"Is it a weekend away *with* the wife and children, or a weekend away *from* them?"

Daniel smiled. *If only.* "Neither. Just to break the routine."

The nametag on her apron said *'Carol'*. She tried to be considerate. "If you don't mind me saying, you really don't look your best. Are you fighting something off?"

He toyed with the glass in his hands, wishing it was full again. "I'm sure a doctor would say I just need rest, but that's a lot easier to say than it is to do."

"You can't put a price on your health."

"Be that as it may, sometimes it's easy to forget."

She noticed a crooked chair at the next table and paused to straighten it. Daniel sat still and tried to gather himself, unable to grasp why something inside was nagging him for a whiskey.

"You know," said Carol, pausing. "Those leftovers are still in the kitchen. They're a little cold, so I can't sell them to you, but between you and me, they're probably still alright. You can have them if you want."

Daniel's stomach tried to answer for him. "Yes please," he said. "That's very kind of you. I'm sure they'll be fine."

She left him sitting in grateful retreat from the bustling crowds, then returned after a short while with two loaded plates. "If this doesn't tide you over," she said, "then I guess there's no helping you!"

Both dishes overflowed with an obscene quantity of food. Heaps of bacon, sausages and black pudding. Four people could have feasted on it, but Daniel had it all to himself.

And he couldn't have been happier.

Unceremoniously, he dug in with a fork and began to shovel the food down his throat, scarcely pausing for breath. Carol had fried some eggs to help balance the plate, which were almost scolding hot, but he ate ravenously, with a voracious appetite.

It was over in minutes. Filled to his absolute limit, Daniel leaned back on the chair and clutched his stomach, barely able to sit straight. He groaned with a mix of contentment and discomfort, which brought the waitress back out of the kitchen.

"How was that?" she said. "You look much better. You'd pass as a normal colour now."

"This was all I needed," said Daniel, though he could feel fresh sweat forming on his brow. "It's so often the way after a night of drinking."

The waitress nodded. "You should take it easy. Why don't you just enjoy the sunshine for a while?"

He stood awkwardly and tested the readiness of his legs. "The sunshine isn't really my kind of thing, but I appreciate the thought. You've been kind to me."

Carol's face creased into a warm smile. "I'm glad to be a help," she said. "Be sure to get that watch of yours fixed. You never know what else you'll miss if you keep running late."

Carrying the extra weight of all that breakfast, Daniel shuffled out of the restaurant. The commotion on the road showed no signs of slowing down, but he didn't feel an urge to join it, content to ignore his life for a little longer.

At a set of lights, he crossed over to the promenade and stole a glance at the beach. There was something about the salty air purging his lungs, more cleansing than a shower would have been. He found the gentle walk helped to settle the food in his stomach, and he ambled aimlessly, savouring each step.

Eventually, though, the heat got to him. Daniel felt a pinch beneath the muscles on his chest – heartburn, inevitable as the exercise tangled with his digestion.

When he came to an empty bench overlooking the sea, he sat down to rest, watching children playing on the sands below. A young couple trudged up stone steps beside him, exchanging banter without thought or malice.

He and Isabel hadn't laughed like that in months.

Restless fingers toyed with his broken watch, hoping it would work again. Roman numerals glinted in the bright sunshine as golden hands spun round and round. She had bought it for him, and it was now a fitting memorial to their relationship.

Broken, irreparable.

His body felt just as bad. Daniel could feel it punishing him for weeks of neglect. He was clammy and hot, his body stealing energy from the sun and turning it against him, forcing him back off the bench in search of shade.

The mounting traffic on the road had worsened – angrier, grumbling engines and blaring horns. He could see it curl into the distance, reaching around the coastline. Daniel felt a lump in his throat and a sudden, debilitating claustrophobia. Trapped, no way out without a long and bitter struggle.

He doubled back towards the hotel, finding it increasingly difficult to walk straight. The sun on his back stung his neck as it started to burn, and he bunched his hands into fists, struggling to keep calm. Needing more than anything to be far away from there.

Just then, a car engine roared above the chaos. *Another troubled voice.* Down the line of traffic, someone was trying to force their way out of a parking space. Not gently, nor politely. Their silver hatchback snarled and cursed, the driver boiling with rage.

As desperate as Daniel was.

Distracted, Daniel stopped walking, and double yellow lines by the curb afforded a clear view of what happened next.

A break appeared in the traffic – no more than four vehicles long – and the driver tried to fill it. He shot out of his parking spot, tyres screeching, trying to match the speed of the others. But at that moment, the same traffic slowed, and the driver was too focussed to realise.

He lost control. Daniel could see him grab the steering wheel and twist it around, narrowly avoiding the cars in front, veering over the road and thundering towards the pavement.

Right at Daniel.

Daniel's legs froze, rooted to the spot. He could see a woman in the passenger seat, staring into his eyes, their terrors locked together as the gap between them vanished.

Tyres struck the steep curb, and the ground shuddered as the force of the impact knocked the wheels sideways, pushing the vehicle in a new direction. It slid across concrete paving, missing Daniel by inches. *So close that he could have touched it.*

The rush of air pushed him backwards, and he lost his footing, landing hard on one knee. Behind him, he felt the ground heave as the car ploughed into a lamppost, but Daniel couldn't turn to see it.

He had problems of his own.

Suddenly stripped of breath, a pain shot up his jaw, locking it closed. Daniel panicked, rooted to the spot, feeling as though his ribcage was folding in on itself. Something tore up his left arm to the center of his chest and forked like a bolt of lightning, making every last muscle seize up.

He could tell he was biting his tongue, but couldn't feel it, and couldn't stop it. He tried to scream through barred teeth, clutching at his chest as though he could squeeze life back into it. Lungs cried for air as tears poured down his face, stretched beyond his limits.

Daniel collapsed, unable to maintain a resistance. *Losing the struggle.* As the skin of his cheek came to rest on worn concrete, his eyes drifted into the distance, coming to focus on a woman standing a hundred yards away.

She was watching him.

Suddenly, she was all he could see – a long, green coat that sank down to her knees, sodden brown hair across a pale face. She looked on from a safe distance, an observer. *Like she didn't even care that he was dying.*

Daniel tried to reach out for her – *to hold on to life* – but he had no strength to fight with. Instead, his arm collapsed uselessly on the pavement and he caught a last, long glimpse of the watch on his wrist, golden hands frozen where he had been playing with them before.

3:14am.

And that was his last memory.

11|VISCERATION

Daniel felt a strange sensation, one he had never known before – an unnerving detachment, easy to pretend he wasn't lying with his face against the concrete, dragged to the ground in broad daylight.

Letting out his final breath.

Surrounding noises grew muffled – the screech of braking traffic and the gasps of a halted crowd. Even the sunlight seemed to ease off, releasing him from insufferable warmth, despite a cloudless sky above him.

From a distance, the woman in the green coat watched him slip away, and with the carnage of the car crash only a few meters behind him, they must have been the only two people who knew what was happening.

Colours dimmed and then everything faded – concrete, seafront, sun and sky. Daniel found himself adrift in an empty space, freed from the shackles of reality.

Floating in nothingness.

He could still hear the waitress' crackly voice. *You can't put a price on your health.* In the endless black, he pursed his lips to speak, but any sound he made was swallowed by an overwhelming silence.

Then, stripped of the outside world, every sense went suddenly haywire. Daniel was bathed in light from all directions. Static in his ears took him to the edge of tolerance and his skin tingled, as though he had been cast onto a bed of nails.

Yet none of it hurt.

Sound and feeling came together and the colours – the sensations – took the form of distant memories, unlocking experiences he had long forgotten. Daniel returned to the world, not just remembering, but *reliving* his life from start to finish, and somehow all at once.

He saw his childhood – the countryside where he was raised. He saw his adult home, with Isabel inside it. He was a toddler, a teenager and everything between, all at the exact same moment, like his brain was releasing everything it had stored away and pouring it into the darkness.

The final cry of his dying mind.

He could smell Isabel's perfume among countless other scents. Morning heather, sweat, and grease. He felt his hand brush against the soft cheek of a lover, sand running through his fingers, warm water down his arms. All at once, yet none of it mixed together.

Each experience was cleansed from his body, and as it went, he could almost feel the hole it left behind, the void that grew inside him. The first real burst of panic made him try to snatch them all back – to keep something of his identity intact while the rest was flooding out.

Focus, he told himself. *Don't forget who you are.*

Then it was over. The last of his memories vanished. He looked down at short, stubby hands, trying to concentrate on each tiny muscle. He couldn't move any of them. He tried to breathe, but there was no air. Seemingly, no need for it.

Daniel parted from his body. Slowly and silently, he became aware of himself from the outside, floating in the midst, arms suspended and useless.

He embraced the release, free for the first time. No muscles to weigh him down, no emotions to bear, just peace, and he found he wanted to become part of the nothingness. A quiet world without light or sound.

Daniel watched his body drift away and thought a last goodbye to his failed heart and his swollen gut, to his sunburned skin and the hands he had used for thirty-one years. But just as he found his peace, an object appeared in the distance.

Something was out there with him.

Daniel could see it clearly in the crisp vacuum. *Another body drifting helplessly.* The serenity faded as it drew closer, and Daniel became aware of gravity pulling him in.

Without being able to resist or brace himself, they collided. The ghostly shroud of dark was peeled away and he was stunned by another burst of blinding light. It wasn't a bit like the first. This time, it hurt.

A second barrage of sensations struck. Heat, cold, happiness, waves of tiredness and spurts of energy. His old memories returned – pulled in at the same time he was – and fresh ones came cascading through the chaos.

He was in a car one second, then a waiting room the next. The sudden movement made him nauseous, flickers of light and dark, the cycle of day and night. It left him dazed and shaken.

Terrified.

Then the moments stretched out progressively. He was in each place for almost a second, then two or three seconds. He felt pain in his lower back, saw a lounge and a kitchen in endless repetition, meals served up in front of the television.

Daniel was afraid the sheer pace would catapult him into something, hurtling uncontrolled through a life he didn't recognise. He tried to shout, a stifled sound that bled out feebly.

And the next thing he knew, he was awake again.

***

Daniel sat bolt upright, screaming his head off. He was back in darkness, but he could feel a soft mattress and realised he was in bed, warm and comfortable, finally at rest.

And he was still alive.

He gripped his chest, feeling traces of the pain he thought had killed him, reaching out with his other arm to discover a bedside table, with the face of an alarm clock looking back at him.

3:14am.

The same time he had seen on his broken watch. The last thing he saw before he passed away.

Daniel turned on the bedside light and it stung his eyes, pain as though he hadn't used them in days. His vision was blurry, eyelids crusted with sleep, but Daniel could tell he was in a large bedroom with magnolia walls and a red carpet. The curtains were a shade of copper.

He had no idea where he was.

Something touched his arm and he almost jumped out of his skin when he realised he wasn't alone. A slender woman sat up beside him in the bed, tired eyes like puffy slits. She was fair skinned, with jet black hair and a look of concern.

"Are you alright?" she said. "What's wrong?"

A wave of shock coursed through his veins. He had never seen her before, but there was recognition in her eyes.

"Was it another bad dream?" the woman asked. She was pretty, a striking face that he would have remembered. Daniel's lip trembled as he cradled his face, feeling sweat beading on his forehead.

Then he froze.

Daniel lowered his hands and stared at the fingers – long and thin, a pale shade of brown. He clambered out of bed and stumbled around the room, disorientated and sick. They looked and felt perfectly normal, *but they weren't his hands.*

The woman drew back the covers as Daniel saw a door and bolted towards it. He staggered onto the landing and into a bathroom, rushing in with awkward steps, coming right up to the mirror.

A stranger's face was looking back.

He quivered. It was the reflection of a man a few years younger than himself, with short, brown hair and naturally dark skin. Daniel looked deep into those reflected eyes, heart racing. They were unfamiliar.

The woman appeared at the door and rushed to his side, so quickly that it startled him. He swallowed his stomach and tried to steady shaking hands.

"Are you alright?" she said with soft and deliberate words. "Please say something."

Daniel turned, her face blurred to his vision. "What the hell is going on?"

His voice was deep and croaky. He looked into her eyes and saw fear, an expression that intensified when she saw his own. There was something about it. Something he recognised.

"Andrew," she said. "You're scaring me."

He turned back to the mirror and raised his hands to his face, touching thick skin and morning shadow.

Who the hell was Andrew?

She took his arm and squeezed it gently, trying to calm him down, but as she did, a sudden wave of tiredness washed over him – an unnatural feeling, more like an attack.

Daniel's legs gave way and he fell forwards, colliding with the glass. His wide-open eyes were thrown into their reflection, and she gasped as the mirror cracked.

Once more, everything went dark.

***

The next time Daniel became aware of himself, it was daytime. He drifted around in a haze of confusion to find himself alone in a sitting room, spread across a beige fabric settee. His legs were raised and cushions had been piled beneath his head.

This time, he could see properly. Daniel sat up slowly and looked through a large window into the garden behind it, twenty meters deep and fenced in by a thick hedgerow. The lawn was a lush green, sparkling after a spell of rain. Two small trees book-ended an empty flower bed, and their long branches shivered in the wind.

An empty feeling in his chest made him check his pulse – weak and erratic, threatening that the slightest knock could set him off. Through the glass, he could almost smell fresh air, unable to fathom why he was still alive to do it.

Daniel inhaled slowly, holding the air as he counted to ten. Then he looked down and opened his palms. *Dark skin and a criss-cross of wrinkles, much deeper than his own.*

He pressed them together. They felt so real – they *were* real – but he couldn't comprehend what was staring him in the face.

Daniel was suddenly a completely different person.

He pulled himself off the settee and onto the prickle of short carpet, standing delicately. He noticed a mirror above a false fireplace and stared at the reflection. The stranger was taller than him, with hair maybe two inches long and thick across the scalp. They were handsome, with brown eyes and an immovable cloud of stubble across their chin and neck.

Daniel didn't need to wave his hand or touch his face to be sure it was him. He just knew. The man in the reflection had somehow drawn him in, and all of Daniel's wishes to leave his stressful life had come horribly true.

He noticed pictures on the mantel, wedding photos. His host appeared to be the groom, and the bride was the woman he had been in bed with. The one who called him Andrew.

His wife.

Legs felt weak, unable to support his weight. Daniel sank back onto the sofa. *Surely this wasn't possible, no more than an elaborate dream.* He was somehow inside Andrew's head.

And why was he suddenly so tired?

***

Daniel spent days in such turmoil, a prisoner in a life he could neither control nor understand. Disorientation kept him in perpetual panic, rarely still for long enough to catch his bearings.

He often woke up screaming, lying in bed next to the woman with the jet black hair. Then one night, he found himself in a bedroom along the hallway, separated where he wouldn't disturb her.

Estranged with his hysteria.

Whenever he found himself in the living room, Daniel looked out at the garden, and through watching the plant life, he managed to get a handle on the passage of time.

Summer rose and then faded almost instantly. Trees turned brown and shed their leaves, the lawn carpeted in yellows and oranges.

He awoke one afternoon to find the glass steamed up with condensation and frost coating everything outside, turning the grasses white and the hedgerow into a spiny cloud of crystallised branches.

Daniel missed six months in minutes. Winter brought longer nights, and he seemed to have less time in control. He skipped Christmas completely, hurtled through February and March.

A year must have passed before his journey ended. As the world warmed up, he came around on a dry and heavy morning. Right away, he felt a new vigour – less turmoil, more sobriety – and Daniel knew.

This time, he finally had control.

It was another bedroom – somewhere strange, with a pale wooden floor and thick, dark curtains. His vision was blurred, but he could see a clock on the bedside table. A bright green display.

Seven o'clock in the morning.

Daniel felt unusually energised, and he immediately rose to check himself over. He was topless, wearing a loose-fitting pair of pyjama bottoms that hung low around his waist. His stomach was small and tight, a far cry from the bulge he was used to hiding.

On the table, Daniel found a pair of glasses and put them on. Everything came into brilliant focus. *Every crack on the wall, every scratch in the woodwork.*

It took him a moment to adjust, walking down a long, narrow hallway to a minimalist lounge. It all looked somehow familiar, though he had no memory of ever having been there before.

A shiny, dark leather sofa stood on a cardinal red rug over a tiled floor. Kitchen cupboards ran down the nearside wall. There was an emptiness to it, an echo that made the room feel hollow, anything but homely.

There were no pictures anywhere, nor any sign of his supposed wife. Instead, Daniel saw a large window with a grand vista of the city centre. He was several storeys up, staring at a large car park, coloured vehicles in place of petals. Not a tree in sight.

It gave him a restless urge to take his first breath of the outdoors. Excited, Daniel threw on a t-shirt and some shoes, then with a mixture of awe and bewilderment, stumbled out of the building into summer sunshine. Warming rays beat down, but it didn't feel uncomfortable. Andrew's body seemed to like the heat.

He staggered down the pavement, getting used to all the physical differences. Legs were longer than his own, and although a kind of instinct told him how to move, Daniel kept missing beats in his stride, wrestling with his own reflexes.

There were people everywhere. The city centre was densely packed, high rises casting shadows over busy roads. He tried to distance himself from a growing bustle, reminded too much of the seafront.

Which, to Daniel, only felt like an hour ago.

He stayed close to the walls and doors, locked so early in the day. Daniel saw excruciating detail through eyes he wasn't used to, trying to savour each sensation – the glasses pressing down on the bridge of his nose, the sunlight on his face.

Innocent laughter drew him to a schoolyard, and he watched parents wave their children off at the gates. Daniel never had the chance to start a family, but had always wanted to.

An altogether different set of emotions swept over him. He thought of the people he had left behind, the people he cared about. *Isabel and his father.* Daniel had died miles from both of them, embroiled in petty arguments which had seemed so important at the time, but pointless now.

It left a bitter aftertaste to his bygone existence, something he just couldn't leave as it was. Daniel had a chance to set things straight, to pick up where he left off, perhaps even make a fresh start.

He carried on walking, but within a few yards, a strange fatigue spread through his legs, something like pins and needles. Daniel realised he had used up all the energy he had, pushing too hard to adjust in a single day.

His body still needed rest, and lots of it. This was all too soon. He had to to muster more strength before he could face his loved ones, and he never should have strayed so far from the bedside.

Daniel cursed out loud and turned, retracing his steps through the city. All the way, he was dogged by rousing tiredness and a swathe of detachment, growing more weary with each precarious step.

He returned to the flat and let himself inside, lacking the coordination to close the door behind him. Staggering into the bedroom, he peeled off his t-shirt before collapsing back onto the mattress.

He felt lousy. Limbs gathered mass, pinning him over the covers. He knew he would sleep for hours, but for once, he understood it was important.

To stand any chance of a future, he needed to build on the strength he had gained, develop instead of squander it. In the brightness of the morning, his eyelids refused to stay open for a second longer and he drifted away.

Willing himself to wake up again soon.

As he went, the last thing he heard was the front door swing shut – a loud, almost deafening slam, almost like a gunshot. The sound reverberated in his head, but even that couldn't shake him.

And once more, everything went dark.

12|ENOM

Daniel's old body – his body by birthright – was a heavy thing. It was only through walking as a thinner man that he came to realise those short, unwieldy legs had always struggled, turning him away from needless exercise.

Worsening an already weak heart.

He could feel his poor health with every step. Beneath his shirt, Daniel's round stomach jiggled as he walked along the pavement, chest heaving up and down. His ankles were sore from tight leather shoes, ill-prepared for walking such distances.

Nothing felt like his fault. Isabel had colluded with the doctor, pressuring him into walking to the office every weekday, even hiding his car keys. The reward for his strain was a tarnished diet and exhaustion, ensuring he got nothing out of life but the things he most hated – work, sweat, and no time for his girlfriend.

He pushed onwards. To Daniel, two miles was a marathon, and he focussed on familiar patterns to keep him going – scars and cracks on the pavement, overgrown hedgerows.

The sight of his yellow front door spurred him on from a distance, and he hurried down the final stretch. His waist-high front gate had been left swinging open, and when he went through, the door was unlocked. Both told him the same thing.

Isabel was already home.

He entered to a wide hallway, marred by aged décor he never could stand – a paisley carpet and striped wallpaper. He kicked off his shoes and felt damp socks tingle, sighing with relief.

Almost instantly, there was movement elsewhere in the house. Daniel went down to the living room, strangely nervous. The open space felt small, undermined by a low ceiling. A long rear window looked into a cramped garden, shadows gathering as the weather worsened.

"Hello?" he half-whispered. Daniel heard a sigh from the master bedroom and looked in through the open door. Beneath ruffled bedclothes, Isabel lay spread eagle on the mattress, wearing nothing but a pink nightdress.

"There you are," he said as he came to the doorway. "A sight for my sore eyes."

"You're very early," said Isabel with a croaky voice. She sat up and ran her hands through ruffled blonde hair. "I wasn't expecting you here for ages yet."

"I think maybe you're running late," said Daniel. "It's half past five. Have you been in bed all day?"

"No," she said. "I got in after I came home. It's short hours on a Friday, remember? What brings you home so soon?"

"I decided to take back some of the extra hours I've been working," Daniel said as he flexed his toes. "Plus I'm getting better at the walk. Forty-six minutes."

Isabel cleared her throat. "Well either way, you've still caught me by surprise. Are you hungry? I'll be ready to eat by the time I'm done cooking."

"No," he said. "I filled up at lunch, and this stupid diet won't let me indulge. I'll try to hold off. I was thinking we could go out somewhere."

Isabel smiled, showing rows of near-perfect teeth. Daniel hadn't seen that expression in weeks, and instead of warming his heart, it felt oddly misplaced.

"Give me a minute to put some clothes on and I'll see you in the living room," she said, kneeling up on the mattress.

"What are you doing in bed, anyway?" asked Daniel. "Are you feeling okay?"

"Just tired," she nodded insincerely. Isabel's hair looked windswept, clothes in a heap on the floor.

He frowned. "Am I missing something?"

She dealt him a look that warned against stating the obvious, and it cut right through his good intentions. *He wasn't supposed to have come so early.*

"He's been here, hasn't he?"

"Don't start," said Isabel. "Please, just don't."

Daniel's palms started sweating. He had suspected for a while, but this was the first time it had stared him in the face. He turned and walked back into the living room, as much as he could do to put one foot in front of the other.

She pulled on a lilac dressing gown and followed. "I'm sorry you had to see that," she said, still trying to flatten her hair down. "For what it's worth, I've tried to keep it from you as much as possible."

The weight of the world crashed down on top of him. Daniel collapsed onto the couch and stared blankly into space. "How long?" he asked.

"A month or so."

"And I suppose all the time I've been spending out of the house works perfectly for that, doesn't it? Long enough to have him here before I'm back."

"It isn't like that, Daniel," she said. Her tone was factual. "Today was the first time, and we didn't exactly plan it."

"Has he gone, or is he hiding in the bathroom?"

"Please don't," she said. "I tried to tell you, but you're hardly ever around. I can't exactly have this conversation with myself."

"You still should have found a way," he said.

"Well, perhaps you're right, but *you* shouldn't be acting so surprised. Did you honestly not know?"

Isabel didn't look remorseful or even upset. Instead, her face conveyed intolerance. *You brought this on yourself,* it told him without the need for words.

"I just thought we'd work through it," said Daniel.

"No, you didn't. You ignored our problems like you do everything else, and it only made them worse. We couldn't live in silence forever."

Daniel tried not to look at her. "That's no excuse for you cheating on me," he said.

Isabel growled. "Why do you do this to yourself?"

She turned and marched into the bedroom, slamming the door shut behind her. Left alone in the lounge, Daniel stared blankly at the four walls that held him in. In the blink of an eye, his perception of the house was transformed – no longer a place that required a little work to be homely. Now it just looked dark and miserable.

He sank into the cushions, but then the bedroom door flew open and Isabel came marching back out. He could see the anger raging in her.

"You know what? I'll be damned if I'm going to let you play the victim," she said. "I'm a good person, and sometimes it's like you expect me to fail. Did you ever stop to think that just maybe I've been finding this harder than you have?"

"Of course you haven't," he said. "It's my heart that's in trouble!"

"I'm not talking about that," she interrupted. "Or maybe I am. It's how you've done what the doctor suggested, but not a thing more. There are countless other ways to exercise besides walking to the office. Take a look around you!"

She pointed at the faded wallpaper, but Daniel just shrugged. "We both know how bad a job I'd make of it."

"That's my point exactly," she said. "You won't try anything unless it's on your terms. This was supposed to be a home we built around us, but after a year, nothing's changed."

"If it was all so unbearable then you should have told me."

Isabel's voice was calm and low. "I keep trying, Daniel. You shut off when I broach the subject because you're never ready to hear it. We haven't functioned as a couple for a long, long time. All I did today was move on."

"Is that what you call it?" said Daniel, watching the floor.

"I didn't mean-..." She stopped herself and recomposed, loosening the tension in her muscles. "You know what? You should move out."

Nothing could have prepared him to hear those words. Daniel's eyes met hers and saw no emotion. The passion they had shared was gone, and what stood in its place turned his world upside down.

Isabel was no longer in love with him.

**

Andrew Goodwin's body roused from sleep, rolling over and peering toward the curtains. Blurred vision watched the light creeping over the top with a sense of wonder.

Daniel looking out through borrowed eyes.

He was lying on the bed, more-or-less how he had fallen sleep, as though he had been unconscious for five minutes or twenty-four hours. Hairs on his bare chest stood on end, sending a tingle down his spine as his arm brushed against them.

Daniel felt stronger than he had the day before, well rested. He rolled off the mattress and peeled back the curtains to find another cloudless sky, feeling keen not to waste any time.

He raided the chest of drawers for a t-shirt and walked barefoot to the kitchen, cool tiles on the soles of his feet. The cupboards were mostly empty, but he found some brown bread and made toast, which he had with black coffee. Hot caffeine rushing through his system.

Wide awake, Daniel climbed in the shower and cleaned himself – head up, staring into space rather than down at that alien physique. He discovered a small tub of contact lenses in the medicine cabinet and put them in clumsily with those spiny fingers.

Having hair was a strange sensation. It took some time to style it right, and he needed perfection. After yesterday's wastage, Daniel fully intended to make contact with the woman he loved.

And let her know how he felt.

A brief hunt around the flat revealed Andrew's keys under the bed, where they must have slipped from his pocket the day before. Daniel went outside with them, where a warm wind did little to diminish another beautiful day, walking through the car park taking deep, rich breaths.

He pressed the fob on Andrew's key ring and listened for a car unlocking, finding a bright red Honda Civic parked neatly at the back. Daniel slid inside onto a leather seat, perfectly adjusted for his new frame, as it obviously would be.

Feeling energised, he started the engine and worked his way into heavy morning traffic, crawling through the city center. Luckily, he knew the roads, and although he lost his bearings in the smaller estates – a hole in his memory where he had forgotten past routines – he eventually found the little bungalow with the yellow door.

Daniel's former home.

He pulled up on the pavement, just out of sight of the kitchen window. Before him, the road stretched into the distance, and he watched the minutes ticking by, hoping desperately that Isabel still followed the same routine she had once made him copy.

Walking home from work for lunch.

While he waited, Daniel put the radio on, hearing the same old tunes that didn't care how long he had been away. He found unlikely company in the newscaster's drone – the same unending conflicts, the same mundane scandals.

Time passed slowly. Searching through the car, Daniel found an empty notebook in the glove box, and used it to make a map back to the flat. But here, he face a new kind of problem.

Andrew appeared to be right-handed, whereas Daniel could only write with his left. Whichever way he held the pen, either the body or the mind wasn't used to it. Daniel couldn't make it go where he wanted it to, leaving illegible scribble all over the page.

He gave up in frustration, emasculated. *How far would he get without being able to write?* Clammy palms grew more uncomfortable as he sat messing with his unruly hair, feeling each second slipping by.

When she appeared.

Even from a long distance, Daniel knew it was her. There was something in the way she carried herself, the way her hair reflected the sunlight. She wore a long, grey skirt and a black cardigan that was fastened at the front, striding down the pavement with the kind of bravado others would mistake for cockiness.

Isabel.

Her boots clopped loudly as she approached. Large eyes shone a brilliant blue, and for the briefest moment, their gazes locked. She looked away just as quickly, however, as two stranger's eyes might meet across a crowded room.

Isabel walked right past the car, unnervingly close to him. She had changed her hairstyle – shorter and more rounded to her face. Her clothes were all new, hugging a trim figure closely.

Daniel couldn't move from his seat, paralysed by the sight of her. Isabel opened the front gate and walked up to the house, making it indoors before he summoned the strength to get onto his feet and come after.

In the stark light of the clear morning, and with his stomach in his throat, he dealt three loud rasps on the door. There was a click as it slowly drifted open, bringing him face to face with the woman he had loved for years.

It was petrifying.

"Hello?" she spoke with quizzical tone. Daniel's heart skipped two beats as he fought to overcome a natural, yet harrowing reaction – she didn't recognise him.

"Hello," he replied, lost for words. After a long and awkward silence, she spoke again.

"I'm sorry to be rude, but do I know you?"

"You won't," he said. "At least not at the moment. There's something I think we should talk about."

"Has something happened?"

"No, everything's fine," he said. "I'm sorry if I seem a little shaken, but I used to live here."

"Oh, I see," she said. "Did you leave something behind that you'd like back? I think the washing machine was here when I moved in, but if you take nothing else, have the carpet."

She smiled, and it went someway to soothing Daniel's nerves. He looked down at the worn paisley.

"I haven't missed that at all," he said. "And I'm surprised if you still have the same washing machine. It always used to get slime all over my clothes."

"It's just a case of how you use it," she said. "You weren't the only one to have that problem."

Isabel leaned against the doorframe, and he could see over her shoulder, down the corridor and into the lounge. He found himself checking for movement, but she caught him staring.

"I'm Isabel," she said.

"Pleased to meet you." Daniel just wanted to speak his name, but the truth sounded so preposterous.

"I'm sorry I can't invite you in," she said. "Maybe a walk around memory lane would be good for you, but you see, I'm about to head out myself."

"Oh," said Daniel. "Do you really not have time?"

"I'm afraid not. You could come back later on, if you like? I might be in after seven."

Daniel hadn't seen the evening in a long time. "I'm not sure I can do it," he said. "Maybe some other lunchtime?"

She smiled. "You can always try your luck."

He needed more than a stolen minute to make his confession. Feeling he had no choice, Daniel retreated to the pavement, and she closed the door without waving him off.

He was strangely glad off it. The chance to lower his guard. Daniel hadn't been remotely prepared for how difficult it would prove to talk to her again. They had been lovers once, but he lacked the right words to make it that way again.

He returned to Andrew's car, deflated. It had always been more than just a physical attraction. They were drawn to one another's souls, and that much was no different about him. He just needed to make her see it, but he didn't get the chance for another try.

A vehicle approached from behind – a black Range Rover, tall and imposing, headlamps almost as high as his rear window. It stopped Daniel in his tracks, and he watched in disbelief as the driver's door opened and a man climbed out.

Daniel recognised him right away – average height, with short, fair hair and a stocky build. A shudder ran down his spine as the man walked to the front gate and swung it open.

The gate Daniel had only just closed.

No sooner was he by the door, than it opened from the inside. Isabel practically threw herself at the man, coiling her arms around his neck and planting a passionate kiss on his lips.

Daniel swore out loud. He couldn't believe – *refused to believe* – what his eyes were telling him. She led the man inside and drew the door closed, an insipid smile plastered between his ears as he helped to push it shut.

Daniel had hoped to never see him again, and straight away, knew how difficult he would make it to become a part of Isabel's life.

He was a menace, the worst thing that ever happened to Daniel.

His name was Ryan.

13|CHOES

The squeal of an alarm clock shattered a poor night's rest. Daniel's eyes flickered open to an instant panic, barely realising the covers were off him, the curtains were open.

And he was alive for a third morning.

Daniel stabbed out blindly for the alarm, feeling his heart leap inside his chest. For a moment, he feared it would trigger another heart attack, until common sense took hold. It was, after all, a different heart now.

He had been dreaming, reliving the day of his death over and over, those last turbulent seconds as the car swept past him on the pavement and his heart gave way.

He went through it all again in cruel detail. *The plate-loads of greasy breakfast which he funnelled into his mouth, the prickly heat from the pouring midday sun, the woman in the long green coat who watched him collapse, and the purgatory that followed.*

Now, he was back in the bedroom of Andrew's flat. Daniel stood and looked out of the window at a blue morning, sight blurry, contact lenses having fallen out during the night. The colours echoed his feelings – empty and cold, smothered by harsh facts that fouled his resurrection.

The world had moved on in his absence, and Isabel was with somebody else.

Daniel turned and walked listlessly down the hallway. His old life was finished, and all he had to show for it were the people who loved him. He hadn't considered they might not love him in return.

Floor tiles pinched his feet as Daniel busied himself with anything he could find, mechanically cleaning, washing, tidying – things he could do without needing to think.

Here's to doing you a favour, he thought of Andrew. Daniel wiped down the sink until it sparkled, and only when he had no distractions left was he confronted by just how wretched he felt.

Tears started to stream down his face. Every last hint of Daniel's identity had been stripped away. He hadn't cared at the time because he thought he wouldn't need it again, but there he was, still around, battling what he now knew of the afterlife.

There wasn't one.

Death really seemed to be the end after all. Daniel had seen it. Every misfortune that had plagued him in life had no comeuppance. It was just bad luck. He had died at the age of thirty-one, in what should have been his prime, and there was little chance he would get anything to make up for it.

He felt alone, hollow, and it took all of his strength to keep moving. Daniel had to force himself to dress and leave the flat. There was still another place he could find hope, a part of his life which couldn't be so easily overwritten.

Someone who would never have another son.

***

Daniel had been raised in a simple world, miles from the nearest town, surrounded by hills and dense forest. His biggest mistake was to leave it, assuming there was something better elsewhere.

With no other family, his father had eventually followed, chasing neither bright lights nor excitement, but his only child. Daniel felt guilty for abandoning him there, stranded far from the world they had both preferred. Alone, perhaps as much as Daniel had felt since his rebirth.

Clammy hands gripped the steering wheel of Andrew's Honda Civic, heading out of the city. Grey roads blended together, one junction after another, neither fetching nor distinct.

Daniel watched the people he drove past, wondering how many of them were like him. *Was Daniel unique, or did everyone who lived so poorly receive a second chance?*

He went on for miles, eyes flitting idly from drivers to pedestrians as he drifted across the lanes. He was a stone's throw from his destination when, suddenly, one car emerged from the others. He recognised the license plate and sat up in his seat, amazed by what he saw.

It was his.

The only car he had ever driven, still roadworthy, and moving past him in the opposite direction – a metallic-green Austin Maestro, barely holding itself together.

Daniel laughed. One cracked wing mirror pointed downwards and the other was held on with duct tape. Rust was covered in layers of dirt. Though battered, it was a vehicle that had helped to define the man he used to be, and now – behind the wheel – it seemed his father had taken over the mantle.

Even through the grime on the windscreen, Daniel recognised him. Excited, he turned around and followed, tailing the car to a supermarket further up the road. Wisps of smoke churned out through the exhaust pipe, but the engine sounded surprisingly healthy, life still left beneath the bonnet.

He watched his father park in a disabled space by the entrance, while Daniel stayed distant, pulling into the furthest spot he could find. In silence, he looked on as the old man took great effort to climb out of the vehicle and stand.

Nothing could have braced Daniel for the sight that met his eyes. Hunched over and frail, his father was wasting away, a shadow of his former self. Silvery hair had fallen out almost completely, and deep wrinkles streaked across his face.

It was a harrowing sight. He looked like he had aged a decade since Daniel had last seen him, clothes hanging off a fragile frame. Daniel suddenly wondered just how long it had actually been since he had died. *A year couldn't have affected his father so badly.*

Almost immediately, Daniel's feet urged him out of the car and he rushed over the tarmac. "Excuse me," he called, and his father looked up. No recognition, just a blank expression.

Daniel cleared his throat to speak again, but from nowhere – to his astonishment – a stranger stepped between them. *And they knew who Daniel was.*

"Oh, hello," said a woman with a dry and husky voice. "You're a bit far off the beaten track, aren't you?"

She looped her arm through the handle of an empty hand basket, looking Daniel in the eye. "I'm sorry," he said, dismissively, "but I don't think I know-..."

"You don't need to apologise," the woman interrupted. "I'm sorry as well, for missing your call last night, even if it was pretty late."

He baulked. Something about her was instantly familiar – long, blonde hair and soft, red lipstick. Daniel was so taken aback that her words were slow to register.

"I didn't call you last night," he said. "I slept right through the evening."

"Yes, you did. You rang at something like four in the morning. It says so on my phone, and it seems an unlikely accident."

The hairs on the back of his neck stood up. *Andrew must have done it.* Daniel almost slapped his forehead. A huge part of him just assumed that Andrew had gone forever, thirst for life clouding the obvious.

Trapped in the nighttime, the two of them had merely swapped places.

He let his father walk right past him as the woman looked him over. "You look tired," she said. "Did you forget you'd called me?"

"I'm fine," Daniel replied, trying to assume the role of a man he didn't know. "Maybe I did call you, but it wasn't intentional."

"Are you busy?" she said. "You should buy me a drink to apologise for ignoring me all week."

"Even if I had the time," he said. "I'm afraid I don't have my wallet with me."

"Okay, I'll pay for the drinks, but I'm buying some of your time in the process."

She put a hand on her hip, making it clear he shouldn't argue. "Fine," he relented. "You lead the way."

The woman took him indoors – to a canteen by the tills – and he followed without question, wondering why he found her so familiar. She ordered coffee for them both, seeming to know how Andrew liked it, then took to a small table by the window.

"So where have you gone to?" she said. "You've been very quiet these last few days."

"I've not been feeling too great," said Daniel, sliding onto a plastic chair to face her. "I've mostly just been sleeping."

"Did you forget we were meeting up last night? I tried to call you more than once."

"This thing has really wiped me out, otherwise of course I would have been there."

She sighed. "Well, you were dragging your feet in the car park, so I guess I believe what you're saying."

Daniel smiled politely, trying to be humble, glad not to be used to Andrew's longer legs quite yet.

The woman raised her drink and pursed her lips, blowing tiny ripples across the surface. "You know it's my birthday next week," she said.

Daniel suddenly noticed a silver wedding ring on her finger and put his hands under the table, realising Andrew wasn't wearing his.

"Do we have any plans?" he asked.

"Actually, we don't. What I mean is the opposite – I'll be busy myself. But I'm free the weekend after, if you want to get together."

"Can we just see how it goes?" said Daniel.

"Well, I'm busy for a good while after that, so we should be clear. It's always hectic for me at this time of year, and it's easy to lose track."

"I know exactly how that feels," he said. "Since I've been off, I'm not even sure what day it is."

"Thursday," she said. "I'm assuming you know it's July."

Daniel nodded, pretending it was obvious. The more he thought about the time he had missed, the more he felt unsettled. He took a mouthful of hot drink to steady his nerves, and she saw steam coming from his mouth.

"Hey, slow down," she said. "You'll do yourself some damage. What's the matter?"

"Sorry," he said, trying to hold his façade. "My life has really come off the rails lately."

"You look pale. Are you sure you shouldn't still be in bed?"

Sobriety flashed across her face and the expression was instantly familiar. Daniel realised where he had seen her before, though it had been from some distance. His jaw dropped open.

The woman who had watched him die.

Though her hair was the wrong colour, she had the same nose and the same eyes. It took him right back to that day by the sea. This was the woman who had stood on the pavement and done nothing to help.

It struck him like a freight train, and Daniel felt a tingle in his chest. He gulped down the rest of his drink, reaching the bottom before she was even a third of the way through hers. The kick from the caffeine was like an addiction, sending a cool flush through his bloodstream. But something was gravely wrong.

Because, with it, Daniel felt tired.

From nowhere, his head grew heavy, and a sudden fatigue threatened to put him to sleep in the middle of the café. Panicking, Daniel jumped to his feet, knocking the table and sloshing the woman's drink over her hands.

"Be careful!" she gasped, but he couldn't hear her. Midday was approaching, much later than he had been awake so far, and it seemed his time was almost over.

Daniel staggered across the café, hoping the motion would wake him up, but every step felt like pulling his legs through wet cement, only to have them refuse his weight when he brought them back down.

He stumbled into the aisles, running his hands along the shelves in search of something – *anything* – that could bring him back before it was too late.

He spied drinks at the far end and hurried towards them, tiredness spreading like a cloud of fog, making it hard to concentrate. He collided with someone's trolley and bounced off it, crashing into racks of wine bottles, feverishly running his hands across labels until he found something he thought could help.

An energy drink.

More caffeine.

In the middle of the shop, surrounded by an audience, he opened the can and guzzled the contents.

Sticky, yellowy liquid poured out of the corners of his mouth as the rest rushed down to his stomach.

Almost instantaneously, there was a rush like a slap to the face. He felt more alert, but it wasn't absolute. Tiredness still vied in the background, and he needed something more drastic to keep it at bay.

Over his shoulder, Daniel saw a pharmacy counter and knew what he wanted. He turned and took off down the aisle, one leg wide awake and the other like a lead weight.

At the counter, two attendants were embroiled in heated discussion with a customer, their backs to the dispensing room. Distracted.

He sped up, heaving his leg as he propelled himself into the open. The rush of blood past his ears made him deaf to the argument, but he saw angry faces and prayed no one would see him.

As quickly as his legs would allow, he ducked through the open doorway and out of sight. Inside, he was alone with the dispensing desk, and hurriedly scanned along rows of prescription medicines.

It wasn't hard to find what he wanted, something he had good cause to know all about.

Adrenaline.

Daniel stuffed his jacket with blue plastic injectors and glass ampoules, taking as much as he could carry. Then, without pausing to think, just as quietly as he had broken in, he turned and stumbled through the door.

By a miracle, he made it back between the aisles without anyone calling after him. He tried to lose himself in the crowd, clutching the drugs beneath his jacket, pushing his way through to the store entrance.

Daniel ran passed the checkouts and down to the disabled toilet, shutting himself inside. As soon as the door was closed, his leg gave way, and had it not been for the safety bar on the wall to grab onto, he would have careered to the ground.

He managed to ease himself onto the toilet seat. In the narrow, box-like room, Daniel dug a hand into his pocket and pulled out a glass ampoule, smashing it against the sink. The top broke off with a crunch as liquid sloshed over the sides.

Daniel took a needle from his pocket and tore the plastic wrapping with his teeth, pulling the sheath off the tip. He held his breath and drew some fluid out, before stabbing it into his thigh with stiffened hands – right through his trousers, forcing the drug into his system.

Immediately, a surge of awareness ripped through his body like a bolt of electricity. The fatigue was wiped clean away, erased in a cold shudder.

And just like that, he was wide awake again.

Daniel sat back on the toilet seat, the cold cistern on the back of his neck. He could almost feel the liquid spread around his system, replacing exhaustion with a powerful urge to get moving.

He drew the needle back out of his leg. He had taken half of the contents into his body, half a syringe now coursing through his veins. He felt so much better, more in control. The empowerment alone made it worthwhile.

Daniel closed his eyes and counted to ten, rubbing his thigh to help move the drug before he put weight on his legs. There was feeling in them again, sensitivity. He eased up onto his feet and laughed nervously.

He felt normal.

Aware he was on borrowed time, Daniel left the cubicle and returned to the café to find the woman had gone. He couldn't blame her – not after his behaviour – but he needed answers, and wished he had at least caught her name.

He made a quick search of the supermarket, but every second set of eyes were staring at him for causing such a disturbance, and he lost his nerve. Better to leave it there for now.

He retreated to the car park, stopping only briefly to check the date at the newspaper stand. *Two years after he had died.*

Daniel had spent twice as long in Andrew's mind as he thought, locked in turmoil. The embers of his life had faded long ago – his father now withered and alone, Isabel having long since outgrown her grief.

He was isolated, cursed rather than blessed with a second chance at life. Daniel retreated to his car and sat behind the wheel, now aimless, afraid to do anything else in case the tiredness came back.

Clouds started to gather in the sky, a storm to break the good weather. The only thing for it was go home and sleep, hoping to continue building strength.

Daniel prayed it would get better, unable to salvage his old life with a few hours at a time. His second birth was agonisingly slow, rapidly becoming some much less than a blessing.

It was a disaster.

Something he was no longer sure he wanted.

14|EMAINS

Daniel woke on the morning of the fourth day with a burning question inside him. Something had happened during the night that he didn't understand, something new and disturbing.

It concerned his dreams, innocuous flashbacks of a lifetime long forgotten, happy days with loved ones, voices from the past. Nothing uncommon, but everything in them was entirely new to him.

They had to be Andrew's dreams, and it set him off thinking – *just who was this person whose life he was stealing?* Daniel was making him a martyr simply to continue his own existence, yet knew nothing about him.

The bedroom that morning was a state, dirty clothes emptied out of the hamper and strewn across the floor. It looked like the place had been ransacked, like Andrew had lost control in the middle of the night.

Daniel woke up half on the bed, legs trailing across the laminate. With a swell of guilt, he felt compelled to tidy up, using it as an excuse to rummage through cupboards, searching for ways to better know the man he was so entangled with.

It proved useful. He came across a mobile phone in one of the bedside drawers, and found a jar of loose change stowed away in the kitchen. There were no pictures hanging anywhere, no keepsakes or notes. Nothing that told him who Andrew was.

As though Andrew had never really lived at all.

Most of the answers Daniel found came from one drawer in the kitchen, crammed with the sort of things everyone accumulates, but no one can find a use for. Manuals and cables, batteries and old keys.

Amongst them, he found a book – a year-old, leather bound diary. It was a record from the period in which Daniel had been trapped in Andrew's mind. The pages folded open to June, and Daniel flipped through them, trying to learn what he could.

Most entries were terse reminders. *'Therapist'*, *'Hairdresser'*. An ominous day in November read *'Moved out'* but neglected to give any detail. There were mentions of a woman's name – *'Katie'* – but no indication of who she was.

Andrew's wife, or the woman Daniel had met in the supermarket?

Only one page had been filled out fully – the address list at the front. Andrew William Goodwin had been born a year after Daniel, making him mid-thirties by now. His home address had been overwritten so many times, it was barely legible, and the next of kin had been torn out completely.

In its place, Daniel found four photographs tucked between the pages, the only ones in the entire flat. All were of the same woman, with shoulder length black hair and full lips. Andrew's wife, the woman Daniel had been in bed with on the first night of his reawakening.

Brown eyes sparkled as she smiled at the camera. One picture had her in a ball gown, another on a campsite. The third was a beach on holiday, and the last one showed her and Andrew together – their wedding picture, the one Daniel had once seen framed on the mantelpiece in their living room, now stuffed in a drawer.

He lowered it with a trace of sadness. They looked happy, *so what could have happened to reduce Andrew's life to that lonely, empty place?*

Was it him?

Daniel put the pictures back in the diary and respectfully stowed it in the drawer. Andrew had been humanised in his eyes. They seemed to both be empty shells. He tried to shake his guilt for stealing Andrew's body and hoped that, ultimately, the decision as to which of them survived would be out of his hands.

Daniel didn't think he had it in him to condemn an innocent man.

***

Now that he had discovered adrenaline, things had turned in Daniel's favour. He no longer needed to fear the tiredness at the end of each morning, able to push it back until he could return to the flat.

Prolonging his day, perhaps even for hours.

Well rested, and with boosted confidence, he returned to his father's suburb. Bright morning sunlight cast long shadows, and overnight storms had made the air fresh and crisp.

Daniel cradled a box of syringes as he sat in the car and looked towards his father's tiny house. Weeds had grown between cracks in the flagstones and a creeper ran amok down the wall, threatening to envelop the building if left unchecked.

His old Austin Maestro was there, parked on a short driveway with oil seeping onto the ground. It looked worn out, yet too proud to ask to be put out of its misery.

Daniel could relate to that.

He opened the door of Andrew's Civic and felt the morning air pinch his bare forearms. Daniel was worried how his father had been living in the two years since his death, needing to be sure the old man could cope before he made his confession.

Fortunately, they had a point of common ground his father would likely share with a stranger. Daniel crossed the pavement and walked down the driveway, nervous, but determined. He rang the doorbell, and it took a few minutes before he saw movement through the mottled glass.

A figure came shuffling towards him, latches turned, and the door drifted slowly ajar. Standing before him was the man he had seen in the supermarket the day before. A man who barely resembled the father he knew.

He wore a dressing gown that Daniel recognised, hanging from his body like tatters where it once fitted tightly. He looked poorly slept, staring blankly at the stranger on the doorstep. *Just as Isabel had.*

This time, however, Daniel was prepared.

"Hi, Mr. Lawton," he said. "My name is Andrew Goodwin. I was a friend of Daniel's, and I was wondering if I could talk with you for a while?"

It was a tenuous attempt at getting inside, but Daniel knew his father. In such a withdrawn state of life, tenuous was all it took. Daniel wasn't surprised when his father stood to one side and pushed the door wide open.

"Of course," he said, extending a hand which Daniel shook gently. "Please come in. I'll take you to the lounge where we can sit down."

His father led him down the hallway. Daniel noticed he kept his left hand raised, always bridging the gap between his thigh and the wall. It was an action Daniel had performed himself many times in the past few days.

Afraid of falling over.

"I'm sorry to intrude unannounced," said Daniel. "Your son was on my mind, and I thought it might be nice to reminisce."

"Call me John," said his father. They turned into the lounge and Daniel took an unpleasant lungful of stale air. Nothing in the house looked to have been cleaned in months, and a threadbare carpet released plumes of dust with every step.

Two leather armchairs stood proudly in the middle of the room, stiff and sun-bleached. Daniel was pleased to see they were still there. He used to sit in that lounge, years ago, and talk with his father for hours.

"I'm afraid I don't recognise you, Andrew," said his father, lowering himself into one of the seats. "How long had you known my son for?"

"We worked together when he moved to the city. A few of us were wondering about him lately."

"That's nice," said John. "Were you at the funeral? I'm afraid Isabel sorted most of that out."

Daniel sat on the other chair, which creaked as it accepted his weight. "I missed it," he said, "but that wasn't her fault. Do you still see her?"

"Not at all. We were never very close. She and Daniel went through the wars before he died, and I didn't think it right to keep in touch."

Daniel shifted his weight, trying to cushion his rear end. "I knew quite a bit about their problems," he said. "She probably regrets a lot of it nowadays."

"Maybe." His father showed more than a hint of doubt. "If you ask me, what he needed was a clean break. If he'd done that, he might still be with us."

It felt instantly strange for Daniel to hear his father speak of him so coldly, an emotionless retrospective on issues that were fresh in Daniel's mind.

"If you don't mind my asking," Daniel said, "did they work out why he died?"

"Heart condition, nothing more sinister. It used to run in the family, so I guess he was predisposed."

Daniel hadn't known that. "Could he have done something about it?"

"Certainly," his father continued. "Daniel had warnings from the doctor, but I don't think they ever sunk in. He always thought he was too young to be in any real danger."

"He would have said he just succumbed to all the pressures in his life."

John Lawton leaned forwards. "Something you have to understand about my son, God love him, is he made things more complicated than they needed to be. Instead of talking, he'd just shut people out and wallow."

"A lot of it was bad luck, though..."

His father smiled. "Now you're starting to sound like he did. To be fair, the timing was unfortunate, but he spent too much time trying to ignore his problems instead of tackling them head on. I told him a hundred times."

"For what it's worth," said Daniel, "your son did listen to you. He just got caught up in everything that was going on, and I suppose that made it harder to communicate."

John picked himself back out of the chair, his arms trembling as they took his weight. "Would you like to see him?" he said.

Hesitantly, Daniel allowed his father to take him to a small room opposite the lounge, crammed with furniture. In the center, a large, oak table stood with six broad chairs around it, no space to pull them out and sit.

It would have been an heirloom, but there was no one to inherit it now, destined to be sold off by whomsoever took the property when his father died.

John Lawton used the backs of the chairs for support as he edged around the room. In the corner, beside the window, was a bureau, itself an antique. Through glass doors, Daniel saw shelves racked with books that hadn't been opened in years.

He followed, coat scraping along the wallpaper. On the bottommost shelf, he saw a small wooden box with a sealed lid. His father ushered him over to read a plaque on the top:

Daniel froze rigid, a horrible churn in the pit of his stomach. John had shown him to his own ashes. Without realising, his father had brought him face to face with his own grisly fate.

The blood drained from his skin. The plaque read '*At Peace*' as if it had any clue what he had been through. Daniel picked up phantom smells of salt on the air and felt pain in his chest.

"My son didn't really have a favourite place to scatter the ashes," his father said. "In the end, I decided he would be best off staying right here with me."

Daniel couldn't take his eyes off the wooden casket. His corpse had been incinerated and stuffed inside it. He leaned against the table, white as the ghost he was.

"Are you alright?" his father asked, inadvertently breaking Daniel's line of sight. It snapped him back to attention.

"Yes," Daniel managed a broken smile. "Sorry, I was miles away." *Like someone just walked over his grave.* "Is this everything that's left of him?"

"Physically, yes," said his father, "but there are a few other keepsakes."

In the cupboards beneath the bookshelves, he showed Daniel a compartment loaded with mementos from his life, the little things his father couldn't bring himself to throw away. Reminders of his son.

"You can look through them if you like," he said. "You might find some things in there that you remember. My favourite is this..."

He produced a file bound in cracked, red leather. Daniel's name had been inscribed on the front in gold lettering. It was a photo album, his entire life condensed into pictures. If there was anything in this world he could consider a legacy, that was it, right in front of him. He instantly wanted it for himself.

"Would you like me to put the kettle on?" his father said. "We can go through it over a cup of tea. You could even be in a few of these pictures and I hadn't noticed."

"That would be wonderful," Daniel said, impatient to muse on his life. "I hope you don't think I'm pushing you into something you'd rather not do."

"Of course not. It's good to talk about him every once in a while. That's how we keep him alive."

The old man squeezed past and left the room. Alone, Daniel placed the album on the table and thumbed through it. For the first time since coming back, he felt a sense of belonging, something that seemed to add purpose to his existence.

He smiled. The other items in the bureau were no less enticing. He found postcards he had sent from abroad, and a pile of business cards from his old job. He pulled a couple of them out and put them in his pocket.

A record of his name.

Rooting through the compartment, Daniel found a collection of personal effects. The spare keys to his car were there, as was his wallet, with trimmed and folded photographs still inside.

Near the bottom of the pile, he found his broken watch – a silver strap with a black face, hands still frozen where he had been messing with them before he died.

3:14am.

The same time he had first woken up after his death. The metal was cold and hard, and it made him shudder. *The last thing he had seen with his own eyes.* He slipped it quietly into his pocket, unable to part with it.

"Do you take any sugar?" his father called from the kitchen.

"Yes please," Daniel called back. "Two of them."

He slid his favourite picture out of the wallet – Isabel and his father, standing either side of him. Daniel stowed it with the watch and put everything else back, moments before his father appeared at the door.

"Daniel used to take two sugars, as well. Are you sure I can't tempt you down to one?"

"I suppose you always tried to wean him off it, too?" he said, with a grin. "One will be fine."

He picked up the photo album and edged around the table to join his father in the lounge, guilty for the things he had taken. Those pieces of his life stood as the only keepsakes either of them had, and both would have cherished them equally.

"Did I notice Daniel's car parked down the side of the house?" asked Daniel.

His father served up a pot of tea before he eased back into his chair. "Yes it is," he said. "I knew how much he loved it, and somehow it seemed fitting to keep it."

"I'm surprised it still works."

"Some days it doesn't go so well, and I can appreciate how that feels."

Daniel felt a swell of concern. "I know it's not my place to say, but is there anyone looking after you?"

His father smiled dismissively, opening the photo album. "Now, you didn't come here to talk about me, did you?"

Daniel knew all-too-well how much his father hated to be fussed over, and rejected any questions he didn't want to answer. Instead, Daniel gave the old man what he wanted and focussed on the photo album, going through each picture, one at a time.

They were there for hours. Daniel forgot all about his confession as they talked, finding it easy to overlook the fact he was trapped inside a borrowed body, living a life that was technically over.

They exchanged stories until his father tired, repeating his anecdotes. Eventually, Daniel put down the photo album and finished his drink. "I think perhaps we've done this enough for one day," he said.

His father nodded. "You're probably right. It's been nice, but I'm getting too old for all this excitement."

Daniel stood, and as he waited patiently for his father to pull himself to his feet, he noticed something about the light outside – it was growing dim.

Night was coming.

Somehow, Daniel had managed to stay awake for the entire day, and still, he didn't feel remotely tired, surviving on nothing more than tea and familiar surroundings.

John Lawton sluggishly escorted him to the front door. "Thank you so much for having me over," Daniel said as he stepped outside. "I know it probably seemed a strange request, but I enjoyed our conversation."

"The pleasure was all mine," his father said. "Perhaps you could come around again soon? We should finish the album now we've started."

Daniel nodded. "I promise to call ahead this time." He reached into his pocket for the mobile phone he had found in Andrew's drawer, then allowed his father to dictate a number he already knew by heart.

Thin clouds started to gather on the horizon as the evening air cooled. Uplifted, Daniel got into Andrew's car and started the engine, deciding to drive with no destination in mind and revel in the extended day.

Travel helped him to think. His alertness gave him hope for recovering his former life, and Daniel decided to drive past the little bungalow with the yellow door, just to see if he could catch a glimpse through the window.

Only three things stood in the way of what he wanted – his own fear of an honest confession, the man whose body he was stealing, and Ryan.

The man who had stolen Daniel's love.

Ryan was a wretch, a man who deserved no mercy, someone who needed to be ousted from his position, as quickly and painfully as possible.

Daniel drew to a halt outside the bungalow, keeping the engine running. The road was deserted, and the silence made him think all the more of the time slipping through his fingers.

If he was going to stop playing games, it needed to be now.

He was too weak to make such a preposterous admission to Isabel's blue eyes, but there were other ways to do it. Daniel fished out a business card from his pocket and scrawled Andrew's number across the back, along with the words he couldn't say in person.

'I am Daniel Lawton.'

Heartbeat racing, he got out of the car and ran across the road, letting himself through the open gate and up to the yellow door. He closed his eyes and thrust the card through the letterbox, holding onto one corner as a last means of retrieval.

She wouldn't recognise him, or even believe him at first, but once she heard his story, Isabel wouldn't be able to deny it. He let the paper slip from his hand as the bristles of the letterbox sucked it into the hallway.

No going back now.

One way or another, the truth was coming out.

15|ESPAIR

The little bungalow with the yellow door was no stranger to arguments. Once a place of love and peace, it fast became a venue for torment.

In the days leading up to Daniel's death.

Even in his old body, Daniel struggled to sleep. Morning sunlight ended a fractured rest by forcing his eyelids open, and as thunder clapped through his skull, he realised Isabel was standing over him, hands on hips.

"What time did you come in last night?" she said. Weeks had passed since they had broken up, and she was running out of patience.

"Good morning," he croaked.

"Are you listening?" She raised her voice. "I said what time did you come in?"

Daniel realised he was spread across the settee, never having made it to the spare bedroom. "I have no idea," he said. "What time is it now?"

"*Half past eight.* Shall I assume you spent another night drunk instead of looking for a place to rent?"

It was a rhetorical question. She could smell the alcohol on his breath. Daniel's walk home from work had become a pub crawl, moving from bar to bar, throwing out all semblance of control.

Self-destructing.

"I've been keeping an eye out for houses," he said, "but I'm not moving just anywhere. It has to be right."

"You need to hurry up. Forget what it's doing to me and take a look at yourself, for God's sake."

Daniel leaned forwards to feel his fat stomach groan. The television garbled in the background as he pieced his night together.

Burgers and beer. So much for the diet.

"Can we talk about this later?" he said. "It's not a good time for me."

Isabel perched herself on the facing armchair and rubbed her hands along the upholstery, ruffling tiny fibres. "Daniel, you only keep making it worse when you drag this out."

"I don't see why I'm expected to move at all," he said. "This is my house as much as yours."

"One of us has to go," said Isabel, "and we both know you couldn't afford to stay here on your own."

"Neither could you without someone to contribute, or shouldn't I ask about that?"

She stared at Daniel coldly. "Ryan's told me what's been happening at work. You may not believe me, but I'm worried about you."

She spoke as an adult would to a child. Daniel tried to wet parched lips as he corrected the time on his watch. *Golden hands on a black face.*

"You look terrible," she said.

"Are you pretending to care?"

Isabel stood and wiped down her skirt. "Of course I care." There was sadness in her eyes. "You may not understand, or want me to anymore, but seeing you like this is difficult."

He felt a lump in his throat which he hoped was imaginary. As she turned to gather her coat, he realised that, for all the punishment he was putting himself through, she looked better with each passing day.

Behind her, Daniel suddenly noticed a figure by the bedroom door, someone else in the room. His jaw dropped, and everything changed as he realised there had been three of them in the house last night.

Ryan had stayed over.

Isabel's new partner wore a business suit with a crisp, blue shirt. The straps of a rucksack trailed behind his back as he tried not to draw attention to it.

"It's time to head in," said Ryan, voice quiet and sympathetic. Daniel must have looked awful to warrant that.

"You can probably tell I'm not ready." Daniel replied.

Ryan cleared his throat, and it was Isabel's turn to hide in the shadows. "Should I tell them you got caught in traffic?" he said.

"Tell them what you like," said Daniel. "I don't need your help." He felt betrayed by a man he had known for years, abhorred by the gall of a colleague he once thought of as a friend.

"Well, I'll have to tell them something," said Ryan. "Try not to be too much later."

"Get out of my home."

Ryan didn't waste any words, glad of the send-off. He took Isabel down the hallway and pulled the front door closed behind them.

The walls shook, leaving Daniel alone, hunched over on the sofa. But it wasn't over. Ryan would be waiting for him in the office, watching him judgmentally, knowing what he had become.

Daniel had been ousted from his life. It was only a matter of time before he was forced to move out completely – to move on, with a new house and another job. Everything he had built over the years was destined to be handed to another man.

His home, his world.

Daniel felt a burning need for justice, for Ryan to pay for the mess he created, but he couldn't find the strength. Sat nursing a hangover, he didn't have a clue what more he could do to stop it.

So for now, he would resign himself to another drink.

***

Daniel's death only added to his problems, whereas it solved most of Ryan's. Lying in Andrew Goodwin's bed, it was all Daniel could think about – how he had been forced into another man's life, creating a second victim of Ryan's cruelty.

Someone else with nothing to lose.

All the lights were on in the bedroom, meaning Andrew had been awake in the night. And it was worse – Daniel stirred to find the mobile phone resting in their shared hand. *As though Andrew had been trying to call for help.*

It was a setback, one with frightening possibilities. Daniel had only just given that number to Isabel, writing it on the business card that went through her door. He hadn't considered Andrew might take the call instead of him.

If he wasn't careful, Andrew could a way to tip the scales in his favour. After all, he would have more people on his side. He couldn't exactly have less.

Not that either of them were up to a fight. Daniel felt like he hadn't slept in days, and as he pulled himself up and stumbled to the bathroom, his face in the mirror confirmed that – swollen, tired eyes, and ghostly pale skin.

The sudden movement brought on a sharp headache, and he shut his eyes tightly, rubbing his temples.

When it had a wholly unexpected effect.

Something popped into his mind – an image, stronger than inspiration, like a flicker of white light behind his retina. It willed him back into the hallway, where he peered into the bedroom.

There was a video camera on the floor.

It lay behind the long curtains, pointing at the head of the bed. *Recording.* Andrew must have been trying to figure out what was going on, and the thought was so strong, it had lingered in his mind. A memory now shared between them.

Daniel ducked back into the room, avoiding the lens until he could turn the camera off. It proved all of his suspicions. Andrew was shifting from a hindrance to a threat, one that needed to be pacified as soon as possible.

He plugged the phone in and dressed while it was charging. He needed someone on his side before

Andrew did something he couldn't prevent, and Isabel was his best chance of a sympathetic ear.

Even then, the chance was slim. He checked the call log before he left and found that, although no one had got through to Andrew yet, people had been trying. Daniel needed to move fast.

He needed allies now.

***

A lush village common had proven popular in the sunshine. Mothers watched as children played on green grass that rustled in the breeze of a pleasant mid-morning.

Daniel knew the area like the back of his hand. Beside them, a short row of shops ended with a tiny bank on the corner.

The place where Isabel worked.

He approached the front door to find a modest queue, waiting patiently to be served at one of two counters. Right away, he caught sight of her behind the safety glass. Still working there, so long after his death.

She wore black, dressing smartly for her job, and she had her glasses on, something she only ever did after a rough night. Daniel studied her face as he waited – her polite smile, the wisp of hair that escaped her ponytail and trailed down the side of her face.

She noticed him before she came free, though she didn't acknowledge it. Eventually, she beckoned him to the window with a muted smile.

"Look who it is," she said, voice softened by the glass. "The man whose house I inherited. Have you been back around since we talked?"

Daniel shook his head. "I've been too busy, but I was hoping we could pick up where we left off."

"While I'm at work?" she said with an innocent smile.

"I'm here to find out when you break for lunch, so we don't waste a second."

She shrugged. "I'm busy again, today. I spend most lunchtimes with my fiancé, so it's him you'd have to argue with."

His heart pounded in his chest. Daniel looked down at her hand and saw a platinum ring with a sparkling diamond.

Isabel was engaged.

"When did that happen?" He tried to hide his shock.

"Months ago. Listen, don't take this the wrong way, but do we know each other? You come across as familiar."

"There's a reason for that, but it's not easy to explain, which is why I put that note through your door last night."

Her smile faded. For a moment, he could have sworn recognition flashed across her face.

"I thought you'd been too busy to come back over," she said.

"Did you read it? I'm surprised you haven't called."

Isabel shrugged. "I don't know what you're talking about. Ryan might have picked up the post this morning, or else it'll still be there."

Again, Daniel's heart skipped a beat. "Are you sure? The name would have been familiar."

She looked concerned and withdrew, a hauntingly familiar motion that took him back to the weeks before he died. "What is your name?" she said. "Maybe I remember you."

He couldn't speak it aloud, not there. It wasn't fair on either of them. Instead, he bit his lip, and the awkward silence changed her manner completely.

"So, there's a queue slowly building up behind you," she said, "and I'm at work, so please tell me it's a coincidence you've found me here, and there's something else I can do for you."

Daniel reached into his pocket. "I need your help. I've forgotten the PIN number for my bankcard and I've run out of money."

Isabel cleared her throat, reluctantly providing service. "I can't give you the number over the counter, but I can have it sent to your address. You could make a cash withdrawal to tide you over, if you need to."

"Yes, please. Give me as much as you can."

He put the card through the mail slot and Isabel scanned it, tapping on the keyboard as she frowned. "Andrew Goodwin," she said. "The name's not familiar. Where did we meet?"

"It'll take a while to explain."

She sighed, then put a slip of paper through the slot. "Just sign this while I get your cash."

He stared blankly at the paper. "Isn't there another way?"

"Just sign it, please."

Daniel swallowed hard. He didn't have a clue what Andrew's signature looked like. He had never seen it. Daniel shut his eyes and tried to concentrate, but there were no sudden flashes of inspiration, no fleeting glimpses of how to do it.

He put the pen in his right hand – the one Andrew wrote with. Unable to back out without raising suspicion, Daniel relaxed his wrist and let it guide him. *A huge, over-the-top curve for the capital 'G'. A trailing end to the letter 'n'.*

He fed the paper back through the slot and uttered a silent prayer. But to his surprise, Isabel filed the receipt without giving it a second glance, keen to hurry things along.

"Here you go." She bundled an envelope full of money into the slot. "Is that all I can help you with?"

"I think so," he said. "I mean what I said. I really do want the chance to explain myself."

"I don't know if that's such a good idea," she said. "Maybe we should just forget it."

Daniel shook his head in disbelief. "You need to read the note before you say that."

"Maybe," she conceded. "But until then, please don't follow me around."

He beat a hasty retreat, marching straight out onto the pavement before his luck got any worse. The sunshine heightened the sweat on his brow, the breeze adding a cool edge to air.

Isabel was engaged.

He struggled believe it. Things couldn't have gone any worse in there. Now, she was more than just oblivious. She was cautious, and it would take even more to convince her who he was.

The surrounding crowds grew thick around him as the day advanced. Just when he thought his bad luck was over, Daniel looked down the pavement and saw a face among them.

Ryan was heading to the bank.

There he was, strolling towards him with a cocky gait and a glazed, contented expression. *The expression of a man in love.* Daniel couldn't take his eyes off him, and it was inevitable that Ryan caught him looking.

"Can I help you?" He said as he approached.

Daniel was through playing games. "I heard you checked the post this morning."

Ryan flipped. Before Daniel could react, he leapt forwards and gripped the collar of his shirt.

"That was you, wasn't it?" he spat. "Putting notes through my door and trying to scare me. Why are you here? What did you say to her?"

The park was full of watchful eyes, but Ryan didn't care, shaking Daniel so hard that his senses were addled.

"Just the truth," said Daniel.

Ryan tightened his grip. "Daniel Lawton is dead and buried. There's no cause to drag him up again unless you want something."

Daniel gagged, his airway blocked. "She has a right to know who you really are."

Ryan raised the heel of his hand and smacked Daniel on the nose, so hard that Daniel slipped through his grip and crumpled to the ground. He scraped his arms on the concrete.

"If you so much as speak to her again," said Ryan, "I'll track you down and make you wish you'd never bothered. Is that clear?"

Ryan picked him back up and Daniel nodded, dazed and powerless.

"Now walk away."

Doing as he was told to, Daniel stumbled blindly down the pavement, away from the bank. He didn't look behind him until he was safely locked in Andrew's car, and by then, Ryan had disappeared.

The money in Daniel's pocket did little to ease his despair. He felt sick to his stomach. Even after all that time, Ryan still had it in for him, clinging to the life he had stolen.

Daniel had to find a way around him, to get to Isabel without him being able to intervene. To turn Ryan into the enemy he really was.

Daniel stiffened his resolve.

If it came to it, Ryan wasn't the only one who could use violence and threats.

16|DENTITY

The next morning came suddenly. A cool breeze drifted across Daniel's face as scant rest withered to reveal a cold surface against his skin.

Certainly not a pillow.

He leapt to his feet. Bright morning sunlight flooded his eyes, and it took a moment to think straight. It wasn't Andrew's bedroom, nor anyone else's.

He was outside.

Daniel had been sleeping in a flowerbed with thick, squat bushes. He turned to see a semi-detached house in what looked like a quiet estate. He was in someone's garden, half-hidden by a row of shrubbery.

Andrew had taken him out of the flat.

Clothes were covered in black soil, dripping off in clumps. He had stiff legs, sore calf muscles, a tight stomach, and a pounding headache.

Andrew must have finally snapped, reacting to the time Daniel had stolen from him. Daniel had a fleeting glimpse of walking the streets in the dead of night, running as though trying to escape.

It looked different in the daytime. He stepped over a white picket fence onto the pavement, trying to find his bearings. Cars were parked in every driveway, curtains drawn in every window. A street enveloped in silence.

Daniel tried to concentrate – to draw memories out – but all he saw in his mind were streetlamps. He checked his pockets to find no money, no wallet.

No keys.

He dropped to his knees, scratching through the flowerbed. Andrew wouldn't have come outside without some way of getting back in. *Surely not.*

He turned over clods of earth and swept away branches, but didn't find so much as a coin or scrap of paper.

He swore, and the commotion caused a rattle from inside the house. Suddenly, the front door flew open, and a man came storming down the step towards him – late thirties, carrying a hefty weight he wasn't afraid to throw around.

"What the hell do you think you're doing?" he shouted.

Daniel immediately stood and tried to kick the soil flat, brushing it from his thighs. "I'm sorry," he said. "I lost something in your garden."

The man came to the edge of the lawn and towered over him. Daniel braced himself for violence, but as soon as they were up close, the man stopped dead.

"Oh my God," he said. "Are you alright?"

"My keys fell out of my pocket," said Daniel. "I'm so sorry about the mess. I was trying to find them."

The man winced. "Have you been attacked? How long have you been out here?"

"I don't remember," said Daniel. He lifted a hand to his face, worried what he looked like, and the man ushered him towards the house.

"You'd better come in and sit down. Have you called the police?"

"No," said Daniel. "I don't think so."

Daniel allowed himself to be led indoors, still clueless where he was. A wide, well lit hallway led through the kitchen to a large conservatory, and the man sat him at a dining table, bathed in direct sunlight.

"No doubt you could use a drink," said the man. "Just take a moment and I'll find the house phone."

"Please," said Daniel, "I just need a moment to pull myself together and I'll be fine."

Footsteps came thumping down the stairs, and a curious head poked through the doorway. Daniel recognised the person at once – the woman he had seen at the supermarket, the one Andrew appeared to be involved with.

On sight of him, her face fell, and Andrew's reason for being there suddenly became much clearer.

"What's going on?" she asked, portraying no further sign of recognition.

"This is my wife," said the man, then turned to address her. "Cheryl, I found this gentleman outside. I think he's been attacked."

Daniel had seen that name in Andrew's call log. *Cheryl*. It felt familiar, just as she did. *Like they had known one another for a while...*

Cheryl walked into the conservatory and pretended not to know him, scanning his face with distant concern. "What happened to your eye?" she asked.

"It's not as bad as it looks." Daniel replied, awkwardly. "At least I don't think it is."

She went to the freezer and addressed her husband. "I can look after him," she said, taking out a tray of ice. "You'd better head off, or you'll be late."

She placed an affectionate hand on the man's chest, trying to keep Daniel from seeing. Cheryl kept a warm smile on her face until her husband agreed, closing the front door as he left.

Then her demeanour changed completely.

"I don't remember inviting you over," she said.

Daniel tensed. "I'm sorry. I didn't realise where I was."

She banged the tray of ice against the counter, loosening cubes which she bundled into a dishcloth. "What's happened to you?" she said.

"I had a fall."

"Did you trip over those legs you keep dragging?"

"Something along those lines," he said.

She handed him the cloth and he pressed it to his eye, still unclear what his injury looked like. Her sympathy was muted.

"I wasn't sure I'd see you again after your behaviour in the supermarket the other day," she said. "You just wandered off and left me sat there."

"I had a funny turn," said Daniel. "I came back once I felt better, but you didn't wait for me."

"Of course I didn't." She turned to the cupboards, showing her back to him. "And when you rang me again last night, I honestly thought you were going to hurt yourself. Is that what you've done?"

The ice burned his skin. "I don't remember much about it," he said.

"So it's drink," said Cheryl. "There's a trace of something on your breath."

"It's not that, either," he said. "I can't elaborate until I understand it better myself. This is something I have no control over, and there are other men involved."

"Be honest with me, Andrew – are you up to something illegal?"

He looked her in the eye. "Believe me, this is not my fault."

"Then you should go to the police."

"It's too complicated," he said. "I'm not sure the police would be able to help."

"You could be wrong. You said you were trapped in the flat, too, but you clearly aren't."

"Did I really say that?" he said. Daniel knew Andrew had spoken to her, but not what was said.

"Yes, you did. And the fact you don't remember only makes things worse."

"Maybe the latch was stuck," he said, dismissively. "Things like that always seem more serious at night."

Cheryl poured him a steaming cup of coffee and sat down. The sunshine caught her hair, making it look like tiny sparks were shooting from her scalp.

"I'm worried about you," she said.

"It won't be like this for long," said Daniel. "I'll find a way to fix it, and things can go back to normal."

"I'm not going to tell you how to run your life, but I think you should get the police involved."

Daniel cradled the coffee cup in his hands, but didn't want it. Bad things had happened the last time he drank coffee. "I won't stay here long," he said. "I need to sort this mess out."

She cleared her throat. "You shouldn't be here in the first place. I've told you before not to come over."

"Why? Because of your husband?"

Cheryl curled her lip and looked away, disliking the reminder. "That's not the only reason, Andrew. Your behaviour in the last few days has made me realise a few things I'm not sure about."

"Such as?"

She grimaced, as though the walls would remember her words. "I've practiced this in my head a hundred times, but it's still hard to say. I'm hoping you'll understand if I try to be honest."

"Cheryl," he interrupted, "this isn't the time to say things you're not sure about. I'm sorry. I wish I could explain, but please don't put yourself out there for me right now."

She stopped in her tracks. "You don't want to hear what I have to say?"

"Not at the moment. Look at me. I know I can't tell you what's going on, but it's serious. Don't get involved."

Cheryl looked hurt, but it was necessary. "Maybe you're right," she said, averting her gaze. "Forget I brought it up. Anyway, you've seen where I live, so I suppose that's progress, right?"

A lock of hair drifted over her eyes, and she brushed it away with an elegant flick of her wrist. He tried to picture her with darker hair, standing on the promenade as she had been on that terrible day.

"Why do you keep looking at me like that?" she asked, self-consciously. "You're staring like I've done something wrong."

Daniel cleared his throat. "There's something else I need to get off my chest. We've met before, two years ago. Something awful happened to me, and I can remember you there at the time."

She didn't need to think. "You mean the crash?"

His legs stiffened. "So I'm right – it was you?"

"No, it wasn't. I haven't been south of London in my entire life. But you've told me about it before. I've seen the scar on your back."

Daniel was slow to catch on, dumbfounded. His head shook in disbelief. *Andrew had been in the crash that triggered his heart attack.*

"What else have I told you?"

Cheryl shrugged. "You explained how you lost control of the car, and the damage it caused meant you couldn't walk for a long time afterwards."

He put a hand on the table to steady himself. *The car that slid right past him, the silver hatchback that had pulled out of moving traffic.*

She froze when she saw his face. "Have I said something wrong?"

"Tell me everything else I said to you."

"You're scaring me, Andrew."

"What else?"

Her face flushed red. "I don't know. You said your marriage collapsed because of it, and you haven't seen her in months."

"Why was I down there in the first place?"

"It was a holiday. Don't you remember?"

A cold shiver ran through his veins and things started falling into place. Waves of memories were unlocked from experiences he and Andrew had shared.

He heard screams – *felt them* – saw blue sky, shattered glass, and horrified faces. Daniel saw his own body from the outside, viewed through the windscreen of a car.

Those now-familiar hands on the steering wheel, those same frightened eyes in the rear-view mirror.

Andrew had been driving the car that swept past him. Daniel could see it now. He recognised Andrew's ex-wife in the passenger seat. Ever since Daniel had first woken up in bed beside her, he knew he had seen her before.

Daniel felt a weight on his chest as his heart stumbled.

"What's wrong?" Cheryl looked him over with a trace of fear, but he wasn't listening. Daniel had been living inside the man responsible for everything that had happened to him, whether it had been intended or not. Ryan was harmless by comparison.

Andrew Goodwin had killed him.

"I need to go," said Daniel.

Cheryl wasted no time. "I'll call you a taxi." She gladly left the room, confused and unnerved.

Alone, Daniel fought to remain calm. It changed everything, each lingering shred of pity and regret. Andrew had taken Daniel's life, and somehow fate had seen fit to turn the tables.

An eye for an eye.

He saw a new direction. By any means at his disposal, Andrew Goodwin had to be wiped off the planet. It simply wasn't fair to grant him anything less.

Daniel thought of nothing else until Cheryl returned, and they sat in silence as they waited for the taxi to arrive. Fuelled by sudden hatred, Daniel would use Andrew's own life against him.

Cheryl – *Andrew's lover* – would help Daniel to get home and make sure he was alright. There would be a neighbour – *somebody, anybody* – who would let him back into the building, where he would force his way into the flat.

Daniel could then use Andrew's possessions to force him out. Ryan had intercepted the business card and chosen to deny what it told him, but Daniel would try harder. There was another way to tell his tale without choking on the words.

Andrew's video camera.

He could rehearse, make it perfect. His confession and history, everything he remembered until the moment he died. He would give Ryan and Isabel something they couldn't argue with, make it irrefutable.

Then, together, the three of them would find a way to end the life of Andrew Goodwin.

17|MPTINESS

Daniel found Ryan's black Range Rover parked in the same old space, outside the same old office. He knew precisely which window Ryan would be sat behind, able to keep a watchful eye on his vehicle.

It was early in the afternoon, but Daniel didn't feel the least bit tired. Anticipation had him too far on edge, more alert than he had felt in a long time.

Nervous.

In his hands, he kept a tight hold of Andrew's video camera. He had recorded a ten minute confession – a collection of stories that he hoped would prove his identity beyond all reasonable doubt.

Not that Ryan was reasonable, but by intercepting the business card, he had presented himself as a litmus test. *A dry run, a chance to test the footage on a man who didn't matter.*

The car door opened with a warm clunk, and Daniel stepped onto the road. He had parked far away from Ryan's window. The car was too distinctive to be missed, and Daniel needed the distance to gather his strength.

He perched close to the building door, and when ready, stepped into the open. It was only a matter of seconds before Ryan came rushing out.

"You again?" Ryan stood in a shirt and tie, one foot frozen in the doorway. His jaw hung open.

"Don't fly off the handle this time," said Daniel.

"I thought I told you to keep your distance." Ryan took Daniel by the arm and strode away from the office. He tried to stand tall – to look strong – but his face told a different story. "Why are you here?" he said.

"To make you appreciate what I wrote on the card," said Daniel.

"I get the message," said Ryan, "I just don't care. You're abusing the name of a man who's not around to defend himself, and you're going to stop."

"But I don't need defending," said Daniel. "It's me, right here."

Ryan shook his head, dismissively. "How did you find me?" he said.

"I used to work here," said Daniel. "That's the same reason I know where you live."

Ryan's eye twitched. By all means, he wanted to lunge forward and attack, but couldn't with his colleagues so close. "Listen," he hissed, "tell me who are you, and what you want from me."

"You know who I am."

"Not a clue," said Ryan. "I was friends with Daniel for years, both in and outside of work. I knew everything about him, and I swear he wouldn't know you, either."

Daniel held out the camera.

"Now, that's where you're wrong."

***

The first time Ryan watched the footage, he did so in silence. The second time, he was full of questions. By the third time he went through it, Ryan had gone back to saying nothing, gravity sinking in.

"I only know half of those stories," he said, "but I don't doubt the rest of them."

He and Daniel sat in a bus shelter, still in sight of the office. Both men had lowered their guard.

"No one could know that much about me," said Daniel. "Not even my father."

"Did Daniel keep a diary? Is that where it comes from?"

"It's me, Ryan," said Daniel. "I can't explain how it happened, but it's me."

Ryan kept his voice lowered, even though they were alone. "How could you possibly ask me to accept that you're him, right there in a stranger's body? It has to be a trick."

"For Christ's sake. It's not!"

Ryan stood up and glanced around him. "Let's suppose you're right, not that I believe it for a second. You're a grown man, so what happened to the whomever was in there before you?"

"His name's Andrew, and he's still here."

"What does he think about this?" said Ryan.

"I don't think he knows."

Ryan put a hand on Daniel's shoulder, ushering him away from the building. "Now, how would that be possible? Surely it's obvious."

"I've only been back for a few days," said Daniel. "He hasn't pieced it together yet."

They reached the curb, but Ryan carried on walking, escorting Daniel across the road. "You know what I think?" said Ryan. "I'd say there must be something wrong with you, something missing in your own life that you're trying to fill with a dead man's."

Daniel tried to slow down, but Ryan tightened the grip on his shoulder, pushing him towards the car.

"Ryan," said Daniel. "Wait..."

"Just get back in your car, Andrew. Drive away and find something more constructive to do with your time." He spun Daniel around and pushed the video camera into his chest. "That's the last I want to hear of it."

"You have to understand," said Daniel. "This isn't bitterness about you and Isabel. It's about my identity."

"Goodbye, *Andrew*."

Ryan folded his arms, making it clear he wasn't open for discussion. He waited as Daniel unlocked the car and put his foot inside, the door acting like a shield between them.

"Let me prove how well I know you," said Daniel. "Ask me something no one else could answer."

"No." Ryan's expression held fast, but Daniel didn't give up.

"We used to go to the pub after work on a Thursday," he said. "Years ago now, before Isabel and I started seeing each other."

Ryan took a step back from the car, arms still wrapped across his chest. He said nothing.

"Okay," Daniel continued. "You were sleeping with the boss in your old department. That's why you had to leave."

"That's enough," said Ryan.

"Can't you see how important this is? If I can't convince you who I really am, then what chance do I have with my father and Isabel?"

"None whatsoever," said Ryan. "I'm warning you not to bring her into it."

"You can't ask me to do that," said Daniel. "You know she's too important."

Ryan grabbed Daniel's hair and pushed him down, forcing him into the driver's seat. Given no other choice, Daniel shut the car door.

"You're scared it might all change if I come back," said Daniel.

"Don't be stupid!"

Daniel started the engine and held the camera up. "It's all on here, Ryan. When she sees it, things will be different. You're not the only one who loves her."

"Alright, that's it." Ryan snarled and pulled the door handle. Daniel panicked, and before Ryan could reach inside, he hopped over the gearstick and climbed out of the other side of the car.

There wasn't time to think. Daniel turned and fled up the pavement, threading his fingers through the camera's hand strap, willing his tired legs not to fail him.

"Come back here," yelled Ryan, giving chase. "Give me that camera!"

Fear made Daniel blind. He ran to the end of the road and piled off the curb into oncoming traffic. A dozen vehicles slid to a halt with a deafening screech as he pelted between them, refusing to let himself be caught.

Ryan wasn't so fortunate. With no grip on his work shoes, he ran straight into the side of a van, knocking the wind out of his lungs. Struggling to right his balance, he lost sight of his target.

Giving Daniel an opportunity.

At the far pavement, Daniel ran headlong into a copse of trees, puffing and panting, well aware he couldn't outrun his tail on even ground. He buried himself deep amongst thick bushes and lay low, kneeling on cool soil.

He swallowed his breath and held it. Through gaps in the branches, he saw Ryan come through the traffic and pause, looking left to right, refusing to give up the chase.

Daniel's lungs screamed for oxygen, face glowing red, watching silently as Ryan chose a new direction and set off again, putting faith in blind luck.

Daniel had escaped. On a count of five, he let a long breath between his lips. The camera was still in his hand, intact. He closed his eyes and listened as the traffic moved away, stealing a moment to recover.

Even the confession hadn't been enough to convince Ryan of his identity. That made two failed attempts to win him over, and it shattered what was left of Daniel's confidence. His last remaining chance was to be even more extreme, to use force instead of reason.

Too late to back out now.

Daniel's breathing returned to normal, and so did his heart rate. Crouched down and secluded, he felt the faintest tingle at the back of his neck, and realised with horror what it meant.

Sleep.

Calming down from the chase, his body was commanding him to rest, putting him under so that it could recover before Andrew took control.

Daniel felt his weight leaning into the vegetation and slipped to the ground with a thump, the bushes shaking as he collapsed.

He searched his pockets and realised they were empty. The syringes were back in the car. Trembling arms gripped clumps of branches as he fought a powerful urge to lie back and drift out of consciousness.

Suddenly, the branches parted. The commotion had drawn attention, and Ryan had heard him. Without so much as a second glance, he bent down and smashed his fist into Daniel's face.

The blow connected with his already-bruised eye, intensifying the pain. It pushed Daniel back from the brink of passing out. Ryan grabbed his arm and twisted it out of shape, forcing the camera out of his numbed hand.

"This is mine now," said Ryan.

Daniel struggled to speak. "Isabel will believe me," he winced. "You know she will."

"She won't, because she'll never know about you. Even if your story was true, Andrew, I wouldn't let that happen. She's been through her grief already."

"It's not your decision to make." Daniel found himself leaning into Ryan's hold, teasing the pain to stay focussed.

"Well, it certainly isn't yours," said Ryan. "And since we're as good as married, you can bet your life I'll protect her as I see fit."

"Just listen to me," said Daniel.

Ryan gripped the video camera in his free hand. "No, you listen to me," he said. "Your lies end here. If I see you again, I'll kill you. Got it?"

Stripped of choice, Daniel nodded in agreement. Ryan let go of his arm and stepped back onto the pavement, taking the camera with him. But Daniel couldn't leave it there.

Sleep was still coming.

Before Ryan could react, Daniel scrabbled out of the bushes, stumbling back into the road. Brakes shrieked as traffic swerved to avoid him, a miracle he wasn't knocked down.

The tarmac seemed to twist beneath Daniel's feet as he hurried back down to his car and wrenched the door open, collapsing into the passenger seat. With laboured movements, he clicked open the glove box and grabbed one of his syringes.

There were seconds to spare. Daniel dug the needle into his leg, praying to strike a vein, heaving down on the plunger with all the strength he had remaining.

Immediately, cool, raw shock dragged him back from the brink of unconsciousness. Daniel felt a rush of liquid through his veins, electrifying his nerves.

Making him feel alive.

The darkness was instantly subdued, pushed back for a few hours more. Adrenaline once again saved his day from an abrupt end, giving him a last reprieve to finish what he had started.

The chance, however, had passed. Daniel looked up to see Ryan return to the office, somewhere he couldn't follow. Ryan wouldn't come back out for hours, and Daniel couldn't wait that long.

He was on borrowed time.

Daniel banged his hands against the steering wheel in anger, then stopped himself. Getting worked up only made things worse. He had to be more stoic, learn how to ration his remaining strength.

Because if Andrew learned that trick first, a huge advantage would be lost.

There was less urgency than he cared for. Ryan was protecting Isabel, and didn't want her to watch Daniel's confession. Another day would make no difference to what she knew of him.

Daniel had to rest – succumb to sleep, and in doing so, put himself back at the hands of Andrew Goodwin.

Though Daniel grimaced at the prospect, it didn't render him helpless. He could throw Andrew off the scent, take steps to keep him trapped in his nocturnal prison.

The car keys could be hidden, the money confiscated, and he could go further. For the first time, break the silence.

With shaky hands, Daniel was going to write to him.

Andrew,

By now I'm sure you know things aren't how they should be. You can't change that so stop fighting. Stop wasting time. Stop trying to run.

Just stay put. It will all be different soon.

18|ACRIFICE

Daniel heard a crunch, smashed glass. He was on his feet before he knew it, turning towards the sound. Dazed and disorientated, he realised it was a new day.

Night had been and gone without him even realising.

He was in an empty bedroom. The curtains were a deep, metallic orange, and faded paper on the bare walls showed where pictures had once hung in the sunlight.

Daniel took a moment to adjust, unsure if he recognised it. In his mind's eye, only seconds had passed since he had fought with Ryan, and he was still reeling from the blow to his eye socket.

Now, it seemed Andrew had moved him again in the night. *First Cheryl's front garden, now this.* The man was more than just an obstacle.

He was becoming a real threat.

Looking over his shoulder, Daniel saw a door leading onto a narrow landing, cold and blue. His attention was instantly drawn to a bathroom at the end, where the light was on.

He had been there before – the mirror he had peered into on the first night of his rebirth. The first time he had seen his new reflection.

This was Andrew's house, or had been once. Andrew must have come there seeking refuge, and he hadn't come empty handed. Beneath a dusty, full-width mirror sat a porcelain washbasin, and Daniel discovered where the crunching sound had come from.

It was full of broken glass.

Andrew had taken the metal safe box that Daniel kept under the bed and brought it to the unfamiliar house. He had then used the box to smash its contents to pieces. Glistening liquid poured from smashed vials and broken ampoules.

All of the adrenaline, wasted.

Daniel tossed the box onto the floor and rifled through the broken fragments. Only one syringe had survived intact – safe inside its plastic wrapper – but it was empty.

Panicking, Daniel used it to suck up every tiny pool of the yellow-tinted substance, struggling to fill it even halfway, scarcely able to believe what he had been reduced to.

Just half a shot, then it was all gone.

Daniel buried his face in his hands, peering between spiny fingers at his reflection. He felt a swell of hatred boiling over, swift and insurmountable. *Those unfamiliar eyes and unkempt hair.*

Andrew Goodwin was ruining everything. Daniel smacked the side of his head with the palm of his hand, trying to beat his opponent from his skull. He snapped and threw himself headlong at the mirror, crashing into the glass. It folded with a crunch, forming cobweb-like fractures.

Wounding both men.

Dazed, Daniel tripped over his feet and stumbled back onto the landing, tumbling to the floor. Deep pressures were released, and a sudden flood of pictures gushed through his mind.

Daniel saw through Andrew's eyes – climbing into the Honda Civic and reversing out of the car park, escaping from the flat in the darkness. He saw how Andrew had driven to that empty house. *Katie's house.* As he thought about it, Daniel knew the name. *Katie, Andrew's ex-wife.*

And this time, Daniel's stolen memories carried more than just images. As he lay on the floor in contortion, he felt waves of emotion as well. *Paranoia and desperation.*

He realised how Andrew was feeling, not so much a conniver as a man at the end of his tether, someone wholly out of control. Daniel hadn't realised how badly the man had been affected.

It was good.

The pain subsided, and Daniel came back to his senses with new wisdom. Andrew could still be controlled. Daniel just had to assert himself, to be more clever in his approach, turning Andrew's fear to his advantage.

Daniel climbed to his feet, and again, looked in the mirror. Between concentric cracks, he saw himself differently. With pale skin and a bruised eye – so unruly and gaunt – he had become a blank canvas. No longer Andrew Goodwin, but not quite Daniel Lawton. Someone new.

He could work with that.

Daniel picked up the safe box and took stock. At least Andrew hadn't thought to empty it. The wallet was still in there, along with the bank notes he had managed to get from Isabel two days before.

He found the mobile phone, and on sight of it, discovered someone had been trying to make contact. There were four unanswered calls, all from that morning – one from a blocked number, and three from a mobile phone. His heart fluttered at the thought of Isabel, but he knew better. Only one person had cause to be so persistent.

Daniel rang the number back, and it connected almost instantly.

"There you are." Ryan's manner was different on the phone. Calmer.

"What do you want now?" Daniel asked.

"To talk," said Ryan. "I've had all night to mull over the things you've told me, and I have more questions."

"Are you serious?" said Daniel. "You attacked me. Why would I want to come near you again?"

"Because if everything you said was true, then you'll need me to believe you. I'm guessing that's worth any risk."

Daniel snarled, unable to deny it. "We went through this yesterday. How do I know you're prepared to listen this time?"

"You have my word."

"Alright then," said Daniel, with a sigh. "I can come to the office right now, but we have to stay in plain sight so I feel safe. And I want my camera back."

Ryan lowered his voice, as though others could hear him. "The office is no good. I'll have to come to you."

"You mean to my home?" said Daniel.

"That's right," said Ryan. "I can be there in an hour. Just give me the address."

Daniel was instantly wary. The flat was his only sanctuary. They needed somewhere neutral – open, overlooked, and yet still private.

Standing on the landing of Katie's house, Daniel looked through a long window at a suburban street. Something rose proudly above the rooftops in the near distance.

The familiar spire of a church.

He had a better way to deal with Ryan.

***

An indecisive summer yielded unpredictable weather. One minute, the sky was clear, and the next, it was covered with cloud.

In transition between the two states, patches of white were intercut with vast strips of blue. The sun would beat down for minutes, only to have it smothered, and an ominous chill cast over the landscape.

It suited the location. Daniel stood on cut grass, surrounded by burial plots and decades-old headstones. The church towered overhead, sun shining through stained glass windows, bringing colour to pale stonework.

No more than a handful of visitors wandered amongst the graves, enough to keep Daniel from feeling alone. He waited restlessly as Ryan's black Range Rover pulled up at the roadside, and Ryan ambled casually over.

"Looking for your headstone?" Ryan wasn't smiling, full of disdain.

"I was cremated," Daniel replied. "You know I don't have one."

"You're right: I do know that, but you shouldn't. Who else have you been talking to?"

"None of your business."

Ryan held out the camera. "You should know I've made copies of the footage."

"I'd expect nothing less," said Daniel, "but do you believe it yet?"

"Your confession? Of course not. It's the rest of the tape I'm more concerned about."

Daniel frowned, and instinctively stepped behind a pitted headstone, keeping a shield between them. "What do you mean?" he asked.

Ryan shook his head. "I'm not surprised you don't know what else is on there. *A certain car crash.* It's right near the end of the recording. You filmed the whole thing – the truth, not just your version of it."

Daniel looked down at the camera. Andrew had left it recording on the bedroom floor, days ago. Daniel had helped himself without thinking to check what was on there already.

"Andrew filmed the crash?" he said.

"Yes," said Ryan. "That's exactly what you did. Now, I've seen you mount the curb and kill the real Daniel Lawton. You mowed him down in cold blood."

A sudden breeze snaked through the graveyard. "It can't be what you think," said Daniel.

"It couldn't be anything else," said Ryan. "You should be locked up, and I'm here to make sure that happens."

Daniel raised his hand defensively. "Hang on a second," he said. "You told me you'd listen."

"Save your breath. It wouldn't change my mind. You're trying to steal a man's identity to extort the ones who loved him."

"There's another explanation." Daniel was growing short of breath. "I didn't know Andrew had filmed the crash, but it actually helps to prove my point."

"I'm not the one you have to convince," said Ryan. "We're going to the police station together, you and I. We'll show them what you did. I don't know how you've managed to get away with it for so long, but it goes no further."

"Ryan, I'm begging you as someone who used to be your friend. You've already taken everything I have-..."

"Don't act like you know me," said Ryan. "You're insane! The only reason I haven't already gone to the police was I needed to look you in the eye first, and now I can see the fear. You know you've been caught."

Ryan curled his lip, and Daniel knew it was pointless to plead for sympathy. Ryan was a man who would exploit every advantage to his own ends.

Daniel had to run.

He turned on his heels and shot across the graveyard, clutching the camera tightly. A straight line took him to the rear gate, a route that Daniel had been careful to learn.

And he had left the gate swinging open.

"Get back here!" Ryan gave chase, instinctively following. Even blackmail was worthless if Daniel disappeared, and he had a substantial head start, thirty yards in front by the time Ryan matched his speed.

Ryan lost him around the corner for almost three seconds, struggling to keep up with the change of direction. Katie's house was less than a minute away, and Daniel covered the ground almost effortlessly, buoyed by resolve. He could feel his heart rate soar, but controlled his breathing, eyes steadfast and cold.

He saw Andrew's red Honda Civic parked in the driveway, reminding him which house to turn into. Well ahead of his rival, he loosened his grip on the camera and launched it into a bush by the window.

It sank between the leaves, hidden from sight. Daniel stood by the open door and readied himself as Ryan came hurting up the gravel and threw himself into the air.

Together, they crashed through the front door and into the hallway. Daniel gasped, turning as he landed. Ryan grabbed the back of his head and forced it to the ground.

"Where do you think you're going?" Ryan shouted into his ear, hatred burning in his eyes.

Daniel heaved himself along the floor, carrying the weight of both men. Ryan tried to dig his heels into the ground – to stop him in his tracks – but Daniel had too much determination, calling on a reserve of strength he didn't know he had.

Hidden power from his borrowed body.

Daniel raised his elbow and flung it over his shoulder, catching Ryan's jaw. Ryan tried to grab hold of his arm, but Daniel was indomitable.

He used the shift in weight to roll Ryan off him and clambered back to his feet, hobbling down the hallway and lunging through the door. He grabbed something he had laid out on the kitchen counter earlier.

A piece of brick.

As Ryan rushed towards him, Daniel span around and sent it flying through the air. The blow connected directly with Ryan's scalp with a crunch. Blood splattered across the wall and he stopped dead in his tracks, head bobbing, then collapsed at Daniel's feet.

In seconds, it was over. Ryan's chest rose and fell – not dead, but out cold, and unlikely to recover in a hurry. Daniel steadied himself on the wall and tried to swallow his panic.

This was how it needed to happen.

Ryan couldn't be allowed to roam free, and the police would lock Daniel in prison for the evidence against him.

There was another way. Wasting no time, Daniel stooped down and grabbed Ryan's arms, dragging him into the lounge. The room was empty – abandoned by its owners – but Daniel had discovered a tool shed in the garden and helped himself to some useful items.

A plastic chair and a roll of twine.

He sat Ryan facing the window, looking out into the garden. Long ago, Daniel had used that view to gauge the passage of time, looking out to see the seasons change. The garden was once well-tended and vibrant, but now sagging branches draped over a forlorn hedgerow, flowerbeds choked by spreading weeds.

Cold and unloved, even in the summertime.

It seemed fitting that Ryan should be in the same position. Daniel put him on the plastic chair, then bound his wrists together through the slats on the back, making it so tight that no man could feasibly undo it themselves.

The blood running down Ryan's face had started to crust, and his head was slumped into his chest. As wretched as he looked, however, Daniel found it hard to feel any pity.

The man was an animal.

Daniel could feel his own heart starting to slow, but he was ready for what followed. Without hesitating, he took the mobile phone out of his pocket and let it slip to the floor, where he rose the heel of his shoe and smashed it onto the screen.

The handset was crushed to pieces, *revenge for the wasted adrenaline*. Daniel could survive without a phone, whereas to Andrew, it was a lifeline.

As Daniel's legs started to grow heavy, he drew the curtains closed and turned on the ceiling light, hiding from any prying eyes. Then he sat on the floor and leaned against the radiator beneath the window, facing his captive.

With a sense of grim necessity, Daniel took hold of the outlet pipe and wrapped the rest of the twine around it – over and over again, tying his wrist down, so tightly that it hurt.

There wasn't time to consider how to get loose again come morning. Ryan still refused to accept who Daniel was, and there was only one way he could think of to prove that Daniel Lawton and Andrew Goodwin were different people.

Daniel would show Andrew to Ryan.

The two men would be secure, and they could do nothing but talk. Once Daniel was back the next day, he and Ryan could work together to get free. All that mattered was the end result.

Restrained, Daniel let his head fall back against the wall and waited for sleep to come. He shut his eyes and concentrated, trying to detach from the line of distinction where Daniel ended and Andrew began.

Andrew needed to understand how dangerous Ryan could be for them both. With no means to write a note, Daniel tried to reach out from within, to somehow breach the divide.

As consciousness left him, Daniel pleaded to where Andrew sheltered in the corners of his mind. "Andrew," he called out inside his head. "Are you there?"

He strained so hard that he mouthed the words in real life.

"Listen to me," he whispered. "There are things you need to know..."

19|ATRED

The night passed in the blink of an eye, a frenzied nightmare that threw Daniel back into the waking world with a falling sensation.

He immediately felt a hard floor beneath him – kitchen tiles.

He was still in Katie's house.

The entire left side of his body was numb, paralysed where he had been lying awkwardly on the floor. He felt a large swelling beneath his scalp that throbbed like he had been bashed with a lump hammer.

It was a bright new morning. Daniel tried to draw out Andrew's latest memories, but while doing so, he discovered a piece of torn wallpaper lying beside him, with writing all over it.

Daniel,
I found the man you left for me and let him go. You can't hope to control me all the time, so if there's something you want then just tell me what it is. We need to talk.

Jesus, Daniel thought. Panic swept him onto his feet and he rushed to the lounge.

Ryan had gone.

The plastic chair stood empty in the middle of the room, unravelled twine in a heap across the carpet. Daniel felt a twisting pain in his stomach as he tried to figure out how the two men had managed to get loose.

And the note had called him by name, something Andrew wasn't supposed to know.

With no time to think, Daniel rushed out of the house and thrust his hands into the bush by the front door, feeling for the camera and car keys he had stowed there. Ryan had likely been free for hours, and there was no telling what damage he could have done in that time.

Daniel needed to give chase.

Beneath a glaring sun, he started the car and took off, driving headlong towards the bank. He raced through red lights with reckless disregard, weaving in and out of traffic.

It took seconds to reach the village green. Daniel pulled over by the pavement and dove outside. As he stumbled through the entrance, Isabel saw the bruises on his face and stood up from behind the service counter.

"You shouldn't have come here," she said.

"I know you don't want to see me," said Daniel as he approached the safety glass. "There's something you need to look at."

He placed the video camera in the slot, and Isabel stared from a safe distance. "What is it?" she said.

"Just talking. Things I've been trying to tell you all along."

She reached cautiously down and retrieved it. "Will you go away if I watch this?"

He thought before he answered. "If you still feel the same way, I won't have a choice."

"Okay then," she said, "but you can't stay here while I do."

"You'll have questions," he said.

Isabel shook her head. "Go outside, or you can forget the whole thing."

He complied and retreated slowly, his raised hands trembling. Isabel watched as he let himself out of the door and stepped back onto the pavement.

It was done. After a week of wasted chances, she was finally going to see the truth about him. With a cocktail of emotions, Daniel turned towards his car, when he noticed something in the distance.

A hauntingly familiar shape, standing out from its surroundings.

Ryan was there.

The black Range Rover had been parked eighty meters down the road. Daniel had seen it enough times to know it at a glance. Unable to see the driver, he hurried back to the Civic and sought shelter, sitting in the passenger seat and adjusting the rear-view mirror so he could watch the pavement.

He lay low, with his heart in his mouth. Daniel took the last remaining syringe out of the glove box and held it close, knowing that once his guard was lowered, the tiredness wouldn't be far away.

Two minutes passed slowly. Craving distraction, Daniel reached under the seat for something he had hidden there days before – the photograph he had stolen from his father's house.

Me, Dad and Isabel, March 4ᵗʰ

Somehow, in his father's company, Daniel had managed to stay awake for several hours. He tried to remember how calm and comfortable he had felt, tried to return to that contented state.

After his violent morning, however, it couldn't have worked. A warm shiver spread quickly up Daniel's spine. *Drowsiness.*

With no other choice, he held the syringe so the tip pointed down at his leg, teasing the plunger until a single droplet of liquid formed on the end. He could feel his eyes drifting closed as he stabbed the needle into his thigh and pushed the plunger down.

Instantly, fatigue was peeled back for another few hours. When Daniel looked again, the photograph had slipped from between his fingers.

And it was fifteen minutes later.

He removed the syringe and hauled himself out of the car, rushing back into the bank. Isabel was sat behind the counter with a stern expression. This time, she didn't back away.

"Did you watch it?" Daniel asked as he ran over.

"Watched what, exactly?" she said. "You taped yourself sleeping for two hours?"

Isabel shoved the camera back into the slot.

"I don't understand," said Daniel.

"Neither do I," she spat. "Is this a joke? All the effort you've put in just to show me something so pointless?"

He picked up the camera and played it from the start, but all he saw was Andrew, fast asleep in his bed. *No confession.*

"Now, you said you'd leave me alone if I watched it," said Isabel, "and I'm going to hold you to that. Don't come back, or I swear I'll call the police."

"Wait," said Daniel. "That isn't what I wanted you to see. There was more."

She leaned over and spoke into the microphone on the counter, making sure everyone heard her. "There's a button under this desk that can have the police here in minutes. I'm not asking you again. Leave now."

"Can you please just listen to me for a second?"

"*Leave.*"

Daniel backed off, no choice. Distraught, disbelieving, he pulled open the door and staggered outside. This time, he found Ryan's car had come much closer, and Daniel could see him behind the wheel, broad shoulders hunched down.

"What did you do to the tape?" Daniel roared, storming over. "Where's my confession?"

"I deleted it," Ryan said, calmly. "You know what would have happened if she saw it. I'm just sparing the feelings of the woman we both love."

"You had no right to do that."

"Of course I did, Daniel. You just don't see it that way."

Daniel paused. "What a second, what did you call me?"

Ryan smiled. Even though his face was covered in dried blood and bruises, he didn't seem in the least bit weary. "Circumstances have changed a bit," he said.

"Your friend Andrew and I had a heart-to-heart last night, as you might have gathered."

"So do you believe me now?"

"It seems more reasonable with every minute. Get in the car and we'll talk."

Daniel took a step back. "So you can take me to the police station? No thanks."

A small group of people crossed the road, and Ryan beckoned Daniel closer. "Don't imagine you have a choice," he said with a hushed voice. "Andrew told me where you live, so it wouldn't be very hard to bring you down. Right now, I just want to talk, but not while Isabel can see us. Get in."

Daniel looked over his shoulder. There were faces peering out through the windows of the bank. "I don't have any reason to trust you," he said.

"You're the one who tied me up, so the feeling is mutual. Now be quick, we don't have all day."

***

Ryan took them away from the bank, driving slowly down the road with no clear destination. It made Daniel nervous.

"How long have you been like this?" Ryan kept taking his eyes off his driving, looking Daniel up and down.

"Two years," said Daniel, "but I wasn't awake for most of it. The last eight days is all I remember."

"How did Andrew do this to you?"

Daniel cleared his throat. "You tell me. You're the one who spoke to him."

"Yes," Ryan nodded. "I suppose that's a problem you both face."

Daniel gazed out of the window, watching the turns. "Does he realise what's happening yet?"

"He knows something's wrong," said Ryan, "but I don't think he's seen the full picture. Seems every bit as distressed as you are."

"I still want Isabel to know I'm alive."

"You could have just come clean the first time you saw her, instead of going so cloak-and-dagger."

"And how would that have sounded?" said Daniel. "She would have slammed the door in my face."

Ryan's driving reflected his mood, and as he became agitated, he accelerated. "You know I don't have a reason to like you," he said, "but let me give you probably the best advice you could have right now: *Give up.* It's been two years, and whatever torch you carry for Isabel won't be matched."

"If that were true then you wouldn't have erased my confession and made me look like an idiot in front of her."

"You can't blame me for being protective," said Ryan. "Something like that would devastate her."

"Well, then I suppose you've backed me into a corner. What exactly do you want?"

Ryan slowed down and stared at him. "Isabel hasn't seen my face today, but when she does, I'll have to explain where these bruises came from. How I tell that story is up to you."

"You want me to back off?" said Daniel.

"I want you to be realistic. We all watched you destroy yourself once, and I'm trying to stop you repeating past mistakes. Daniel's dead, let him go. If you stop trying to pour your heart out then I can help you be a part of her life."

"And what do you want in return?"

Ryan smiled. "The same thing anyone would want – to know how you did it."

Daniel squirmed uncomfortably. "I don't know how it happened. It just did."

"Something must have triggered it," said Ryan. "A thought, a will, even a prayer?"

"I can't answer that."

"Then let's jog your memory," Ryan turned the wheel, and Daniel panicked as he saw signs for the motorway.

"Where are you taking me?" he said.

"Back to where it happened," said Ryan.

"That's hours away," said Daniel. "I won't be awake for that long."

"Then maybe Andrew can help me, instead."

"And if we both refuse?" said Daniel.

A creasing smile spread across Ryan's cheeks. "Then maybe I could convince him to go to the police, instead. You should know I've already stopped him doing it once."

***

Ryan drove for over an hour without saying a word, and Daniel sat obediently in the passenger seat. The mere thought of their destination made him want to turn and run – the place where he died, the spot on the seafront where he had collapsed and let out his final breath.

What if something happened when he returned there?

Ryan didn't share his apprehension, speeding down the motorway with conviction on his face. Daniel glanced at the speedometer to see he was doing over a hundred miles per hour.

"You would have liked your funeral," said Ryan, breaking the silence. "Your father spoke."

His words took a moment to register. "I'm surprised you were even there," said Daniel.

"Isabel didn't want to face it alone," said Ryan. "Don't hold it against her."

"Just tell me honestly – how did you two start seeing one another, without my knowing?"

Ryan changed lanes and slowed down to concentrate on his words. "It was when you had your first heart murmur. She rang your desk phone to let everyone know, and left her number. Things just developed after that."

"So you started seeing her while I was in and out of hospital?"

"Only as a friend, but I suppose you could say that." He laughed. "It's funny, I was jealous of you back then for being with her, and now I'm jealous of something else you have."

"You went behind my back," said Daniel.

"Everything was above board," said Ryan. "The only grey area was that you two were still living together after you broke up, but even that sorted itself out eventually."

Daniel raised his voice. "A long time ago, I used to think of you as a friend, but since then, you've stolen pretty much everything I had. What amazes me is that you still don't seem to be satisfied."

Ryan changed lanes again as the car continued to slow down. He took his eyes off his driving. "Listen, I honestly couldn't care less about you right now," he said. "Two years ago, there was a shred of guilt, but I got over that, and it's been a lot better not having you around. We're even planning to sell that wretched house and bury your memory for good."

"You wouldn't dare," said Daniel.

Ryan swerved onto the hard shoulder. Gravel and stone chipped the undercarriage as they slid to a halt. "Stop living in the past," said Ryan. "You have something I want, and I can help you in return. Cooperate and we all see the benefits, or you can get out of the car right now and kiss goodbye to everything."

Ryan leaned past him and opened the passenger door. "You can be in Isabel's life or you can disappear today. It's your choice."

Daniel could feel his face flushing red. "You mean I'd get to watch from the sidelines while you make a new life with her?"

"It's the best you can hope for. You were weak then, and death hasn't taught you a thing. Just look at your bungled confessional tape."

"It was the only way."

"There were *hundreds* of ways," said Ryan. "Did you really think a recording would be good enough for something so important?"

"I would have liked to see you come up with better."

Ryan sat back in his seat. "Well, maybe one day that's what I'll do, and who knows? Maybe me and Isabel will make you a tape of our own while we're at it, show you what you're missing."

Daniel lost control. Before he knew what he was doing, he leapt across the seat and clasped his hands around Ryan's throat. Suddenly all the anger, all the emotion seemed to vent itself at once. Hatred flowed through his hands.

"You don't deserve her."

It would always be that way. Ryan would always find a way to steal the upper hand. Daniel wanted him to pay for the love he had stolen, and for setting him on the downward spiral that claimed his life. There was blood on Ryan's hands, and Daniel wanted revenge, to take back all he had lost.

Daniel wanted him to die.

20|XPLOITATION

Daniel couldn't tell what had happened on the seafront all those months ago, whether fate had planned to sweep him off the planet then changed its mind, or if Death, itself, had somehow made a mistake.

All he knew was that two people had driven him to his heart attack – one through misery, and the other by direct action.

The first of these was finally getting his comeuppance.

Daniel's hands were locked tightly around Ryan's throat, digging deep into the hard flesh of his neck. Cars rushed past the side window, but Daniel held position, clear of what needed to be done.

It felt good to have purpose. Even the exposed nature of the motorway hard shoulder couldn't stop him. Blood vessels burst as Ryan's eyes bulged out of their sockets, staring with horror at Daniel channelling his rage through screaming, red-raw muscles.

Ryan arched away from the seat, trying to push back, but Daniel kept pouring on determination, venting more and more hurt.

If only they had never met...

Ryan's oesophagus gave way with an audible crunch, and with waning strength, his fate was sealed. Brown eyes glazed over, and Daniel knew what they would see next. The surrounding world would fade to black, and he would float through a vast emptiness. Beyond which, Ryan wouldn't care about anything.

A passing wagon shook the car as Daniel lay the body back against the seat, pausing for a moment to catch his breath. There was finally peace in the vehicle. No more arguments, no more hurt.

Ryan wasn't going to be a problem anymore.

Daniel let himself out for some air, standing on the hard shoulder, nursing stiff hands. There was a sense of fulfilment, and he embraced the freedom Ryan had threatened to take from him – a newfound calm, looking down through the windscreen at the slumped and cooling corpse.

He felt no repulsion. If anything, he warmed towards the newly deceased for what they shared together. Where Ryan was heading, he would perhaps understand Daniel a little better.

The police, of course, wouldn't see it that way. Once Isabel learned Ryan was missing, she would know where to start looking, and nothing would convince her of Daniel's innocence.

The body had to go.

With a deep breath, Daniel reopened the door and bundled Ryan's corpse onto the back seat, laying it flat across the leather. Every passing car had a brief glimpse of his fumbling efforts, but no one realised what was going on.

He sat behind the wheel and fastened the seatbelt. Trembling, restless, fearful, and exalted, Daniel rejoined the traffic and made a beeline for the countryside, searching for anywhere secluded.

He was an hour from home, on unfamiliar roads. Daniel followed his gut and found each turn took him deeper into isolation. He could feel his heart rate slowing after the assault, so he turned on the air conditioning, trying to stay awake.

Recycling the stale stench of death.

As the lanes narrowed, Daniel paid less attention to the white lines down the middle of the road. He put his foot down, taking corners blindly.

Over the crest of a hill, the view opened out. Greenery stretched into the distance, fields and hedgerows. In the basin of a wide valley, thick forests surrounded the shimmering surface of a rippling lake.

Sunlight flickered off the water, stealing Daniel's focus. With his eyes on the distance, he had a sudden lapse of concentration. And in that moment, something happened.

An object appeared, *six inches from his nose.* He saw the wrinkled bark of a tree, and Daniel realised he was no longer moving, or even in the car. He heard billowing branches and turned around.

He was in a forest.

In less than the blink of an eye, he had been pulled from the roadside and cast deep into the heart of the woodland. Not a car crash – he wasn't injured or bleeding. *Someone or something had seized control while he was wide awake.*

Disorientated, Daniel steadied himself on the tree and looked up at a thick canopy of lush branches. A blue hue fell over the world that could only have been born of morning. Impossible, unless the night had been and gone.

His clothes were now streaked with dirt, and huge patches of damp soaked right through to the skin. Panic swelled into his sickly gut and he tasted bile in his mouth.

The car was nowhere in sight.

Daniel's feet pulled him into action, trying to find his bearings. Neither the undulating gradient of the forest bed, nor the still and silent air, gave any clue in which direction he was heading.

He wove between trees and thickets, hands scraping across rough bark. Out of control, he hurtled into a clearing, skidding over loose soil and onto a narrow stretch of faded tarmac.

A road.

He followed it blindly, guided only by instinct. The hard surface below made every impact shudder up his knees as he felt his heart racing, pushing him to the limit.

A hundred yards down the lane, he passed a dirt track that snaked back into the trees, and stopped. Andrew had been there, *he knew it*. The tree line parted like a deep, foreboding cavity, and Daniel felt loose gravel shift beneath his feet as he ventured inside.

It was the right place to look. As he edged into the dimness, he saw a large, dark object with steel spindles. Daniel ran towards it, placing his hand on cold metal. Ryan's car, abandoned.

Trembling, he put his face to the glass and peered through the window.

The body wasn't there.

Daniel caged a scream. Andrew had hidden the car and the body in two different places, leaving the freedom he had murdered to maintain hanging desperately in the balance.

The doors weren't locked, and the keys were in the ignition. Without wasting a second, Daniel leapt into the car and reversed down the track. There was a lingering odour inside that flooded his nose, wrenching his gut, and it triggered more recollections.

Andrew Goodwin had tried to dispose of Ryan's body by dragging it into the lake.

With the pedal to the floor, Daniel swung onto the road and sped away. Andrew had left the corpse floating in the open, startled by people walking around the shoreline.

It wasn't long before Daniel discovered muddy tyre marks, only a few hours old. He pulled over and followed the trail of evidence Andrew had left, pushing through ten meters of spiny branches until he abruptly arrived at the lakeside.

No sign of the body.

The air was calm, and he could see far over the smooth waters. Broken reeds showed where Andrew had entered the water, but Ryan's corpse was nowhere to be seen.

Daniel stormed down the embankment and stood teetering on the edge. The heel of his shoe sank into soft mud, icy water rising to his ankles.

He plunged knee-deep into the lake. Clouds of sediment billowed beneath the surface, and goosebumps rose like studs along his forearms.

Daniel pressed on through the cold with gritted teeth, sinking into oily silt. Feeling under the surface, he found tangles of weeds, debris brushing against his frozen fingers.

Ryan's body had to be down there. Cold and desperate, he widened his stance, denying the horrendous probability that he might never find it.

Water rose to his chest, sending shivers up his spine. Daniel's hands turned so numb that he could barely lift them back out of the water. Breathing heavily, he lost his battle with composure. It couldn't end like this.

Overwhelmed and abhorred, he had nowhere to turn. He scanned the water, hoping for a miracle, when he caught a sudden glimpse of something by the trees – a splash of green, strong against the pastel shades of morning.

A figure appeared on the bank, watching him wade in the water.

The woman who looked so much like Cheryl.

The woman who had watched him die.

Daniel's heart all but stopped at the sight of her. She wore a green coat – the same one he remembered from that distant day – and she was staring at him with similar concern.

He started towards her, careful not to make any sudden movements. She was average height for a woman, and looked a similar age to Daniel. Wind lifted the edge of her coat and he saw bare legs, bare feet.

He came to the shore and rose slowly out of the water, the sun casting a breath of warmth over his drenched clothing.

Yet she was the one who couldn't stop shivering.

Water poured from his sodden sleeves and splashed over the mud, softening the soil. "You were there," he said, nervously. "You watched me die."

The woman swallowed hard, mottled brown hair glistening with sweat, *and she nodded up and down.*

"Did you make me like this?" he asked.

She drew a breath, but the words she mouthed were impossible to hear. Her forehead creased – not frustration, *desperation*, pleading to be heard. Instead, she pointed to the trees, and Daniel could make out something in the undergrowth – a bundle of arms and legs. It was instantly clear what he was looking at.

She had pulled Ryan from the lake.

Daniel ran over. The earth around Ryan's body had turned to sticky mud that squelched beneath Daniel's shoes.

"I don't understand," he said. "How did you even know he was here?"

The woman smiled, but her eyes were sad. Daniel had struggled to lift Ryan when he was dry, let alone with drenched clothing. He didn't understand how she had managed.

Shaking and bewildered, Daniel bent down to look closer at the body, when something caught him by surprise, something so shocking that he lost his balance and came tumbling to the ground.

Ryan's chest rose and fell.

He was alive.

Daniel stumbled back on his elbows, staring up at the woman in the green coat. "What have you done?" he said.

A sudden wind howled as he hurried to his feet. Ryan was breathing, no question about it. "What the hell's going on?" said Daniel. The woman didn't even attempt to speak.

"Why won't you talk to me?" he yelled.

Instantly, she vanished, flicked out of existence as if she had never been there. There was no time for disbelief. Daniel had seen so much that he needed no convincing. She was another like him – another lost soul, trapped by Andrew's aura. Another ghost.

There had been three of them all along.

And now there was a fourth. Ryan had returned from the dead into a body that had been strangled and submerged. Daniel watched the shallow breaths – *watched Ryan cling to life* – and his hatred turned to regret. This was some sort of dark miracle, the cruelty of life where there should only have been death.

One more person with whom he shared this ghostly affinity.

Daniel rolled him over. Ryan's pale skin was as cold as ice, and it seemed unlikely he would survive for long. But Daniel wouldn't put him out of his misery for a second time. He couldn't live with that burden.

Daniel took a firm grip and dragged Ryan into the trees, away from the lakeshore. He couldn't bring himself to take Ryan to a doctor. Instead, he heaved the body towards a shelter he had seen among the trees – a small, red-brick building with a flat, white roof.

Somewhere to keep him while Daniel took care of his business.

This was an opportunity, and in more ways than one. Without Ryan in the picture, it would be easier to make Isabel see the truth. No more threats or interference. For as long as it took to win her back, Ryan would have to remain there, alone and untended.

He could only blame himself for that.

Daniel rammed the wooden front door, and it soon gave way. Inside was warm. The steady whir of machinery pumped water out of the lake, and a small window let ample light inside.

There was just enough space to heft the body onto a bare concrete floor, and he let it slump into the corner.

Daniel felt a fever on Ryan's forehead. "Can you hear me?" he asked, to no reply. "You can rest until I'm back. I'm sorry for all this, Ryan. I wish it could be different."

The latch closed with a clunk as Daniel let himself out, and he used a block of wood to wedge the door shut. In some ways, it would have done Daniel a favour to come back and find Ryan dead, solving the problem of what to do with him.

Daniel retraced his steps, smoothing over the tracks with his shoe, more careful than Andrew had been. He circled back to the car and peeled off his sodden shirt, wringing it out, feeling relieved.

He had prevented disaster. The car would have to be disposed of, along with Daniel's clothing, and anything else that could link him to the valley. The day wasn't done yet, not by any means.

Nevertheless, he felt empowered, more awake than ever. With Andrew running scared and Ryan indisposed, his obstacles had been surmounted. For the first time in years, Daniel felt in control.

The sun cleared hilltops in the distance, and he set off, away from the valley. It was over an hour back home and he could use the time to prepare, to straighten his head.

Nothing could stop him now.

21|NNOCENCE

"Daniel?"

Every bone – *every fibre* – cried for sleep, to stop the constant stress as control was handed between Daniel and Andrew, over and over.

Exhaustion was steadily pushing Daniel away, making it harder to stay active without his adrenaline. He managed to stave off sleep until the afternoon, taking steps to cover both his and Andrew's tracks, trying to think of everything.

Leaving Ryan a prisoner by the lakeside.

He slid between the covers as the sun was still beaming through the window, drifting almost instantly into a heavy, dreamless sleep. The very next thing he knew, he was awake again, and as had happened so many times before, something was different.

It was after dark.

Daniel found himself in bed, exactly as he had fallen asleep, as though Andrew hadn't been in control. But for the first time in almost a fortnight, Daniel was in darkness.

He sat up sharply, trying to fathom what it meant. The clock at the bedside read eleven, and he was so blinded by uncertainty that he took a moment to realise someone had just spoken his name.

"Daniel?"

He swept back the covers and jumped to his feet, backing blindly across the darkened room. The voice was distant, distorted, but he knew straight away who it must have been.

Andrew Goodwin.

"I'm here," said Daniel.

"I want to talk with you face-to-face," said the voice, *"but I can't."*

Daniel retreated until he felt cool plaster against his back. Andrew shouldn't have been conscious at the same time as him, unless Andrew had learned something Daniel didn't know. *A way to share control.*

"Don't think for a second that I won't put a stop to this," said Daniel.

The reply came from the hallway. Daniel grew aware of a crack of light around the closed bedroom door.

"Is that Daniel?" said the voice. It sounded like Andrew was eight feet away, detached from their close bond.

"Yes, it's me," said Daniel. "I'm not sure what you're doing, but I hope you realise it won't make any difference to the outcome."

Daniel heard two footsteps, and he could have sworn the voice got louder. *"All I'm trying to do is get my life back,"* said Andrew. *"I don't even think I know you. Why are you holding me here?"*

Daniel laughed with contempt. "Don't pretend you're not guilty," he said. "You're a murderer!"

"Ryan's blood is on your hands, not mine."

"But it's all your fault, Andrew, whether you see it or not. Take my word for it – you've ruined too many lives to play innocent."

Daniel scrunched his eyes up, willing them to grow accustomed to the darkness, disorientated by the voice he just couldn't place. *"Tell me what I'm supposed to have done,"* it said, *"and give me a chance to fix it."*

"It's too late for that." Daniel's legs were trembling. "Neither of us can go back and change it. We have to live with what you did."

"And now Cheryl has to live without a husband, and a man is dead."

"You made you own bed when you started seeing a married woman," said Daniel. "If something's happened to Cheryl's husband, then it's all on you."

"Oh no," said Andrew. *"I may have dragged the body, but I wasn't the one who strangled him. I refuse to believe that. You set me up."*

Daniel frowned at his statement. "Wait a second," he said. "Are you saying you think Ryan is married to Cheryl?"

There was a moment's pause. Daniel could feel the tension in the air. *"You mean he isn't?"*

Daniel revelled in his confusion. After what Andrew had done to him at the seaside, the sense of justice was gratifying.

"You really haven't worked it out yet, have you?" said Daniel.

There was a tense silence in the room, then suddenly, it was bathed in white. Daniel raised an arm to shield his eyes as he realised the ceiling light had come on.

And there she was.

By the doorway – right where the sound was coming from – stood the woman in the green coat. Her face was that same shivering blend of pain and apprehension, the same mottled hair and bare feet.

Daniel's eyes stung from the piercing brightness, but he could tell she was staring at him.

"Where have you gone?" said the voice. They weren't her words, but they came from her direction.

"I haven't gone anywhere," Daniel replied.

Her eyes were wide, unwavering. *"Why won't you come out here and show me who I'm dealing with?"*

"Well, it wouldn't be half as easy as it sounds..."

"For Christ's sake," said the voice. *"Why won't you face me?"*

"Because I can't, Andrew. I'm you."

There was a sudden, loud thump, and the light flickered off. Daniel was plunged back into darkness. "Hello?" he said, voice swallowed by the silence.

There was no reply. Daniel moved from the corner and edged towards the hallway. "Andrew, are you there?"

The thinnest of draughts snaked around his toes. Daniel ran his fingertips across the wall, feeling blindly for the light switch.

And when he turned it on again, he was alone.

Something in the air felt cold, charged with static. Daniel had a dark feeling things were changing faster than he could comprehend. The light was on in the hallway, even though Daniel had turned it off before he went to bed. *As though Andrew had been there after all.*

Daniel moved towards the lounge, when he discovered why the encounter had ended so abruptly – there was someone at the door.

Knock-knock-knock!

Three sharp, loud rasps. He spun around, bare feet rooted to the ground. In that moment, he would have given anything not to have to open it.

"Who is it?" he stammered. Thick wood muffled the reply.

"Andrew? It's me, Cheryl. Can I come in?"

He walked softly towards the door. "What do you want?"

"To talk," she said. "Is this another bad time?"

Andrew put his hands on the wood and peered through the peephole. Cheryl was standing on the other side, wearing a long, black coat and a bright red jumper. Her arms were folded across her chest, drawn up to add volume to her bosom.

Despite himself, Daniel drew the door open, and the second she caught sight of the fresh bruises on his face, she lurched forwards, as if to catch him before he fainted.

"What happened to you this time?" she said. "Are you okay?"

"I'm alright," said Daniel. "It's worse than it looks."

"I've been so worried about you. I know you keep telling me to stop coming over, but you've stopped answering your phone, and I'm afraid you're in trouble. Is this why you wouldn't let me in last night?"

"That's right," he lied, unaware she had been there.

Cheryl hugged him. "I've been worried about you. Can I come in? You'll want to hear what I have to say."

Without giving him a chance to answer, she stooped down and picked up a plastic bag on the floor. Daniel heard the chink of wine bottles inside. She let herself into the hallway and walked to the lounge, seeming to know her way around the flat.

He followed her in. The lights were already on and the blinds closed. She slid off her shoes and unscrewed one of the wine bottles, searching through the cupboards for glasses. "I was hoping you hadn't eaten," she said, pouring, "but I couldn't get out of the house until late, so I suppose I missed that."

"Actually," he said, "I don't think I've eaten all day."

"Oh good, then we can order in. Now sit down."

Cheryl helped herself to ice cubes from the freezer and put some into a tea towel, then she sat him on the sofa, perching on the leather arm to tend to his bruises. Her bedside manner was warmer than it had been in her own house, far from the reminders of her husband.

Being up close helped Daniel to see just how similar she looked to the woman in green. There were, however, subtle differences – freckles on her face, the shape of her eyebrows.

Their eyes met, inches apart. Cheryl leaned in and they shared a soft, passionate kiss. He hadn't known intimacy in years, and he lost himself in her gentle touch and sweet fragrance.

"I'm glad you're alright," she said. "You seemed so sure there was something going on last night that I looked into it, and I believe you. It might be time to go to the police."

Cheryl reached into her jacket pocket and produced the photograph he had stolen from his father's house. She turned it over and showed him the note on the back.

Me, Dad and Isabel, March 4th

"I was trying to find out who Isabel was," she said, "but then I found something by chance. One of my colleagues recognised her from an article on the local news this morning. Her husband has gone missing."

Daniel gasped. *"That was on the news?"*

"That's right," she said, innocently. "Apparently, there's cause to think something bad has happened to him. They're appealing for witnesses."

Daniel shook his head, still trying to work out how Cheryl had got hold of the picture. "What did they say about him?"

"Only that he's missing, but this woman knows more than she's letting on. It's only a few miles from here, so don't tell me it's not connected. I'm going to call into the police station tomorrow and find more answers."

Daniel held his hands up. "Don't, Cheryl. Please don't get involved. Look at the state I'm in and ask yourself if it's safe."

"I can't just stand by and watch," she said.

He leaned up and kissed her, trying to keep her distracted. She instantly reciprocated, as though starved of affection, holding him passionately, running the tip of her tongue down the bare flesh of his neck.

Daniel found her warmth impossible to resist. She ran a hand down his chest as she slid off the arm of the settee, onto his lap.

"I think this should be the night you make love to me, Andrew."

Her hand delved into his bedclothes, but Daniel stopped her, soft fingertips holding her in place.

"What did you call me?" he said.

She drew back, confused. "I called you Andrew. Is there a problem?"

Reality came thundering back. For a moment, Daniel had been carried away by Cheryl's lust, but in truth, she didn't want him. She wanted a man he despised.

"I can't do this," he said.

Her warmth turned to hurt, and she shuffled to her feet. "I thought you wanted it as much as I did."

"I still can't," said Daniel. "It isn't right."

She pattered over to her shoes, wriggling into them as she gathered her coat and purse. "That's what I've told you a hundred times before," she said, "and you did a thoroughly good job of changing my mind. Why is it suddenly so different?"

Daniel shook his head. "I'm sorry, Cheryl. It feels like it's gone too far."

She laughed, a thin snort of disbelief. "What?"

"Maybe we should just forget it."

The hurt on her face was impossible to fake. Overwrought, Cheryl stormed into the hallway, and the walls shook as she slammed the front door behind her.

Daniel sat alone in silence. He could still taste the warm tingle of alcohol from her kiss, but he couldn't have her snooping around. It was better to have her hurt than working behind his back.

Helping Andrew.

Daniel got up and went to the kitchen counter, taking the glass of wine she had poured him and gulping it down. The alcohol tasted good, rare pleasure in a time of remorse.

He had turned to drink once before in his life, but this time, he was in control. Daniel reached on top of the cupboards and pulled down a paper bag filled with small plastic packets.

Sleeping pills.

He swallowed three and washed them down with mouthfuls of wine, emptying the second glass. He could control how he slept, as much as how he stayed awake.

Andrew would bear the brunt of his frustrations. So long as Daniel drew breath, he would take it upon himself to wipe Andrew's existence from the face of the planet. Getting rid of Cheryl was a good start, and in the morning, Daniel would see that Andrew lost his job, his friends, and anything else he cared about.

Daniel would find more adrenaline, and make sure Andrew never had another hour in control. Let him live on scraps of time, the way Daniel had for two years.

See how he likes it.

Even a minute was more than he deserved. After all, Andrew Goodwin was responsible for his death.

A killer.

And killers don't even deserve to live at night.

END OF DAY

PART THREE: HIDDEN CAGE
22|OBRIETY

The air was deathly calm, not a flicker of wind. Maggie made her way up the hillside as pure white snow came drifting down from invisible clouds, spreading evenly across the grass to create a soft, ethereal world.

She didn't feel the cold. Her stripy, woollen hat was pulled tightly over her long, dark hair, and her puffy jacket was zipped right up to her chin. Every inch of her body felt sealed and secure, mittens impervious to the temperature.

Not that the cold would have bothered her. She was an active sixteen year old, restless, energetic. She reached a metal railing at the top of the incline and held onto it, turning back to tease her trailing boyfriend.

"I win," she said. "That was even easier than I thought it would be."

He came puffing and panting after her, with the hood of his winter coat pulled so tightly around his face that he could barely see out. Restricted and uncomfortable.

A young man called Daniel Lawton.

"Just a moment." His voice didn't echo in the thick weather, but Maggie heard it clearly. "Don't go any further."

Daniel didn't mind her being able to run rings around him. Better that than the other way around. The snow underfoot was maybe five inches deep, and she could see the tracks they had left, snaking behind them until the snowfall swallowed them up.

"I can't wait all day," she said. "I'd probably freeze to death."

With a last burst of effort, Daniel finally drew level. They stood side-by-side – one warm and snug, the other cold and breathless. Maggie leaned up and kissed him. It wasn't their first, but it was still something new.

"Happy Valentines," said Daniel, twitching his numb nose.

At the top of the slope was a huge, rounded tower – eighty meters tall, made of grey, weather-worn stonework. A ruined castle keep, dwarfing them both. The snow had no place to settle on its sheer face, so the tower rose out of a white landscape, like a lighthouse from the sea.

"What do we do now?" he asked, shivering.

Maggie looked into his eyes and smiled. "You'll see."

She hopped over the railing onto a walkway around the tower, then followed it skyward, bounding up snowy steps. They climbed above the tops of surrounding trees, and the view opened right out.

They should have been able to see for miles, towards rolling hills in the distance. Instead, all they saw was snow, but it was a striking picture nonetheless. White crystals sank like falling stars, drifting down in endless sheets, giving no clue as to what lay beyond them.

The sense of expanse was amazing.

Daniel caught up with Maggie as she took it in, standing midway up the tower. "It's beautiful," she said. "You were right to bring me here."

He had taken his father's car, too young to officially drive, but bending the rules to impress his girlfriend. His father wouldn't even notice he was gone, and his mother died years ago.

Daniel watched Maggie's profile – her chestnut brown hair stuffed inside that thick, stripy hat. She was another of his secrets. No one knew they were together.

"Isn't it perfect?" she said. Daniel nodded as she turned to him with a playful glint in her eye. "And do you know what would make it even better?"

The snow falling between their faces lessened as she leaned towards him. "What?" he asked.

"If this was where we lost our virginities."

He shuffled awkwardly. "That wasn't what I was thinking when I brought you up here."

"But is it what you're thinking now?"

She took off one of her gloves and started to unzip his coat. The cold sliced right through the gap, onto his warm neck.

"There's no one else around," she said. "Just you and me."

He smiled, nodding nervously. "Okay, then. I'm game if you are."

The steps ended by a stone doorway, and she ducked into the rounded ruin. Inside was just as cold. There was no ceiling, but the snow coming down wouldn't settle.

Excited, she kept climbing. A wooden staircase continued on the inner wall, and it took her towards the top of the tower.

"Are you coming?" she called.

Daniel found her in a raised alcove, with stone benches down either side. An arched window opened to an even higher view of the whiteout, and Maggie stood against a metal rail across its center, leaning out.

"It's like being in space," she said, "only white."

"Space is probably warmer," Daniel hopped up and down as she came back in.

"Don't you think this would be the perfect spot?" she said. "Imagine it right here: You and me, together."

Maggie slid off her mittens and used her bare hands to loosen his hood, peeling it down to reveal a full head of brown hair.

"Take your clothes off," she said, trying to open his coat. As Daniel lost the feeling in his ears, he put a hand over hers. "Do you think we could maybe keep a few things on? It really is freezing."

She shook her head. "That would be tacky. You'd ruin it." To set an example, Maggie undid the fasteners on her jacket. Underneath, he saw the suggestion of her slender shape.

"We should still be practical," he said.

Maggie reached under Daniel's coat to his belt, unfastening his trousers. "Well, you certainly won't need these," she said.

Her cold hands brushed against bare skin as she delved into his clothing. Daniel jumped.

"Jesus," he exclaimed, but didn't try to stop her.

Maggie leaned up and kissed him again. "Naked, please. Do it for me."

He complied stiffly, but she didn't like his progress, so Maggie grabbed his coat and yanked the zipper down, giving him no time to think.

Shocked, Daniel folded up, and he caught her with his shoulder. Maggie lost her footing on the icy ground, and with her hands gripping the collar of his jacket, pulled him along as she staggered back.

They skidded over the alcove. Maggie slammed into the railing across the window. Her thick, padded coat cushioned the impact, but his weight came crashing after, jarring her pelvis into the metal.

And tipping them over the edge.

It was a blur. Maggie grabbed hold of him as they careered through the empty window and out of the round tower. By chance, Daniel caught the railing. For a moment, they dangled against the sheer outer wall, with nothing to grab onto. Icy cold and deathly silence.

Maggie whimpered, clinging on for dear life, when the weight of them both became too much for him.

They fell, arm in arm, plummeting through the icy air. The world spun in streaks of white and grey as Daniel shut his eyes tightly, expecting death.

Something wrenched them apart. He whirled out of control, outstretched palms slamming into something he could grasp hold of.

Branches.

He held them close to his chest until the world stopped spinning. The claustrophobic silence of the still winter's air did little to convince him it was real, that they had just fallen all that way.

This can't be happening.

He opened his eyes to look around. Daniel was in a tree near the base of the hill, suspended nine feet above the ground. His hands were shaking, and he realised he couldn't let go.

Something shivered below him. Maggie was lying on the grass, flat across her back. She had landed heavily, with nothing to break her fall, then rolled down the slope.

She lay staring up at the sky, taking small, tight gasps of the cold winter air. Once again, Daniel shut his eyes, tearing himself away from the foliage and dropping onto the snow covered land.

"Are you alright?" he said, rushing over. She wheezed as she tried to draw air into her lungs.

"Don't move your back if you're hurt," he said, trying to hold her down. Maggie pulled her arms from under his grasp, strong in her desperation. She tugged at her coat pocket, trying to undo the zip.

There was no air in her lungs to speak with, and her quivering lips were impossible to read. Her eyes, however, were pleading.

"Let me get to it," said Daniel as he wrestled the pocket open. Instantly, she plunged a hand inside and pulled something out, sealed tightly in her cold, rigid fingers.

"What's that?" he said. "Give it to me." He tried to take it from her, but she wouldn't let go, or couldn't. He bit down on his gloves and heaved them off, trembling uncontrollably.

Somebody help me.

Daniel grabbed Maggie's fist and tried to prise it open, when all of a sudden, she relaxed. He watched in horror as the panic suddenly drained from her face, her eyelids drifted closed.

And Maggie went limp.

He knew he had to find a doctor or she only had minutes left. Daniel opened her hand and took hold of the blue object she had been clutching so dearly – an inhaler.

Adrenaline.

She had never mentioned having asthma. He held it to her mouth, but she took no breath.

"Maggie?" he said. "Can you hear me?"

He pushed on the plunger and gas hissed between her lips, but she didn't react, colour draining from her face. Daniel didn't have a clue what to do.

He could drag her to the car, but would that only make things worse?

Distraught, he looked up at the window, wishing they had never come there, when he noticed something unusual. Something he couldn't explain.

Maggie had fallen straight down – he could see where she had landed – but Daniel's tree stood some distance from the tower's base.

He frowned. There must have been thirty feet between them, with no wind to have pushed them apart.

So how exactly had he got there when she hadn't?

23|NONYMITY

Death had changed Daniel forever. He was a man with new priorities, savouring each moment as though it could be his last. As though, each new morning, he might not wake up.

He especially savoured the weather – the sensations of heat and cold on his skin, the palette of a cloudy day. He could see the summer struggling to keep its hold on the city. A handful of pedestrians hurried along the pavement, anticipating the heaven's would soon open.

Heaven, however, wasn't something Daniel worried about. He had been there, and found it much more bearable than the moments that preceded it.

A bus pulled over by the pavement, and Daniel hid his face until it was gone. Despite his best efforts, Andrew Goodwin still retained a measure of control, and the man had been awake in the middle of the night.

Daniel had discovered the lounge window smashed to pieces, glass all over the floor, and scattered over the car park below. It was a mark of desperation, but the timing couldn't have been worse.

Ryan had been missing for long enough that the police were starting to search for him in earnest, and without an alibi, Daniel couldn't risk drawing attention.

If he was arrested, it would all be over.

His hand had been forced. The only way to avoid capture was to ensure the police stopped investigating, and that Ryan never spoke against him.

Only one person could make all that happen. Isabel's house stood in shade, dulling the yellow of the front door, and Daniel stood before it with a galloping heart and sweaty palms.

Finally, he had the courage to do what he should have done a long time ago. Finally, he saw no other option.

This was it.

Today, she would see the truth.

***

Isabel had spent her morning perched on the edge of the sofa, staring into space, waiting nervously for the phone to ring. No good for anything else.

The varnish on her nails – only a few hours old – was already picked away, restless hands wanting to be out there looking for Ryan, but clueless where to begin.

She knew who was responsible, but no one believed her, not yet. They wanted evidence – a stolen car, security footage, witnesses. *Blood.* The police were searching in all the wrong places, and Isabel was anxious about what could happen in the meantime.

Brinnnnnnng!

Her doorbell sliced through the silence. In a heartbeat, she was off the couch and sprinting barefoot down the hall. When she got to the door, she almost wrenched it off its hinges, and found Daniel standing on the front step – unclean, with his head shaven close to his scalp.

He looked almost like a different person.

"What have you done to Ryan?" She almost grabbed him by the throat. Only the brightness of the outdoors distracted her long enough to think twice. "Do you hear me?" she said. *"Tell me where he is."*

"I can't do that." Daniel's voice was deceptively calm. "This is too important. I need to come in and explain myself."

"You must be joking," she spat. "You're not going to shoehorn your way into our lives. The day I let you in here will be the day you die."

"I know you're upset," said Daniel, "but it's only because you don't understand what's happened."

Isabel stared with wild eyes, swollen from the tears she had battled all morning. "Tell me where he is, or get away from me."

"Not while I'm on the doorstep," he maintained.

"The police are watching me," said Isabel. "Once they see you've been here, they'll put you behind bars, where you belong."

She grabbed the door and tried to slam it shut, but Daniel put his foot inside and caught it, fighting her back. Scared, Isabel retreated up the hallway, and Daniel stepped unopposed into the house, closing the door behind him.

He found her in the living room, brandishing the cordless phone. "You've got three seconds to get out," she said.

Daniel stalled in his advance. "Just listen for a second," he said. "My name is Daniel Lawton."

She froze. *"What did you say?"*

"It's me, Isabel. I'm trapped in Andrew's body."

Her face was riddled with emotion, but she was nobody's fool. Isabel dialled the phone. Reacting instantly, Daniel leapt forwards and tried to force it from her grip.

"Give it to me," he said.

"Too late. It's ringing."

Daniel tried to wrench it out of her hands, and rather than struggle, she let go. The momentum threw him off balance, sending him reeling to the floor.

Isabel ran into the kitchen, where she shut the door and put her weight against the handle. "Do you expect me to believe you?" she shouted through the wood.

His reply came almost immediately. "Not at first, but the only way I can prove it is by what I know. I can't do that if you won't hear me out."

"Nothing you could say will make a difference."

"We went to Madrid," he said. "A peddler on the street made you buy a necklace you hated, so you gave it to a girl you worked with."

She ignored him, closing her eyes and praying. *God protect me.* In the silence, Daniel rammed his weight into the flimsy wood, flinging her into the kitchen counter.

Before she could regain herself, he was inside and on top of her. "Stop fighting me," he said.

Daniel seized her arms and pinned them to her sides, pressing so hard that her feet almost left the floor.

"Anyone could have known about Madrid," she said.

"Okay, then," he said. "You hated this house within a week of moving in, but you were too proud to admit it to anyone, even me."

She drew a sharp intake of air and screamed in his face. Daniel shut his eyes, but his clutch grew tighter. She could feel her arms bruising.

"Just listen," he yelled back.

Powerless and drained, she sighed. "Alright, just calm down for a moment."

Daniel did as she asked, but he still held her tightly. "Ryan deleted my confession, or you would have heard this days ago. I thought if it was on tape then you might be more inclined to listen."

"You're hurting me," she said.

Daniel loosened his grip. "It was never my intention," he said. "It wasn't."

Despite herself, Isabel's eyes started to well up. "Please tell me what you did to Ryan," she said. "I need to know he's okay."

"He's safe." Daniel closed his eyes. "He's alive, but I can't tell you where he is. Not yet."

Her calm turned to anger. Isabel dug her fingernails deep into his chest, scouring right through the fabric of his shirt.

"Tell me where you took him," she screamed.

The pain made him cry out, but he wouldn't submit, determined to make her see who he was beneath that tearing flesh.

"You can do all the damage you want," he grimaced. "It won't change a thing."

"You're messing with the wrong woman if you think that'll stop me."

Isabel pulled herself free and made a run for the door, but he grabbed her leg and dragged her to the floor. She fell hard, kicking and screaming, landing with a thud.

Quickly, Daniel twisted her wrists behind her back, then dragged her across the living room carpet. Bare feet slid as she tried to grip the fibres.

"Daniel wouldn't do something like this," she said as she struggled.

He cast her into the master bedroom like it was a prison cell, shutting her inside. "Maybe once," he said, "but that was a long time ago."

Alone, Isabel hurried to her feet and dragged her bed in front of the door. As she did, she heard furniture stacked against it from the other side. She grabbed a pair of shoes and slid them onto her feet, making ready to escape, before a shadow fell across her only other exit.

Daniel had moved to the garden. Something scraped loudly along the flags, and she watched with horror as a shelved cabinet was slowly dragged in front of the window.

She hurried to the curtains and yanked them closed, then in the dim light, stood and panted nervously, watching his silhouette through the fabric.

"You're not going anywhere until you listen to reason," said Daniel. His voice was breathless.

"It doesn't matter what you tell me," she said, trying to throw her voice across the room. "You've kidnapped Ryan, and now you've kidnapped me. The police know all about you, so there'll be nowhere to hide."

As she spoke, Isabel scoured her room for a means to defend herself, fully aware that he could come through the glass at any second.

"I'm not hiding," he said. "Ryan was right – I should have told you the moment I came back, but you have to understand how scared I was."

"Well, you should be, because help will be here soon."

He sighed. "No, it won't."

She crept quietly across the floor, watching his silhouette. In the corner of the room, she managed to peer around the curtain. He was rubbing his temple, as though he had a headache, and his eyes looked heavy. Burdened, tired.

"I think maybe we both need to calm down," he said. "I'm going to leave you in there. Catch your breath, and I'll talk to you in a while."

His head dipped between his shoulders, almost like the man was going to pass out, right there in her back garden. Isabel stared from behind the curtains.

Why was he suddenly so tired?

"You're not speaking," said Daniel. "Are you there?"

She hurried back to the middle of the room before she answered. "Yes, but I think we should talk right now. Come on."

He stepped back from the window, shadow blurring. "I don't think so," he said. "Take some time to cool off, and let me know when you're ready to come out."

"You're just going to wait for me out there?" she said.

"Something like that."

He moved out of sight, and silence descended on the room. Suddenly, Isabel felt claustrophobic, a prisoner in her own home. She looked around for a weapon, for a means to call for help.

Nothing but clothes and shoes.

She was trapped, and they both knew it. Isabel listened for footsteps, but couldn't place him. The man could be anywhere – literally *anywhere* in her property – and she didn't trust him not to fly off the handle.

Exhausted of options, she looked for a place to hide. Squatting in the corner of the room, she tried to wedge herself behind the chest of drawers. Her bruised arms slid between wood and wall, and she languished out of sight, somewhere Isabel could conceal how powerless she felt.

A last, desperate chance to be the one in control.

Somewhere he wouldn't see her cry.

24|IGHTMARE

After one more day stranded at the back of his own mind, Andrew Goodwin regained a level of control. And just as two weeks before, when the nightmare had first begun, it was a loud noise that brought him around.

Slam!

Eyes flickered open to darkness, the sound ricocheting through his skull. Muscles tensed as he realised what had woken him.

Banging on the wall.

He was in bed. A hairline crack of silvery moonlight cast itself across the blanket, thick curtains isolating him from the outside world. He could immediately tell that it wasn't his flat. Just the feel of the room was wrong.

Andrew propped himself up on his elbows and rubbed his eyes. For a moment, his mind was blank. He tried to walk through everything he had done, to remember what Daniel had put him through.

Andrew had interrogated a man called Ryan, then set him free, but now the man was dead.

It all came thundering back. *The body on the back seat, the black Range Rover he had driven to the lakeside.* The very last time Andrew had been awake, he discovered that at least two days had passed, not one.

So how long had it been this time?

The wall thumped as someone pounded their fists against it. He felt through the darkness and parted the curtains to see a waist-high fence to the pavement. A full moon shone down brilliantly.

He felt a twinge under his shirt and peeled it off, finding deep scratches all over his chest. Andrew's emaciated body looked wrecked in the moonlight, covered in fresh bruises.

It hurt to take each heaving breath, and the most likely culprit continued to bang on the wall, punching their way through his skull like a jackhammer.

Thump-Thump-Thump!

He turned on the light. All the furniture in the room had been dragged in front of the door. Barricaded, sealed from the inside.

"Can you please stop banging?" he yelled. "I'm awake now."

The noise stopped, long enough for Andrew to gather his thoughts. He cleared the furniture from the door and let himself into a dark hallway, feeling along the wall until he found another light switch.

He wandered into the lounge of a small bungalow. Almost every piece of furniture had been piled up against one of the doors. *A television on a settee, in front of a bookcase.*

It was somehow familiar. As he saw each object, he knew where it normally went in the room, and which way it should be facing.

Looking at each door in turn, Andrew could tell what was on the other side. He could see where the cutlery was kept in the kitchen, the bread and the coffee. The kind of familiarity that could only come from having lived there for years.

Andrew even knew who was banging on the wall, with a clear picture in his mind. Blocked in the master bedroom, there was a woman. Another captive like he was.

A woman he had once seen in a photograph.

"Hello?" he called. "Can you hear me in there?"

The reply was swift. "Yes, can you come in? I need your help."

He hurried over the paisley carpet and heaved the television off the settee, clearing a path to the bedroom door and swinging it open. The room inside was dark, and he stepped in cautiously.

"Are you alright?" he asked.

Thud!

Something huge and heavy landed on top of him, ringing through his skull. Andrew crumpled to the floor, oblivious as someone pushed their way past.

In a blinded daze, he tried to crawl to his feet, but no sooner had his shoulders left the floor than he was pinned back against it.

Isabel knelt on his stomach, a knife in her hand. She pushed the blade up against his chest, threatening to break the skin.

"He's incapacitated." She held a phone to her ear and spoke into it. "I didn't manage to knock him unconscious, but I think he's out of action... Yes, I'll try my best, as soon as I get off the phone."

"What are you doing?" Andrew whispered, head pounding.

She ended the call. "Did you think it was funny, leaving me in there all sodding day?"

"I don't know what you're talking about," he said.

"You don't have to," said Isabel. "Just sit there and be quiet until the police arrive."

Just thinking caused him agony. "I was only trying to help."

She put the phone down and leaned in, pushing the knife hard enough to leave a mark. "Be quiet," she hissed.

The pain helped to bring him around. "You don't understand," he said. "I can't let the police find me."

"What did you expect? You kidnapped my fiancé and forced your way into my house."

Andrew's eyes opened wide. "Look, I don't know what I've done to you, but you have to get away. There's someone watching me, and he'll kill us both if you interfere."

"Just tell me where Ryan is."

He tried to sit up. "You know Ryan?"

Isabel dug her knee into his stomach. "Don't play games. Where can I find him?"

"I woke in a car one night," he grimaced. "I don't know where it was, but Ryan was with me. Someone put us there."

"Who?" said Isabel.

Andrew swallowed hard, trying to catch his breath. "I've never seen him, but Ryan told me his name is Daniel."

Confused, Isabel took her weight off the blade. "Is this a joke?" she said. "You turned up at my bank, *then at my house*, looking like you've been beaten senseless and jabbering on about your confession, then you truss me up in the bedroom, and now you're saying it's not your fault?"

"I know this is hard to understand," said Andrew. "Just look at me for a second. I'm not in control of my life. Please, I can't be here when the police arrive."

She sat back, increasing the distance between them. Something about him wasn't the same. *He was talking differently, pronouncing words with less effort.*

"What on Earth is going on with you?" she said.

"Please, Isabel. I need you to let me go."

Her forehead creased. "Big mistake: If you say you don't remember anything, then how come you know my name?"

Andrew's eyes widened further. *He didn't know.*

The uncertainty drained from her face and she raised the knife. Andrew reached for the handle, but she lashed out in anger.

The blade sliced through his hand. Andrew screamed and convulsed. Without holding back, he struck her in the face, knocking her through the doorway.

Like a shot, he tucked his legs in and slammed the bedroom door, scrambling to his feet to hold his weight against it.

Shutting himself in the bedroom.

The room was pitch black. He felt warm blood gushing into his palm. "Listen to me," he said. "My name is Andrew Goodwin, and I have no idea how I know your name, but I do. I know this house. I can feel places where we've argued and the memory in the walls, but I swear I don't know why."

He put his forehead on the door and closed his eyes. "I'm not asking you to believe me, because I know how it sounds. All I want is for you to let me go before something happens to you. Everyone who's close to me goes missing, or worse."

Andrew turned the handle, and a yellow crack of light broadened as he opened the door. Isabel was on the other side, still wielding the knife.

"Stay away from me," she said.

His arm stung and his head throbbed. "I don't know what the hell is going on," he continued. "If you don't believe that much, then I guess I can't convince you of anything."

Andrew held his hands out to show he meant no harm. Blood trickled down his forearm, dribbling onto the carpet.

To his surprise, Isabel lowered the knife.

"Where did you get that watch?" she said.

He looked down at his wrist – a silver timepiece, with a black face and golden hands. *A watch that had never worked.*

"It just appeared a week or so ago," he said. "Is it important?"

She grabbed his arm, practically wrenching it off his wrist. "Give it to me."

He opened the catch and she pulled it off, cradling it between her fingers. "I don't believe it," she said.

"Every time I take it off, it just seems to appear right back on me."

Isabel's shoulders slumped in disbelief. Her whole demeanour changed, the colour draining from her fallen face as she pushed it back into his hand.

"Read the back."

Andrew turned it over and looked at the rear face. There was an inscription, a piece of clear and irrefutable evidence that he hadn't even thought to look for.

'To my darling Daniel, love Isabel.'

Andrew could see her turmoil of emotions – everything he had struggled with for two weeks, slung upon her all at once.

"I bought this for our second year anniversary," said Isabel. "He swore he'd never take it off. That was so long ago that I'd actually forgotten about it."

She looked at him with new fragility, voice breaking from the upset. "Where in God's name did you find this?"

***

Andrew tried to encourage Isabel to let him go, but she insisted upon tending to his wound, wrapping it in a bandage. *Keeping him alive.*

He leaned against the kitchen counter while she worked. "Do you know how I got here?" he asked.

"You knocked." Isabel kept the knife close by, unsure of herself. "You've been here once before," she said. "Are you sure you can't remember?"

He shook his head. "No, just like a lot of things. Do you know who Daniel is? Ryan seemed to think he was a real person."

She tightened the bandage, and it cut into his hand. "He was real enough once, but that was years ago. He's dead."

"He can't be." Andrew had spoken with him, never face to face, but at least twice now. *Heeded his threats.* Daniel had claimed to be a part of Andrew, as though the two men were interlinked.

"If your story is even remotely true," said Isabel, "then Daniel's the only one who knows where Ryan is. We have to get through to him."

"I don't know how. Daniel just communicates with me when it suits him. The rest of the time, he keeps me in the dark."

Isabel narrowed her eyes, lacking any sense of trust. "Are you sure you don't know where Ryan is?" she asked. "This isn't a game."

"Of course it isn't," said Andrew. "He was in the countryside, somewhere dark. There were trees. I can't remember much more than that. It honestly could have been anywhere."

She read his expression and knew he wasn't telling the whole story.

A siren rang out in the distance. "Is that the police?" he said, standing up. "I thought you called them off."

Isabel took the knife from the counter. "I'm afraid not," she said. "Even if you won't admit it, you're the only lead we have to finding Ryan. If that means we have to drag you around every inch of the countryside to jog your memory, then that's what we'll do."

"I've told you everything I know," said Andrew. "I swear I'd say if there was more."

"Daniel knows more, and that means you do, too."

"I don't understand." Andrew panicked and reached for the door handle, but she was ready for him. The knife came glinting from her hip and caught his arm, slicing into flesh.

Blood started to soak into his clothes.

"I can't let you go," she said, sternly. "Whether you're Andrew or Daniel, you know where he is, *so tell me.*"

He recoiled in pain, and it caused a white flash behind his eyes. Memories came flooding through, released from deep inside.

The woman in the green coat, standing before him by the lake. Unimposing, unassuming. Ryan's cold weight as Andrew dragged him along.

Not towards, but away from the water.

"He's not dead," Andrew shouted, scarcely able to believe it himself. "I can take you to him."

"Explain it to the police," she said. "They'll help us."

He clutched his bleeding arm. "They won't," he said. "Please, Isabel. The police already want me. I attacked one of them a week ago. You have to believe me – I didn't know what I was doing, but they'll lock me up if I don't get away."

"You can still tell them where he is."

Andrew sighed, and as he slowed his breathing down, he chose his next words very carefully. "But I won't, Isabel. I won't help anyone if you won't help me."

She raised the knife. "Are you trying to bargain?"

"Come with me and I'll take you to Ryan. That's the deal."

"How do I know this isn't just a trick?"

"You can bring all the weapons you want."

The siren grew louder, police closing in on the house. Isabel grabbed Andrew's wound and squeezed it tightly. Blood pumped between her fingers.

"Alright," she scowled. "We'll do this your way, but if you put another foot wrong, I swear I'll kill you where you stand."

Andrew nodded, and she released him.

"We have to get out of here right now," he said, taking bandages for his fresh wound. "We'll need your car."

"But I don't drive," said Isabel.

He thought hard, with a mind full of shared ideas. "Well then, I guess it's clear what we have to do next."

25|NJURY

Andrew knelt on a flagged pavement, huddling between a parked car and a thick hedgerow. He glanced nervously up and down the road, dreading any oncoming vehicles.

Even in the streetlight, he stood out by a mile.

Isabel crouched beside him, in shadow. The moon had disappeared behind cloud, and she was almost invisible. Only the sound of her voice reminded him that she was close.

"How's your head?" she asked.

Beneath his prickly scalp, a huge, throbbing lump had risen. "It feels better than my hand," he said. "What did you drop on me, anyway?"

"I balanced a mirror above the bedroom door," she said. "You were lucky the glass didn't smash like I intended, or you would have been dead."

Andrew knew she meant it, but he was still glad of some company for once. Along with his pains and near-constant anxiety, he wasn't struggling to stay awake.

Isabel shuffled on her feet. One hand was wrapped around the knife handle in her coat pocket, though she no longer felt she needed it. Covered in wounds already, Andrew didn't want to come near her.

"Are you sure there's no other way?" she whispered.

"This is all I can think of," he said. "It isn't easy to put into words. I can picture the layout inside, and I know what I need to find, but I've never been there."

They looked at stranger's house – enveloped in darkness, shielded from the pavement by tall trees. Andrew could recall being there before, when he wasn't in control. He knew the texture of the wallpaper, the ruffle of the threadbare carpet, and he could clearly picture the old man who lived inside.

The third person from the photograph.

Ever since the blow to his head, Andrew was finding it easier to draw those memories out. "Once I've done this," he said, "you'll hopefully see I'm not a threat."

Isabel flashed a smile, but it wasn't sincere. She couldn't bring herself to accept Andrew's story. *That Daniel was inside him.* All she knew for certain was that Ryan was missing, and Andrew was the only way to get him back.

He crept out from cover, and she watched him go, wishing none of this had ever happened. Gravel crunched beneath his shoes as he edged down the driveway, guided by his outstretched palms.

The house was silent, deceptively so, lulling Andrew into a false sense of security. In the darkness, rough brickwork snagged his bandage as he stole down the side of the building to a tall gate. *Soft, aging wood and cold metal studs.*

It was unlocked, just as he knew it would be, and he cupped his hand over the latch as he pulled it open, trying to muffle the rusted squeak.

A brief parting in the clouds afforded him a moonlit view as he crept delicately through the back yard, finding the rear door hanging ajar.

Just as he knew it would be.

Andrew ducked inside. Moonlight didn't follow him into the house, but he knew what to expect. *The refrigerator, the cupboard door.*

A stale smell filled his nose and he held his breath, listening for movement. Someone was sleeping in the lounge. He could almost hear them breathing, a faint noise that grew louder as he edged along the hallway.

His fingertips were his guide. Andrew felt the peeling seams of aged wallpaper, tiny bumps on a picture frame, and by the time he found the glossy wood of the dining room doorway, kicked up dust was irritating his tired eyes.

He went in. Curtains were drawn, pitch black. Andrew shut his eyes – useless in the dark – and found it heightened his other senses, reaching out to find a table made of smooth, polished wood.

A soft carpet swallowed his footsteps. He almost grew complacent, and that made it all the more shocking when an object stopped him dead in his tracks.

Something new.

The layout had changed since his last visit. Andrew felt a large piece of furniture in his way – like a cabinet, but lined in fabric. It ran from the table to the wall, leaving no room to squeeze past.

Andrew's confidence was shattered, and he could only see one thing to do.

Turn on the light.

He eased the door shut and felt for the switch, breaking out in a cold sweat as he pressed it. Even with his eyes closed, he was blinded. A thin, paper shade around the bulb made it seem even stronger, piercing through layers of skin.

Andrew steadied himself while his eyes adjusted, fearing the whole time that something might stir in the lounge. The new object was a clothes horse, so heavily loaded with bedding and towels that it felt much sturdier.

He lifted it aside and edged around the room, feeling urgency now the light was on. A glass fronted bureau in the corner bore shelves laden with keepsakes, and near the bottom, Andrew found a sealed wooden chest with a brass plaque.

Here Lies Daniel Lawton

There he was – the man who had tormented Andrew, locked him away, and made him do such horrible things. They had finally come face to face, the only way that they possibly could.

It was a sobering event. Daniel was a real person after all, and very dead. Andrew fought the urge to wrench off the lid and pour the ashes on the floor, taking revenge for everything he had lost.

Instead, he reached for a shoebox he had seen in his mind. There were papers inside – Daniel's passport and birth certificate – and beneath them, Andrew found what he was there for.

The spare key to Daniel's car.

Andrew's Honda Civic had gone missing, taken somewhere that his memories weren't betraying. This was the only way to get out of the city and find Ryan. *The only way to prove Andrew's innocence.*

He held the key in his bandaged palm and put everything back as he had found it, then returned to the door, taking a last look around before he turned out the light.

Click.

Right away, something was wrong. The room wasn't plunged into darkness. A thin sliver of light crept under the door, and Andrew could make out chair legs, the carpet, his shoes...

There was another light on in the house.

"I know you're in there," said a voice.

Andrew's heart skipped. The gash on his arm started to pulse as he slipped the key into his pocket and wrapped his fingers around the door handle, sweaty palm touching cool metal.

"I'm coming out," he said.

Light from the lounge revealed a ruffled red carpet. Standing in the doorway was the elderly man from Andrew's memories – a gaunt and fragile person, with a thick brow of deep wrinkles.

Daniel's father, John Lawton.

"Andrew?" said the man. "What on Earth are you doing here?"

"How do you know my name?" Andrew raised his hands, showing he posed no threat.

"You told me when you came around last week," said John, confused. "Was this why you were showing so much interest in my son? So you could steal from him?"

"Don't jump to any conclusions until you've heard me out," said Andrew. "I have an explanation."

"You look like you're in trouble," said John.

"Heaps of it, and I wish I could say it has nothing to do with Daniel, but that would be a lie."

"Daniel's been dead for two years," said John. "How could it possibly involve him now?"

Andrew closed his eyes. "Because he tried to kill somebody."

John Lawton was dumbstruck, but it quickly turned to anger. "How dare you make such an accusation," he said. "I don't care how well you knew my son. You don't know the first thing."

"I'm telling the truth," Andrew squirmed. "It's too complicated to explain." He eyed the front door, wanting to escape, and rescue came when a third voice interrupted.

"Hello, John."

The old man turned to the kitchen and his face sank. "Isabel, my God. I haven't seen you in years."

She appeared in the doorway, adopting the same calming manner as Andrew. "I'm sorry we lost touch," she said, "but Andrew and I need your help. We just can't explain why."

"What are you doing here at this time of night?"

"Ryan's in danger," she said. "I hate to ask you for this, but we need Daniel's car."

Andrew stepped forwards. "It's only for a day or two, and then we'll explain everything."

The old man thought for a moment, still reeling from the sight of Isabel. "I haven't seen you since he died," he said. "If you really wanted the car, then you could have told me two years ago."

"I'm sorry," said Isabel. "Things have changed since then."

John's head sank. "Fine, just take the key and go," he said. "It's up to you whether you bring it back."

Andrew went to rest an arm on his shoulder, but thought twice. "Thank you," he said. "We'll return it once this is over, I promise."

Neither of them really believed it.

***

The engine of the metallic-green Austin Maestro crunched and wheezed, as heavily worn as its current owner. John Lawton watched from the living room window as the woman he had loved like a daughter took one of the last reminders of his son.

He couldn't bring himself to wave them off.

A cloud of black smoke drifted into the air as the vehicle settled. Andrew wrestled with the heavy gearstick as Isabel wrestled with her guilt.

"You shouldn't be hard on yourself," he said.

"That was Daniel's father," said Isabel. "The last time I saw him was at the funeral. I didn't mean for it to be so long, but I suppose I've just been busy."

"I'm sure he understands," said Andrew. "You can't expect to stay in touch when the thing that binds you together is severed."

"He looks old," she said. "John's changed so much since it happened. I don't suppose he has anyone else in his life."

Andrew slid a hand onto her knee, lending support. She let it stay there. "Once we find Ryan, we'll bring the car back and you can explain it all to him. He'll be over the moon when he finds out Daniel isn't dead."

"Hmm," she muttered, dismissively.

They smelled burning in the air as Andrew turned onto the road and got underway. "Where are we going?" she said.

"The countryside. I can picture it quite clearly in my head – a lake in a valley, surrounded by woods."

"Yes, but how are we going to get there?"

He reached the end of the road and signalled to turn right, but a feeling welled up inside, an urge to go the other way.

A will so strong that he could hardly resist it.

Andrew slowed to a halt, staring at the steering wheel.

"Are you okay?" said Isabel.

"I don't know," he said. "I can't go right."

She looked out of the windscreen. *No other vehicles on the road, just the blue hue of an approaching day.* "It looks clear to me," she said, "but if you think it's a bad idea, turn left."

He let his hands guide themselves, and the wheel turned anticlockwise, sliding easily through his fingers. There was an indescribable sense of doing the right thing, like a rush of endorphins.

They moved through town, scant traffic to slow them down. The same thing happened at the next junction – Andrew's muscles told him which way to go, guiding him out of the city.

Isabel could see the confusion on his face. "Would you like me to drive?" she said. "I can have a go."

"No, I'll do it," said Andrew. "There's less chance of getting lost if I can sit behind the wheel. I'm not sure, but I think-..."

He slammed on the brakes. The car slid to a halt in the middle of the quiet road, straddling both lanes. Isabel was flung forwards into the seatbelt, jarring her neck.

"What is it?" she said. "What's happened now?"

Andrew stared up at the sky, dumbfounded.

"It's daylight."

The first rays struck the tops of buildings. He had seen less than two minutes of sun since this all began, two stolen minutes before he had been cast back into darkness.

"Are you alright?" Isabel asked.

Tired eyes gazed with wonder at the sun rising over the horizon, an experience he thought he might never have again. Hours had passed, and he still felt no tiredness.

Andrew was more than just alright.

He was back in control.

26|EMORIAL

Andrew Goodwin sat by the roadside and cherished the wind on his face, feeling cleansed after weeks of confinement. He ran his hand across his stubbly scalp, finding it hard to get used to.

Struggling to remember himself.

Isabel had been helping him to piece things together, filling gaps in his memory as they drove. It hadn't been easy to hear, but he was finally getting a rounded picture of the truth.

Daniel was in his head – Andrew had no choice but to accept it – hiding where he couldn't be found, taking over when Andrew's guard was down.

What made it worse was the line between the two men was no longer so distinct. Moments of Daniel's life kept merging with his own. Andrew was recalling stories as Isabel recanted them, knowing how they finished before she got the words out.

It was almost voyeuristic to experience Daniel and Isabel's intimacy as a couple, an intrusion on their privacy. It made him grateful for the wind in his face, freeing him from having to think about it.

"Look out behind you," said a voice.

He turned to see Isabel rushing towards him, struggling to balance a hot baguette and two steaming cups of coffee. Andrew took the drinks and set them down.

"We're going to have to share the food," she said. "I didn't have cash for any more."

"Don't worry about it," he said. "My stomach's in knots. I doubt I could keep anything down."

The wound on Andrew's arm stung him sharply. There was a smell in his nostrils that put him off the thought of eating. *Burned rubber.*

She sat next to him and looked down the road. "Have you made any progress?" she asked.

"I'm still working on it," said Andrew. The two of them were in a part of the countryside neither recognised. Instinct had guided him there, but now, it had failed him. Andrew sat on a bench, staring at a crossroads, no inkling of which way led towards the lake.

Lost.

"Daniel definitely would have stopped," said Andrew, looking at the white lines on the tarmac. "I just can't tell which way he turned."

Isabel unwrapped the baguette and tucked into it with hungry mouthfuls. "Can't you just pick a direction and see what happens?" she said.

"We'd be flying blind," he said. "Out here in the middle of nowhere, it could take hours to backtrack if it turns out to be wrong. I'd rather wait here and get it right."

She nodded. "Okay. After what happened at Daniel's father's house, you've earned some leeway."

Andrew watched her eat with muted envy, taking his eyes off the road. She saw something in his jealousy. "You know, Daniel used to give me a very similar look to that," she said.

"It must have been hard to speak to him again," said Andrew.

"I didn't realise I was doing until afterwards," she said. "It's still hard to believe."

"Are you a spiritual person?"

"I believe in God, but there's a difference between believing in something and being confronted by it. Daniel is supposed to be dead, and that's all there is to it."

"Can we be sure that he isn't?" said Andrew. "This thing inside me says it's Daniel, but how can we know it's telling the truth?"

Isabel stopped chewing and shook her head. "He knows things only Daniel could. I didn't see it at first, but no other explanation fits."

Andrew held his drink, absorbing its heat. "Sometimes, I can see through his eyes," he said. "Moments you've shared together. Then at other times, I come up with nothing."

"But you're absolutely sure that Ryan's alright?" she asked.

Andrew nodded. It had only been a few days since he had heaved Ryan's cold carcass out of the car and dragged it to the lake. He could picture it vividly, and he had been so sure that Ryan was dead.

It mortified him to think he was wrong – that Daniel had retrieved him, alive and well, and that Andrew had tried to drown a living man.

"Daniel wasn't the only one who died, you know," said Andrew. "Back at the seafront. I died too – for a minute, so they tell me. I just don't remember it."

Isabel lowered her food. "Do you know why you survived?"

"I'm not sure Daniel's in this alone," he said. "There's a woman, dressed in green. I see her everywhere, and I've got too many memories over her. I get the impression she's trying to help him."

"Who do you think she is?"

Andrew thought of Cheryl, of their striking similarity. He hadn't seen his girlfriend since handing her the photograph under the door, but even as he thought about it, he could see her perched on Daniel's lap, wrapping her arms around him.

Giving the picture back.

Andrew put a hand to his chest to feel the sharp edges through the fabric. It was in his pocket. *Had she known what she was doing?* He realised with a sobering chill that there wasn't anyone he could really trust.

"There's something I need to ask you," he said to Isabel. "Do you still have feelings for Daniel?"

A lorry drove past and they watched it go, rather than share eye contact.

"I'm afraid I don't know you well enough to answer that," she said. "I'm with Ryan now, and that's all that matters."

Andrew nodded, his question answered, and stood. "We should go."

"Did you work out which way we're heading?" she said.

"No, but I think I realise why. Daniel may have missed the junction completely and driven right through it. It's possible – no second thought, no chance of recollection. We'll carry down to the next one and see if it becomes-..."

Andrew faltered in his step, veering towards the road. Isabel rushed up beside him and helped to take his weight. "What is it?" she asked. "Are you okay?"

"It's nothing," he said. "Just a headache. I've had it for weeks."

"Are you sure that's all it is? You don't look very good."

Andrew pulled himself back to his feet, walking towards the car. Isabel trailed behind for a moment and watched his uneven walk, the way he was starting to drag his leg.

He didn't look very good at all.

***

Trusting Andrew's impulse, they drove straight through the crossroads and carried on towards the lake. It seemed to be a wise decision, because at the very next junction, he felt a clear sense of which was the right direction.

And that they were starting to get close.

The winding roads led through valleys and hillsides, and Andrew struggled with the Maestro's stiff steering. Isabel noticed small patches of blood seeping through the bandage on his forearm, and made him pull over to examine it.

"I'm so sorry I hurt you," she said. "I feel terrible."

Peeling back the dressing, she could see the deep gash she had inflicted, crusted over. It looked sore, like it really needed stitches, but all she could do was tighten the wraps.

Still, she felt she owed him something.

"The last time I saw Daniel was two days before he died," she said. "We bumped into one another in the hallway as we left for work. Neither of us said a word. We didn't even smile or nod, just put our heads down and kept moving. I struggled with guilt for months because of that."

Andrew was glad of something to take his mind off their destination. He drove off again, keen to get it over with. "Sometimes," he said, "we can get so caught up in our problems that we lose sight of what's important."

"Are you married?" she asked him.

"I was once," said Andrew. "I suppose technically I still am. We aren't divorced, but she's disappeared."

"How long ago was that?" said Isabel.

"Six months at the most," he said. "She emptied our house and vanished into thin air."

"Do you think Daniel could have been involved?"

"That he got rid of her?" Andrew slowed the car as it occurred to him. "Couldn't be. That was months ago, and it's only been like this for a couple of weeks."

Isabel shrugged. "Daniel's been dead for two years, Andrew. I'm not saying he did something to your wife, but if he hasn't been inside your head all this time, then where was he?"

The roads continued to twist and dip, slowing their progress. Andrew put a hand inside his jacket and retrieved the photograph.

"Did he show you this?" he said.

Isabel took it and fell silent. After another mile, he realised she was still staring at it. "Are you alright?" he asked.

"I've never seen this picture before," she said. "Just so you understand, Daniel wasn't always this hostile. In fact, it's hard to believe he's the same person. You were right – I did love him once, and a part of me always will."

Andrew was surprised at her level of tenderness. "I suppose we have to remember what happened to him," he said. "*Daniel died,* and we can't have any idea what that was like. Perhaps he could be forgiven for his madness."

"He was a good man once," said Isabel. "I don't think he would have harmed your wife, and I don't think he meant what he did to Ryan."

Andrew's wounded hand was shaking as he turned the wheel, though he didn't complain about it. "Katie was always quite offhand," he conceded. "She could have just decided to make a fresh start. Either way, I just hope this is over soon."

"Absolutely," said Isabel.

Silence fell as she stared out of the window, and Andrew looked vacantly at the road ahead, waiting for his instincts to tell him what to do next.

A layer of sweat glistened on his brow, thinking back on his imprisonment. *The shoebox under the bed was Daniel's way to keep track of his new possessions.* It had seemed more sinister at the time, as had the broken watch – *nothing more than an old treasured keepsake.*

And as for the pains in his forehead...

Somewhere deep inside his mind, Andrew heard a violent scream. There was a flash before his eyes, and the steering wheel flew out of his grasp.

He lost control of the car. Powerless, he put a hand across Isabel's chest – just as he had done with Katie, on that fateful day by the sea.

"What's happening?" she screamed.

Andrew slammed his foot on the brake and the wheels locked, but the car kept moving, sliding on a thick crust of mud. They careered off the carriageway into a hedge, saved only as the front wheel slipped into a ditch and dragged them to a halt.

He panted nervously as Isabel stared with wide eyes. "What was that?" she said.

"I don't know," said Andrew. "My eyes... I saw something, like..."

Ryan's cold, pale corpse.

"We must be getting close," he said. "I think Daniel's trying to stop me."

Isabel forced her door open, churning up the undergrowth. Climbing out of the vehicle, something caught her eye.

"My God," she gasped.

She stood looking down at a wide valley, with a deep, thick forest covering the fields like a blanket. In the center was a lake.

"I know where we are," she said. "I've been here before."

Behind the wheel, Andrew felt the same recognition. "I think I have, too," he said.

"But it's been years," said Isabel. "We weren't here since..."

Andrew turned to see a tear in her eye.

"I'd forgotten how beautiful it was," she finished.

He couldn't bring himself to tell her what he saw when he looked at that same view, but it certainly wasn't beauty. Daniel was absolutely right to want them to turn back around.

All Andrew saw was death.

27|ORNING

Breaks in the cloud provided glimpses of sunlight, creating pockets of warmth that were dotted all over the valley.

Andrew steered towards the forest, moving slowly in case he lost control again. The green Austin Maestro juddered as it ran over potholes, and cool air whistled past the windscreen.

The closer they got, the more he could remember of his last visit, and it put him on edge. There was no way he could tell Isabel what he had done for the sake of self-preservation, heading down those narrow lanes with a body on the back seat.

Ryan's cold, grey corpse.

Whether her fiancé had been alive at the time or not, Andrew had still tried to dispose of him, to sink him without a trace. The thought of it spurred him on, a need to set things right.

"Do you recognise anything yet?" Isabel had her own reasons to be restless. Whereas Andrew had proven to be trustworthy all day so far, his past behaviour said otherwise. She couldn't help but wonder which was the real him.

"I think we're going the right way," he said, "but everything looks different in the daytime."

He didn't recognise the road, but it felt right, and he was still trusting his gut. Relying less on what he could see and more on his feelings, it started to grow familiar. Lush, green trees clustered together like walls of leaf and bark, and a wide patch of earth by the roadside caught his attention.

Smooth and level, as though someone had recently tried to cover their tracks.

He pulled over and climbed out, the wind scattering hairs on his arms. In the distance, he saw a thick canopy, and shivered at the thought of the pitch dark forest he had tried to hide in.

Daniel must have woken up there, the moment Andrew fell asleep.

Isabel jumped out of the car and followed, more unnerved by the second. She had been expecting Ryan to be locked in a house, or some other type of building. She couldn't grasp why Andrew seemed to be searching the undergrowth.

"Are we getting closer?" she said, but Andrew didn't answer. He ploughed into the trees, following the sound of lapping water.

"Are you listening?" said Isabel. "Where are you going?"

He pushed through the branches, recalling the heavy weight he had dragged, but finding no trace of his actions. Still, his instincts told him this was the place, and it was enough to steady his nerve.

Andrew broke through to the lakeside. Rippling water stretched for hundreds of meters into the distance, with a thick border of trees that spread up the sides of the valley.

The sun came out for a few seconds, then disappeared just as quickly.

"Please tell me you know where you're going." Isabel came up beside him, but Andrew remained quiet. The ground was thick with unkempt grasses and ferns. He remembered how it felt to stumble down to the bank and plunge amongst the reeds.

Isabel grew impatient and stepped between him and the water, blocking his view. "I don't like where this is heading," she said. "Either show me where Ryan is or stop stringing me along."

"Just be patient," he said, dismissively.

"I'm worried you don't know what you're doing," said Isabel. "If Ryan's out in this weather then there's all the more reason to hurry."

"I'm trying my best."

Her eyes burned. "Try harder. I'm warning you."

An image entered his mind – the knife in Isabel's coat pocket. Suddenly, all he could think about was the power that she held over him, as long as she had it.

Quite beyond his control, a new direction grew inside of him – an instinct, just like he had been hoping for.

His hand twitched.

"You've got ten seconds to come up with something better," she continued, "or we're calling the police. They can search this place in a fraction of the time it would take us."

The wound on his forearm tingled, a reminder that she had cut him twice already, and wouldn't hesitate to do it again. *Unless she no longer had the means to.* The thought spread like wildfire, and Andrew found himself leaning towards her.

Isabel saw it, too. "What are you doing?" she said.

His arms left his side, quite beyond his influence. *An urge that wasn't his.* Isabel took a step backwards, reaching for the knife handle.

"Tell me what you're doing," she said.

Andrew made no attempt to speak, so she pulled out the blade and held it in plain sight. Slowly and cautiously, Isabel edged away from the muddy bank.

Just then, the sun broke through the clouds and sparkled off the waters, flooding Andrew's eyes with light. He snapped out of his trance, using his raised arms to shield his face.

And he noticed someone in the distance.

Someone was watching them from around the lakeshore, making no attempt to hide themselves. He saw long, dark hair, and shoulders that shuddered as though they were freezing.

The woman in the green coat.

Daniel's accomplice.

A cold rush brought Andrew back to his senses and he turned to Isabel. "Don't make any sudden moves," he said. "Just turn around and look behind you."

She kept the knife pointed rigidly at his chest. "And show you my back?" she scoffed. "Why would I do that?"

Discovered, the woman started to drift in their direction, coat lifting as she put one bare foot in front of the other. Andrew took a step away. "It's the woman I was telling you about," he said. "We have to go."

"I'm not falling for this," said Isabel.

"It's the truth, I swear. We need to hurry."

Andrew turned on his heels and rushed into the trees, not caring which direction. As soon as his back was turned, Isabel glanced over her shoulder. The wind across the lake made her eyes water, but she could see all she needed to.

There was no one there.

A cry rang out, and Isabel looked to find Andrew collapsed on the ground. "What is it?" she stepped over cautiously. "Are you alright?"

He clutched his forehead in pain, staring over the lake.

"We have to go now," he yelled.

Isabel shook her head. "You ought to lie still."

"There isn't time!"

Andrew hauled himself off the grass and took her arm, pulling her towards the trees. Isabel went blindly, clutching the knife in her free hand. They hurried through the woodland as he recognised spots of churned undergrowth which had been covered over, branches that had snapped in two.

He saw red brick and knew where Ryan had been hidden. "Over there," he said. "Quickly."

Andrew steered Isabel towards a pump-house, recessed from the water's edge, not much larger than a garden shed. The lock was off, and the door swung open, a low hum from machinery inside. He let go of her arm and catapulted himself indoors, almost tripping over the doorstep.

Ryan had gone.

Dried water marks showed where he once huddled on the floor, but now he had vanished. Isabel didn't realise what she was looking at.

"What's wrong?" she said.

Andrew moved to a small, square window at the back, staring through it with wide eyes.

The woman in green, fifty meters away and closing.

"It's a trap," said Andrew. "She must have been waiting for us to come here."

Isabel tried to peer over his shoulder. "Who are you looking at?"

"The one who's been helping Daniel," he said. "Can't you see her?"

The door drifted closed, as if pulled by a breeze. Andrew rushed over and grabbed the handle. *Locked tight.* He heard a hauntingly familiar sound from all around the building.

Scratching, clattering.

Turning back towards the window, a deep sense of dread washed over him. The woman in green stood behind the glass, staring straight into his soul.

Her expression was determined, unblinking, terrifying. Andrew surged forwards and grabbed Isabel, pulling her towards him, and the second she was clear, the woman put her hand through the window pane.

Without breaking it.

Andrew watched in horror as the she stepped through glass and brickwork, as though it were an open doorway. The transition made no sound – she just passed through like it wasn't there.

As though she were in a different plain of existence altogether.

They had nowhere to run. Andrew felt a draught snake around his legs, the heat of the engines suddenly pulled out of the air. The woman stood before them with quivering arms, her skin devoid of colour.

There was a sudden, violent, unnatural thump inside his ribcage. Andrew dropped to his knee, clutching his chest.

"What is it," Isabel cried. The knife slipped from her hands as she rushed to his side. "What's happening to you?"

Andrew saw the phantom's coat – a green hem, stained in blood which trickled to the ground and disappeared before it struck the concrete. He realised it wasn't a coat at all, but robes.

As in hospital robes.

A searing pain shot up his neck, and Andrew's heart stopped beating. "I can't-..." His words were stifled, jaw clamped shut.

Isabel helped him to the floor, able to see the panic on his face. "Focus on your breathing," she said. "Stay calm."

Her voice in his ear was the only thing to keep him together. Andrew forced his eyes closed – trying to will the pain away – and to his astonishment, it worked. The pain lessened, and a mellow heartbeat rose out of the silence.

When he opened his eyes again, the woman was gone.

Andrew and Isabel were alone in the cramped building. He lay on the ground in a state of shock, afraid to move. "Didn't you see any of that?" he asked with a shallow voice, hands shaking.

Isabel stroked his hair. "I kept glancing through the window," she said, "but I don't think anyone came near it."

"She was in the building, Isabel. *She was standing right next to you.*"

There was pity in her eyes. "You need a hospital," she said.

"This is where Daniel was holding Ryan," said Andrew. "He was locked in. I can feel it."

Isabel's face dropped as she saw the dried stains on the wall. "The door looked like it was broken," she said. "Maybe he escaped."

"Even if he did, then where would he go?"

"I don't know," she said. "*Somewhere.* Ryan's a capable man. He would have thought of something."

Daniel rubbed his chest gently, feeling delicate. He had seen Ryan's poor condition, and would have been surprised if he had moved more than a few yards of his own accord.

"We need to keep moving," said Andrew. "More could come back to me."

Isabel put a hand out to stop him. "No, you've done enough for one day," she said. "Look at the state you're in. You need to rest."

"It's not that simple," he said. "Every time I drift off, Daniel takes control and just wears me out even more. I can't stop it."

"But I can't afford to lose you," said Isabel. "This is hopeless if we don't have your memories."

"There's no time," he said.

She thought for a moment. "Then we don't have any choice but to ask Daniel for help."

"Are you serious?" said Andrew. "Daniel's a desperate man, and dangerous, too."

"It's our only chance of finding Ryan without pushing you over the limit," said Isabel. "We need some answers, and what better place to get them than from the source?"

She helped him to stand, leaving the knife on the ground as she tried to take his weight. High above them, the clouds grew thicker, and they came out of the building into shade.

"I'm scared," said Andrew. "Scared that one day soon, I might not wake up."

"If you don't manage to rest," she said, "things will get worse all the quicker. I'll look after you, and once I know Ryan's safe, we'll find a way out of this."

Andrew straightened up, standing on his own two feet. "Are you sure you'll be alright?"

She nodded. "We don't have a choice."

"Whatever you do, don't let your guard down," he said. "Remind yourself that I won't be the same person."

She slid her hand into his.

"I know you won't, Andrew, but that's okay. You'll still be someone I know."

28|BSESSION

The more Isabel saw of Andrew Goodwin, the more she was convinced of his story. That Daniel was inside him, vying for control.

The claim was so ridiculous – so unlikely – that it simply had to be true. The only thing she couldn't decide was whether that made Andrew a friend, or someone to avoid at all costs.

Someone dangerous to be around.

Daniel held the answers, and she knew just how to get through to him. Isabel had been to the lakeside before, and had the perfect location to make her former boyfriend open up.

It was a place only the two of them would understand, that not even Andrew could know the significance of.

And it wasn't a place of death.

***

Eighteen months before Daniel died, things were different – a simpler time that at least one of them still yearned for. *No heart murmur, no dishonesty.*

Autumn arrived late, and the valley struggled to keep up with the changing weather. A thousand trees shed their leaves almost overnight, carpeting the world in oranges and browns.

Isabel stood between the window and the curtains. She had pulled herself out of bed just in time to catch a vibrant, maroon dawn, an unearthly palette of rich colours.

She wiped nervous palms on her thin nightshirt. Anyone standing in the garden would have seen her bare legs – perhaps more – but she wasn't worried. There was scarcely a soul for miles around, one of the reasons why she had booked that hotel in particular.

No interruptions.

Something stirred behind her. With a playful laugh, Isabel turned and yanked the curtains open, sending unforgiving daylight shearing through the darkness.

"Finally," she yelled. "Happy birthday!"

Beneath a steeply sloping ceiling in the corner of the room, Daniel lay in bed. He groaned and rolled onto his front.

"Oh no you don't," she said. Isabel ran barefoot over a thin, blue carpet and pounced on top of him. "It's time to open your presents."

His face was buried in the pillow, but there was no reaction. She hopped back off him and pulled the duvet to the floor.

"Can I not just sleep?" he said with a croaky voice.

"Sadly not," she said. "Hurry up, I've been waiting for you."

Exposed, Daniel turned over to face the new day, but refused to open his eyes. Isabel knew what to do.

She unfastened the top button of her shirt and climbed astride him, knees sinking into the mattress.

She started to sing. *"Happy Birthday to you..."*

He could feel her bare skin fold around his hips. Daniel couldn't resist a peek.

"...Happy Birthday to you..."

Her legs were warm after a night under the covers. She squeezed her thighs, gently pressing through the fabric of his boxer shorts.

"Happy Birthday, dear Daniel..."

On mention of his name, she opened another button, teasing him with a view of what was underneath.

He smiled. "I thought you just said I'd be in charge of the unwrapping."

Isabel slackened her grip. "Oh, you are," she said, "but not of me."

She slid off the bed and pattered to her suitcase, leaving Daniel in a state of arousal. "Where are you going?" he said.

"Close your eyes."

He did as he was told until she returned and sat cross-legged beside him. "Here's a little something to make up for growing old," she said.

Daniel peered through a slit in his eyelids at a gift-wrapped parcel, the size of a hardback novel. The paper was a shimmering red.

"Do you want me to open it right now?" he said, distracted by her chest. She prodded him in the side.

"Hey, I spent a long time planning this." She buttoned her shirt. "Stay focussed."

Daniel picked up the gift and tore the paper without a thought for ceremony. Inside was a black box, lined in fabric, and he opened it to find his birthday present.

A wristwatch.

The strap was made of silver, with a thin gold band down the center of each link. The face was jet black, with two golden hands that pointed to golden numerals.

He lifted it out of the box and felt something on the back, turning it round to find an inscription in fancy italic lettering:

'To my darling Daniel, love Isabel.'

The weight implied expense. He slid it onto his wrist and closed the clasp – exactly the right size.

"This is incredible." He leaned over and gave her a lingering kiss. "I thought we were planning to save all our money this year."

"I couldn't resist," she said. "Not for your thirtieth birthday. There are some more presents, too."

She turned to leave, but Daniel put a hand on her leg. "Hang on," he said. "You're spoiling me. I wasn't expecting any of this."

Isabel allowed herself to be drawn back over to him. Daniel cradled her face and kissed her again.

"It's called a surprise," she said.

"Well, I appreciate the effort you've gone to," said Daniel. "Let's not rush it."

She smiled. "You should know I've got the whole day planned out in my head."

He ran a hand along her inner thigh. "At least give me the chance to say thank you for my first present," he said.

"I suppose there's time enough for that."

Their lips locked passionately, and Daniel felt the weight of her chest push him down onto the mattress. Isabel's thick head of messy blonde hair folded around them, and for just for a second, they were the only two people in the world.

It was a moment that Daniel would always remember. She broke off his gaze, fingers and lips moving down his chest. Her hair tickled his face, so he lifted his chin, staring at patterns of dried damp on the woodchip ceiling.

Swirling like camouflage.

Eyelids fluttered across his stomach. Daniel lifted his arm and felt the cool pinch of the wristwatch. It brought a smile to his face, more certain than ever that he would love that woman until his dying day.

He wasn't to know just how soon that day would come.

***

Daniel clung tenuously to consciousness, trying to find an anchor. Every twitch reminded him how much his muscles ached. He felt a deep wound in his forearm and his skull was pounding.

A headache that only ever seemed to get worse.

He lay in darkness, enveloped in a thick, unnatural silence, to the point where even a pin drop would have been deafening. All he could feel were a pillow under his head and a soft mattress.

Unwelcome memories flooded into the void, things that Andrew had done while Daniel was asleep. *Pleading with Isabel as she held a knife to his chest, the woman Daniel loved turned into a well of hatred.*

The visions grew more disturbing as they became less violent. Isabel appeared to relax in Andrew's company, tending to his wounds, treating him like a friend. Daniel felt a surge of jealousy, and his eyes flickered open as he realised something else.

Those memories were from the daytime.

And it was now the dead of night.

He tried to sit up, but couldn't, wrists and ankles bound with thick ropes. Instead, he raised his head and saw hairline slits of light around a doorway at the foot of the bed. A faint hue showed him a sloped ceiling overhead, and he recognised it right away.

The hotel room they had stayed in, all those years ago.

Only one person would have known to put him there. Daniel drew a deep breath and spoke out.

"I'm awake, Isabel. You can talk to me now."

There was a thud from the bathroom and the door drifted open. A silhouette appeared in the doorway, long hair and curvaceous hips.

"Hello, Daniel."

Isabel turned on the light and he shut his eyes, ghostly images plastered on his retina. The room hadn't changed in the years since they had been there last.

"Do you finally believe it's me?" he said.

"Yes," said Isabel. "It took some convincing, but I can see that now."

She kept her distance. Daniel could smell fresh perfume – at once soothed by her presence, yet unnerved by her behaviour.

"You can untie me if you want," he said. "I won't hurt you."

She shook her head. "I'm sorry, but you have to stay there so I feel safe."

"Did Andrew put you up to this?" said Daniel.

"Look around you." Isabel's expression was muted, like she was holding her feelings back. "Andrew couldn't have known to bring you here," she said. "Don't you recognise it?"

His eyes were drawn up to that same pattern of dried damp he had seen years before. *Swirling like camouflage.* "How could I forget?" he said. "Did you notice I'm still wearing the watch? My father kept it."

"I saw," she said, "and it's still broken."

"Just stopped," he corrected. "Like most things, we could fix it, if we really wanted to."

He grimaced, a lump on his forehead where something had smashed into it that morning. *A falling mirror, perched above an open door.*

Isabel sat at the foot of the bed, as close to him as she dared to get. "Listen, I'm sorry for the way I've been this last week," she said. "I was too hostile when you came to the bank, much more than you deserved."

He nodded. "You're right to be sorry," he said. "You shut me out when I needed you most."

She found it easier not to make eye contact. "Just so you know, I don't blame you for what you've done. I know it's not normally in your nature to act like this."

"Then why did you bring me here?" said Daniel. "Why this room in particular, when I have such fond memories of it?"

"You know why," said Isabel.

"Then what happens when you have what you want? Will you just leave me to suffer?"

"I don't know," she said. "You have to understand that everything's changed since you died. *Years of pain and healing.* I'm not the same person anymore. My feelings towards you are confusing."

"It's not your fault," he said. "We were torn apart before we had a chance to smooth things out."

"That may be how you choose to remember it, but our relationship was over long before you died."

Daniel shook his head, refusing to listen. "We would have come through it," he said.

"But every time I tried to talk, you'd change the subject, just as you have done a dozen times this last fortnight. Skirting around the truth, feeding me stories."

"I had to," he snapped. "I suppose just blurting out that I was your dead boyfriend would have sounded better?"

"It would have been the truth," said Isabel. "Surely that makes it better by default?"

"Of course not."

Isabel withdrew and stood up, moving from the bedside. "We're looking for Ryan," she said.

"And you thought this room would make me talk, didn't you?" His temper started to flare. "Where do my feelings come into it? *I've died, Isabel. I'm trapped inside the man who killed me.* Why doesn't anyone care?"

"Because of what you've done to other people." Tears formed in her eyes. "You've hurt men who don't deserve it. Andrew's no more of a killer than I am, and you've tortured him. How can you expect me to care about you?"

"You don't know what they're really like." Daniel tugged hard on the ropes and Isabel backed away, worried he could tear through them. "Ryan lies and makes threats," he said.

"You tried to kill him."

"Only because he tried to kill me first. If you only knew what he was capable of-..."

"Then he'd be no worse than you are," she interrupted. "Tell me where you've taken him and let's finish this now. You wanted me to accept that you're back and I do. I can see that. There's no reason to keep him prisoner anymore."

Daniel relaxed his arms, realising his behaviour was getting him nowhere. "I'm not keeping him from you, and I never was. This has gone so far out of hand."

"Where is he?" she repeated.

Daniel looked around the room, remembering how much he used to love that place, and how it was ruined now. He closed his eyes. "Do you remember when the car broke down?"

"After your birthday?" said Isabel. "Arcadia. Of course I do."

"Well, then you know where to find him."

Her upper lip trembled, but she swallowed her anger. Daniel could feel her contempt as she stood up and stiffened.

"Please don't hate me, Isabel," he said. "You've got no idea how it feels to be like this. No one does. All I have belongs to other people now, even my memories."

Isabel went the bedside table and cleared the crockery off a thick wooden tea tray. "There's one more thing Andrew wanted me to ask," she said, ignoring his pleas. "Who is this woman in green who keeps helping you?"

Daniel pulled on his binds, growing nervous as she lifted the tray. "I have no idea what you're talking about."

Isabel nodded. "That's what I told him you'd say."

She slammed it down onto the swollen bruise, and Daniel was catapulted out of consciousness, head slumped into the pillow.

Out cold.

Isabel knew him well enough to see straight through his lies. It didn't matter what he said, the expression on his face always told the truth, even in Andrew's body.

Daniel was lying about the woman in green.

He knew exactly who she was.

29|EMORSE

Isabel left her hostage to sleep until morning, unable to tell which of the two men was getting the rest. She huddled in the corner and listened to their breathing, granting a few hours of respite.

Hoping it would keep both of them alive.

She, herself, couldn't sleep at all, full of regret for her actions. *For screaming, scratching, and slicing with the knife.* Neither man had asked for their entanglement, and they would have done anything to avoid it, even if it meant death.

Sunrise made her keen to escape from the hotel room and never return. Isabel wet a cloth and sat on the bed, dabbing the man's forehead to reduce the swollen lump.

His eyes parted, just the tiniest crack.

"We need to get moving." She spoke softly, but her words were impartial.

"How long was I unconscious?" he said.

Isabel smiled insincerely. "That depends on who I'm speaking to."

The man had stirred so many times in the night that it was impossible to keep track. He tried to raise a hand to his temple, only to remember he was tied up.

"Why does my head hurt so much?" he said.

"That's my fault." She wiped away crusts of blood. "I didn't know how else to put you out."

He lay still for a moment. Isabel could see sweat forming on his upper lip. "I mean it," she said. "I can't untie you until I know who you are."

"It's Andrew," he said.

"And how can I be sure?"

"I don't know." He swallowed laboriously. "It hurts when I try to think."

"That's too convenient," she said. "I need you to convince me it's safe to let you go, and quickly. It's a long way to where Daniel's keeping Ryan."

The man turned his head away, repelled by the daylight. "I remember," he said. "The place where the two of you broke down, three years ago."

"Andrew shouldn't know that story," said Isabel.

"But I can see it," he said. "I don't know, I-..."

Again, the man tried to touch his forehead, wracked with pain. Isabel had no desire to see either of them suffer, but she couldn't escape the fact that – besides a slurring of speech which was easily faked – there was no clear way to tell them apart.

In the end, pity made her cut through the ropes that bound him to the bed. Instead of sitting up, he curled feebly into a ball.

"Can you walk?" she said, but he didn't answer, barely conscious.

Isabel stroked his hair, unsure what else to do. She needed them both to pull through – Daniel for his knowledge, and Andrew for more reasons than she cared to admit.

Without him, she didn't have the strength to face what could have happened to Ryan by now.

What if he was dead?

***

Bruised and wounded, Andrew Goodwin sat in the passenger seat of the Austen Maestro, head against the window. Despite the bright morning and a bumpy ride, he drifted back to sleep, afflicted with a fortnight of endless torment.

Struggling with his own identity.

Untamed hedgerows scraped down the sides of the vehicle. The engine grumbled, causing the glass to vibrate, blending into harmony with the creaking suspension.

Behind the wheel, Isabel was sick with worry. *Afraid that Daniel could turn violent.* Every time the man opened his eyes, she stole a breath, never sure which one of them was in control.

It drew her attention from the road. Isabel hadn't driven in years, and she wasn't finding it easy. The gearstick trembled as she heaved the wheel, determined not to let it get the better of her.

Just one more thing she was trying to hold together.

They drove back towards the city. The lanes widened as trees withdrew to the borders of grassy fields, dissecting the landscape. She had been there before – years ago, returning from Daniel's birthday.

The only time his car had even broken down.

Stranded for hours, it wasn't an experience she would soon forget. Isabel found the turning easily, and the man in the passenger seat came to as he felt the car slow down and manoeuvre through a gap in the trees.

They found themselves on a steep hillside, cut off from the world. *An acre of land with a fortification of shivering branches.* Overgrown gateposts stood at the entrance, with a sign in chiselled lettering.

'Arcadia.'

Isabel drove them up a pitted driveway of worn tarmac towards a building at the summit – a two-storey cottage with large windows and a sloping slate rooftop.

Long since abandoned.

Every pane of glass had been smashed, dripping from the window frames onto a lawn of foot-long grasses and nettle bushes.

The scene hadn't changed since Isabel had been there last. Worn tyres rumbled over fallen roof tiles, peeled paintwork fluttering as a strong wind tore up the hillside.

The driveway curled around the house, and as they neared the back door, they discovered Ryan's black Range Rover.

Isabel's heart skipped a beat.

"There it is," she cried as she slammed on the brakes. Powerful gusts tried to force her back as she flung the door open and fought her way to the other vehicle.

Empty.

She turned towards the house. "*Ryan?*" she shouted out. "*Ryan, can you hear me?*"

The wind absorbed her cries. Distraught, she ran indoors to find every room had been stripped bare, holes in the plaster where the pipes had been looted.

Broken glass glistened on the carpet. Rainfall had seeped through the rooftop, filling the air with the stench of festering damp.

"Can you hear me, Ryan?" She cried so loud that her voice broke. *"Tell me where you are."*

Tears were streaming down her face. Andrew – *or Daniel* – came into an empty lounge to find her standing at the base of a staircase with sunken steps.

"Don't go up there," he said, leaning against the wall. "It looks dangerous."

"What have you done to Ryan?" she asked.

"I can't remember," he shrugged.

Isabel gripped him by the collar. "Show me where he is," she screamed. "You know, God damn it! You can show me."

His addled mind made it impossible to distinguish one set of memories from another. Isabel put a foot on the bottom step and it creaked under her weight.

"Please," said the man. "I honestly don't think he'll be up there." He shut his eyes, wishing they could stay closed.

"There's nowhere else he could be," she said.

"You haven't looked outside yet. Maybe he escaped."

He tried to take Isabel's hand, but she brushed it off, squeezing through the frame of a glassless patio door and into the garden.

"Ryan," she kept calling into the gale. *"Ryan."*

She trampled through overgrown flowerbeds, praying not to find him face down in the grass. Unfit to follow, the man hobbled through the back door and returned to the two cars.

Every time a memory was triggered, it hurt. He felt muddled, as though neither one of his personas had complete control. Pieces of grit stung his face as the wind gathered strength, flinging lumps of stone and slate at the vehicles.

Thump-thump-thump.

Down in the garden, Isabel soon realised there was nothing around her but rubble and weeds. She looked up the hillside to see the man idling against the car, seemingly doing nothing.

"Hey!" She stormed back up the driveway. "Why aren't you searching?" she yelled.

He leaned against the Maestro, letting it take his weight. "I don't know if I'm up to it," said the man, trying in vain to pull himself together.

"The hell you aren't," she said. "The answers are in that head of yours, and I need you to snap out of this and guide me to Ryan."

"I can't," he said. "When I think about him, all I see is darkness."

An endless void, free from pain and complication.

"Do you expect me to believe that?" said Isabel. "Why are you stalling?"

"I'm not," he said. "Please, just let me get myself-
..."

Something glanced off the back of the Range Rover, loud and unexpected.

Thump.

Isabel looked down to see slate and strips of bark all over the ground, but none of it was moving. She turned, aghast.

The sound was coming from inside the boot.

She ran to the Range Rover and put her ear to the metal. "Ryan?" she said. "Can you hear me in there?"

There were three seconds of silence, then two muffled knocks.

"Oh God," she cried. "How do we get him out? Have you got something-... We need to get the door open."

She dropped to her knees and started fumbling amongst the debris, searching for anything she could use as a lever.

"Help me," she cried.

"I don't know how to," said the man.

She jumped back to her feet. "The only reason Ryan's in that car is because you shut the door on him. You need to fix this."

He shook his head and repeated himself. "I don't know how."

She beat her hands against his chest, full of hatred. *"You get him out of there,"* she said. *"Think of something."*

In spite of the aching, he tried. "The keys," he said. "I haven't seen them in days. They must be around here somewhere."

"Where?" said Isabel.

He couldn't think, just couldn't.

She ran back to the Maestro and took the other set of keys from the ignition, throwing them to him. "Concentrate," she said. "Pretend you have to hide those from me. Tell me where."

He looked around him, and in focussing his mind, one place stood out immediately – the wheel arches.

Instinct took him to the front of the car, where he reached down to find the Range Rover key lying on one of the tyres. He unlocked it, and immediately heard Isabel heave open the boot.

Ryan lay curled up inside, clinging to life. His clothes were tightly wrapped around his chest where he had huddled from the night. His skin was ghostly pale, and he was almost too weak to raise his arm.

On sight of him, she almost fainted.

"Oh God, Ryan! What has he done to you?" She took his hand, locking their fingers together. His skin felt cold and wrinkled.

"Is he alright?" said the man.

"Help me lift him," she said. Together, they folded him out of the car and slid him onto the back seat of the Range Rover.

Isabel snatched the keys and climbed in.

"We need to find a hospital," she said.

Her companion clamoured into the passenger seat, checking to see Ryan was comfortable. *Laid out across the back seat, face pale and bruised, exactly as he had been on the night Daniel strangled him.*

Isabel flung the gearstick into reverse. The pedals were so light compared to the Maestro that the car rocketed around, almost smashing into the other vehicle.

"How far are we from the city?" asked the man as she straightened the wheel and moved off.

"I've no idea," she said, "but we'll get there in no time. You just watch me."

The car bounced down the hillside, buffeting over slate and potholes. It knocked something loose, and an object rolled out from under the passenger seat.

The video camera.

As Isabel turned back onto the main road, the man picked it up and examined it.

"I wonder what this is doing here," he said.

"I've seen it before," said Isabel, putting her foot down. "You brought it to the bank."

"Ryan told me there's a murder on it."

"I didn't look," she said. "Someone watched it for me. They said it was just a man sleeping, which I assumed was you."

"That's right," he said. "I recorded it one night, but the camera disappeared. I assumed Daniel had thrown it away."

Curious, he unfolded the screen and pressed play.

Straight to the footage of the car crash.

There wasn't time to look away. He returned to the seaside on the day Daniel had died. *The day both men had died.* Katie's recording showed Andrew Goodwin as he lost control of his silver hatchback and swerved off the road.

Neither Andrew nor Daniel could take their eyes off the screen, both seeing the footage for the first time. Red brake lights filled the picture, and Andrew twisted the wheel, heading for the promenade.

His car bounced onto the pavement with a metallic, deafening crunch, and careered towards a man that Andrew recognised from a photograph – *pale and overweight, standing frozen in the vehicle's path.*

Daniel Lawton.

The sight of him was a shock to both men – his dishevelled, neglected body. The car missed him by inches, without ever making contact.

Daniel couldn't believe it.

Instead, the vehicle sped on, ploughing into a lamp post. The camera was flung out of Katie's hand and the picture went dead. But that wasn't the end of the story.

Andrew could picture more in his mind, unable to escape it. A split-second before impact, something glanced off the bonnet with a thump – a specific, fleshy thud.

It was a fifteen year old boy, running down the curb line. *Jogging.* He was wearing a hood and headphones, zoned out, in his own world. He broke through the crowds without realising what was happening and ran headlong into the car.

The sound was unbearable.

Andrew hadn't been able to face it. In the aftermath of the crash, no one had spoken against him. Because of the jogger's neglect, Andrew was absolved of blame.

Katie, however, was less forgiving. *The only other person who had seen it happen.* When Andrew came to in the hospital, laid out on his front, he could see it in her face – the distance between them. He did the only thing he could think of to avoid his actions.

He pretended to forget.

Whether she believed him or not, Katie kept his secret, but at the cost of his marriage. Though she played along with his façade, she could never look at him the same way.

He couldn't blame her for hating him.

Sat beside Isabel in the Range Rover, he let the video camera slip from his fingers. In one careless moment, his life had been ruined. Since then, Katie had vanished and Daniel had awoken inside him.

Punishment for his crime.

"Are you alright?" Isabel took her eyes off the road as he sat numbly. "Don't fall apart on me now," she said. "I need you to keep Ryan safe."

The man couldn't turn to face the body on the back seat. His muscles had turned to stone.

"I'm so sorry for all of this," he said. "I wish I could go back and make it right."

"Who am I talking to?" she said. "Tell me who you are."

He looked at her with wild eyes. "Isabel, it's me."

His words were slurring, and the panic in his face would have been hard to imitate.

"Daniel?" she said. "Let me speak to Andrew."

"I can't," said the man. "I think something's happened to him."

Isabel brought the car to a screeching halt, sliding across both lanes. The man in the passenger seat stared at her like a rabbit caught in headlights.

"I'm not joking," she said. "Give him back right now."

Daniel shook his head, searching inside himself. Suddenly, his thoughts were crystal clear, no longer conflicted. *One focussed voice inside his mind.*

With the last wave of unlocked traumas, two weeks of struggle had come to an abrupt conclusion.

Andrew Goodwin had gone.

30|RAUMA

Daniel Lawton sat on a short bank of plastic chairs, transfixed by his shadow on the wall. He swore he could see it grow as the sun descended, reaching slowly across the paintwork.

He savoured the sight, refusing to let such moments pass him by.

Treating each day as his last.

Isabel came marching up the corridor towards him, high heels echoing off the hollow walls. Her tired eyes portrayed the hardships she had been through, and the slump in her shoulders contrasted her determined stride.

"How is he today?" Daniel asked, snapping out of his trance.

She walked right past him, making a beeline for the vending machine in the corner. "He's still no different," she said. "They told me he might be able to hear my voice, but it's difficult to find anything to say."

Over the last thirty-six hours, she had learned the code for every type of coffee in the machine by heart.

She ordered an Americano and waited impatiently for it to pour.

"How much longer can he stay like this?" said Daniel.

"If he doesn't snap out of it soon, he's looking at brain damage. He may have it already."

Andrew had been missing for two days, leaving Daniel in complete control. The sense of normality should have been exhilarating, but all he had done in that time was sit obediently outside the patients ward with Isabel.

It had been a long wait.

"Why did you shut him away in such a bad condition?" Isabel asked. She could hardly stand Daniel's company, but needed conversation. *To talk with someone who could talk back.*

Daniel sighed. "It was only supposed to be for a day or so, until I could explain myself to you. But instead of listening, you attacked me."

He lifted his arm to show the deep gash, now dressed in fresh, tightly-packed bandages. The doctor had given him something to relieve the pain, though it hadn't stopped his headache.

"Don't try to make me feel guilty," said Isabel. "You should think it's a miracle I haven't turned you over to the police, and if it hadn't been for Andrew, I really would have."

Daniel hunched forwards, elbows on his knees. Every conversation they had went the same way. "You're still not seeing my side of the story," he said, "Ryan attacked me and I defended myself."

"By strangling him?" said Isabel. "By trying to drown him?"

"After all these years, I should have earned the benefit of your doubt."

"No, Daniel. It's just the opposite – it hurts twice as much that you did it to me." There was hatred in her eyes, and only one reason why she still tolerated his presence. "Let me speak to Andrew," she said.

"You can't," said Daniel. "Like I told you before, he just isn't there anymore."

"I don't believe you. He's a good man, and if you've hurt him too, then I swear I'll make you pay."

Daniel threw his hands up. "There you go, tossing out the blame again. Don't make out like Andrew's a saint. He killed me, remember?"

"I've seen how it happened and it wasn't murder," she said. "It was an accident, bad luck. Andrew didn't mean any harm, unlike what you did to Ryan."

"Don't judge me," he said. "You don't understand what it's like."

Isabel shook with anger. "Don't judge you?" She got up and marched defiantly to a window into the ward, pointing to the other side.

"Look at what you did."

Ryan lay unconscious in a hospital bed, hooked up to an array of machinery. A heart monitor attached to his arm pipped slowly as he fought for his life.

Daniel didn't need to see it. He had looked through that window enough times in the past two days. Part of him wished for an act of God to finish what he couldn't and end Ryan's suffering.

Isabel wiped a frustrated tear from her eye. "I wish you'd never come back," she said. "I really do."

"Don't say that," said Daniel.

"This is such a mess. Why couldn't you just talk to me in the first place?"

"*I tried,*" he said. "I tried so many times that it drove me insane, but you wouldn't listen. Ryan's warped your judgement."

She sniffed, gazing through the glass at her partner. "How is it your business what he says to me?"

"Because my feelings towards you haven't changed," he said.

"Well, mine have." Isabel kept her back to him. "You're just history to me."

Daniel snapped. For him, it hadn't even been a month since they had been living together. Unable to cope, he stormed out of the room, needing to leave before their argument spiralled out of hand.

The whole world seemed to be against him – no one fighting his corner – and what hurt the most was that a part of him shared their perspective.

She's right to hate you, spat a voice in his mind. *Why should she care what you've become?*

He hurried down the stairwell, never breaking his stride. Daniel headed for the lobby and marched through the first door in sight, needing be far from everyone, trying to outrun his thoughts as they turned on him.

No one deserves death except you.

The sun dazzled as it glinted off every passing windscreen. He walked down a busy roadside, haunted by the video footage of his decayed and bloated body. Andrew's car had never touched him – Daniel could see that now. *It was just bad luck.*

A restless, powerful urge made him move away from the hospital, from the chaos he had caused. He lengthened his stride, running from his scathing inner voice.

Since then, all you've done is destroy, it said. *Taking back what you think you deserve.*

The wind rushed past his ears and he turned towards it, hoping to drown out his thoughts. But the voice grew louder, refusing to be silenced.

You spoiled your chance at life, and now you're coming after mine.

Daniel faltered in his step. It was neither insanity nor guilt. Pushing out from hidden depths was a sleeping soul that he hadn't heard or felt in days.

Andrew Goodwin.

"Why won't you just leave me alone?" Daniel cried.

Andrew had been absent for days, nothing more than a memory. *"You're the intruder,"* said the voice. *"You're the one who should be leaving."*

The pavements were overcrowded, so Daniel ducked into the road, picking up pace. Cars swerved as he cut through traffic.

"It was justice that put me here," he said. "It wouldn't be fair if you went unpunished."

"Your lifestyle caused your heart attack," said Andrew. *"You can't blame me for your own neglect."*

Daniel started to run down the white lines in the middle of the road. Pounding elbows narrowly missed passing cars in both directions.

"Just let me get on without you," he said.

"I can't, Daniel. We're too closely tied together. I can see everything you've done, as clearly as though I did it myself. I can see you strangle Ryan."

Passersby watched as he struggled with his sanity. "It wasn't my fault," said Daniel.

"No excuses," said the voice. *"You've ruined my life, just like you ruined your own."*

Daniel roared – anger, frustration. As the surrounding traffic slowed for a crossroads, he ploughed straight through, determined to put an end to it all.

A transit van screeched to a halt, horn blaring. It clipped the edge of Daniel's boot and spun him in the middle of the road, unable to brace himself as a car came from the other direction.

And slammed straight into him.

With a gruesome smash, Daniel was tossed into the air, sent clean over the bonnet. He felt bones shatter, tasted blood in his mouth. *Blazing, instant pain down the side of his body.*

He rolled off the roof, slung to the ground. His gashed arm was now badly broken, but the painkillers went some way to dull the feeling, almost detaching him from the impact.

Onlookers gazed in horror as Daniel stood and clumsily walked away from the accident, blood pouring down his face. Deep within his battered skull, the voice was screaming.

"What the hell did you just do?"

He found solace in Andrew's change of tone. Though it hurt with every step, Daniel pressed on. "You have to accept the blame for what I lost," he said. "What you robbed from me."

"You've stolen my life," said Andrew. *"I never took a thing from you on purpose."*

Daniel caught a glimpse of green and noticed the woman in hospital robes, standing on the pavement.

Her hands were lifted from her sides, and a rising wind shifted her mottled hair.

She looked distraught.

"Leave me alone," Daniel yelled at her.

"She can't," said the voice. *"She can no more leave you than I can."*

The traffic stood stationary, queued up behind the accident. Drivers watching with stunned expressions as Daniel marched between them.

"But I know you can leave me," he said. "You can go back to wherever you've been hiding. This is it, do you understand?"

The woman in green appeared again, further along the pavement. Daniel saw another junction and set off towards it, limping as fast as his wounded legs would allow, moving past the ghostly figure.

Instantly, she reappeared in the distance.

"Stop," said the voice. *"Let's talk this through."*

Daniel tried to ignore it, to drive Andrew from his mind like a rogue thought. It brought out pain behind his temples, a resistance to the very idea.

"Stop!"

The second cry was so loud that it shook his skull. Daniel's legs locked up and he tumbled helplessly to the ground. His head knocked against the tarmac and left him dazed, a jarring pain from his broken arm.

In that moment, it all seemed too much to bear. He had lost Isabel, his only love. He had lost Ryan, once a dear and trusted friend. He couldn't even bring himself to tell his father he was alive, for fear of what it would do to his fragile state.

Daniel Lawton was utterly alone.

He pulled himself back up, rising shakily to his feet. His leg held strong, no explanation for why it had suddenly failed until he tried to move, and realised he couldn't.

His body was refusing to respond.

A quiet descended on the street, crowds watching him intently. Daniel stood rigidly, legs rooted to the spot.

"Let me go," he said.

"So you can kill us both?"

He looked at morbidly-fascinated faces all around, reminding him of the day he died. Strangers that weren't willing to help.

"I'm not kidding, Andrew. Let me go."

The town center seemed to be at a standstill, waiting to see what would happen next. In the silence, Daniel heard the deep blast of a distant horn, and looked down the road to see a solid steel parapet at the sides of the pavement.

A railway bridge.

All he wanted – more than anything – was a way out, to have his troubles taken swiftly off his shoulders. He could think of only one way to make that happen, and if he took Andrew with him, then all the sweeter.

Tense muscles pulled both ways at once.

"I can't let you do it," said Andrew.

"You don't have a choice," Daniel countered. "I'm the one in control now. You've had your chance."

"We can talk about this, reach a compromise."

"I said I'm in control," he cried.

Daniel's leg tore loose, the stalemate broken. He took off down the road, racing between stationary vehicles, running towards the bridge.

"You're not thinking straight."

"This is the clearest I've ever thought," he puffed. "If you won't leave me, then it has to be done. Otherwise, we'll just keep going in circles."

Daniel leapt onto the pavement and fought through the crowd, pushing people aside. Seeing his madness, a long stretch opened out, tightly packed spectators letting him pass.

He skipped over the flags and launched himself at the barrier, getting a foothold on deep rivets. He scrambled to the top and stood precariously, holding his arm tightly to his chest. It pulsated, but only steadied his resolve.

"Please don't do this."

Daniel stood on the top and peered over the edge. The drop was ten meters onto railway tracks, and a train was approaching from the distance. But someone was already down there.

The woman in green.

She stood below him, gazing up. "What do you want from me?" Daniel screamed at her.

"She's trying to help you," said Andrew. *"She doesn't want you to jump."*

The woman's mouth opened and closed, forming words he couldn't hear.

"Leave me alone," said Daniel.

She lifted off the ground and gently rose up, physically drifting in the air towards him.

"Listen to what she's trying to say," said Andrew. *"She only wants to look after you."*

"She stood and watched me die," he cried, watching her beckon him down from the ledge. Tears flooded his face, mixing with the blood on his cheek. "You should have left me," he yelled.

"You owe her your life," said Andrew.

"And what good has that done me? Things would have been better if I'd died two years ago, Andrew. Don't pretend it wouldn't."

The voice in his mind fell silent, letting Daniel search inside himself. Both men had passed away on the seafront, two years before. Yet somehow, both had survived, just as Ryan had survived his drowning.

Daniel realised that his life had gone from bad to worse since then. *The despair, the obsession, the trauma.* There was only one way out – to restore the balance, to put things as they should have been that day in Brighton.

His legs tried to draw him back from the precipice, but Daniel's resolve was far too strong. For the first time in days, he had to power to take matters into his own hands. To control his destiny.

Instead of pulling away, Daniel chose to move forwards, to force his legs to do the opposite of what Andrew and the woman both wanted.

He careered over the side of the railway bridge, screaming with a trembling fear. In his mind, Andrew screamed along with him, but in horror and disbelief.

Bystanders gasped as he fell. Warm air turned cold, rushing past, and Daniel continued to clutch his broken arm – not spreading himself wide with exhilaration, but curled up, *foetal*, screeching in agony.

Ten feet... fifteen feet...

The pain refused to let up, pushing out from deep within his shared mind. It rendered him deaf and half-blind, right up to the very last moment.

Thud.

Daniel Lawton struck the ground with a deafening smack. Bones shattered, hurting more than he could have imagined. The side of his face caught on sharp debris and split wide open, blood gushing out, mixing into the gravel.

He came to rest, contorted and crushed. The approaching train slammed on the brakes, squealing like the man inside his head, making him yearn for release.

Unable to move, he watched it stop. Daniel saw the bloodied hem of a green garment – uncovered legs, pale skin of the dead. *A ghost, watching him slip away for the second time.*

Overwhelmed, his senses shut down. The world around him grew numb, cold, a sensation he had longed for ever since the last time.

He felt released. In his head, Andrew was still screaming, the bittersweet cry of a man served a twisted injustice. *An eye for an eye,* just as Daniel had promised all along.

The sound never made it through his broken jaw, all that energy bouncing around inside him. Instead, the world went black, and Daniel curled his lip, almost to a smile.

White teeth were stained crimson by the pool of blood. He felt peace at last, and as his eyes drifted to the distance, he embraced the growing silence.

Death.

The one thing he truly wanted.

31|FFINITY

"Keep pushing, baby. You're almost there."

Hope was gripping her husband's hand, trying to convey how much pain she was in. *See how you like it*, she was thinking, but couldn't spare a breath to talk through gritted teeth.

She tried to withdraw into her own world, to detach. It made more sense to coach herself, because no one else understood how it felt. She could fill in the gaps.

Get it over with. Squeeze that fucker out of your body.

The midwife knelt at the foot of the bed and kept an eye on her progress, a stranger so close to her most private area. The only real witness to the birth of her son.

Figuring out why Hope had chosen to have the child at home, without medication, seemed like solving a riddle. Right there, spread across her marital bed in an unflattering green gown, she was starting to question her sanity.

The baby had overstayed its welcome inside her. Hope had endured five hours of gruelling labour and just wanted it to be over. The waiting was like torture, but she tried to keep control.

Whether her body liked it or not, that child was coming out in the next five minutes.

Her husband didn't know what to do with himself, tethered to her with his mangled hand. He tried to take her grip in good spirits, but a sweat on his forehead betrayed just how much pressure he was under.

"You're going to have to try harder," he said. "Take a deep breath and go again."

He had been saying such rubbish for hours. All Hope wanted was to take the pain away – with bourbon, or perhaps a blow to the head. She could remember their conversations about it, decisions made in more sober times. Hindsight just made her feel even worse.

No, she thought. *The only way this is going to end is when I make it happen.*

She heaved, a push that used every muscle in her body. She could feel the child shift just that little bit and tried to keep the pressure on. Her lungs were on fire. The rush of blood to her head made her feel faint, but she kept going.

Get out of me, she thought. *For the love of God, get the hell out of me.*

Just then, there was a shift. Something gave way, and the child jolted a fraction further out. But there was another sensation, something wrong. She could feel muscle tear. She could almost hear it, like undoing the zipper on one of her dresses.

Suddenly, her world became that much worse. The midwife – who until that time had uttered nothing but words of encouragement – changed her expression. The husband saw it too, a once comfortable and confident woman almost losing her balance.

Her words were spoken quickly. "Mr. Lawton, I think you should call an ambulance." He froze as the colour drained from his face. "John," she said. *"Now!"*

Hope felt warmth around her thighs, wetness on the sheets beneath her. The midwife straightened up and took a towel, padding it over the duvet.

"Come on Hope, this baby has to arrive now, whether we like it or not." She looked her patient in the eye and saw panic. "Ready? Go."

Hope pushed with every ounce of strength she had left. The pain was almost beyond belief, stinging from deep beneath her stomach. She opened her mouth wide, letting out a tortuous cry.

John ran to the bedroom doorway, standing with the phone to his ear. He drew sharp, worried breaths as he looked at his wife – *at the bed* – and steadied himself on the doorframe.

Blood. Lots of it.

The midwife tried to calm them both down. "It looks worse than it really is, but listen to me – we need to get this baby out. I need another push." Hope nodded, wide eyed and terrified. "Alright then, darling. On three..."

The agony was more than she could handle – a searing, stabbing ache. She faltered on the first heave, but quickly recovered for the sake of her child.

Any pain is worth it to see him safe.

The midwife reached down and put her fingers inside, trying to draw the baby out. Hope thought she could feel a head pass through, or perhaps it was the foot. She just couldn't tell.

All at once, numbness spread, starting to creep its way up her body. Hope almost welcomed it, lacking the strength to fight back. She looked down and saw the bottom of the bed was soaked in her own blood.

John dropped the phone on the floor and rushed over, but by then, she didn't care to look at him. She knew what was happening.

She was going to die.

It almost came as a relief, a compelling release, but she couldn't allow it to happen until she had seen her child.

The midwife still had a hand inside her, trying to force the infant through the last leg of the journey. Hope could feel it coming out. If nothing else happened in her life, she needed to know it was alright.

"Oh God," she said. "Oh God."

Just ten more seconds, enough for a lasting glimpse of her boy. That was all she asked for, but death wouldn't wait. It called to her.

No more pain, it promised. *Never again.*

She tried to resist, to stave off the inevitable. *Don't listen to it, Hope. You can bear any pain for the sake of your child.*

She thought she could stand an eternity of despair if she could just see his face, hear his cry. Her whole life had been building up to that moment, and it was too close to pass up now. With the fading embers of life, she battled death itself.

Draw strength from the pain. Don't ever let it fade. Don't die without seeing your baby.

***

Isabel paced up and down the hospital corridor, trying to walk off her anger. She was thankful that Daniel had stormed out of the room and left her alone. Two more minutes and she would have said something she didn't mean.

Her feet squeaked against the plastic floor. The Americano in her hands was too cold to drink, but she hadn't noticed, lost in thought.

Until she heard a scream from outside.

Isabel rushed to the window and looked down at the road below. Traffic stood still in both directions, and a crowd of onlookers stared at three men in luminous yellow jackets – paramedics running down the pavement towards her.

They escorted a stretcher trolley, and the drink slipped from her hands as she realised who was lying on it.

Andrew Goodwin.

She turned and bolted to the stairwell, feet flurrying down the steps, moving so fast that gravity couldn't keep up. As the medics came indoors, Isabel burst into the lobby.

"Please," she cried. "His name's Daniel. Is he okay?"

The body was strapped down – twisted, malformed, *like he had fallen from a great height.*

The doctors pushed straight past her and wheeled the trolley into an emergency theatre. She caught a glimpse of his bloodied face. *Split open down the side, torn to the bone.*

"What happened?" she called after them.

Nobody answered, and a voice from outside interjected. "He fell."

Isabel turned to see a middle-aged man standing by the entrance, both hands full of shopping bags. He stepped into the building and watched the commotion with gruesome interest.

"Did you see it?" Isabel said. People barked orders at one another from behind the theatre doors.

The man nodded. "He was shouting to himself, your friend. Then he took a dive off a bridge. It must have been twenty feet. I've never seen anyone survive a fall like that."

"Was he pushed?" she asked.

"Not a chance."

Isabel wrenched open the theatre doors and shouldered her way inside. "Let me see him," she said, pushing past the medics. "He's with me."

A nurse immediately turned and tried to usher her back out of the door. "You have to leave," she said.

"Isabel?" At the sound of her voice, Daniel suddenly sprang to life, *as though risen from the dead.*

"I'm here," she said. "What happened to you?"

He writhed in agony, wide open eyes trying to find something to lock onto. "My father," he spat, struggling to speak through his broken jaw. "Who's going to look after my father?"

The heart monitor on the wall suddenly squealed and he collapsed, unconscious, flat on his back. One of the doctors rose onto the stretcher and started to press down on his sternum.

The nurse put an arm across Isabel's chest and forced her through the door. "You can't be in here," she said.

Isabel covered her mouth as she was taken out of the room.

What in God's name was happening?

***

"Happy Birthday, son. Look who's come to see you."

Little Daniel sat in a baby rocker chair, bouncing up and down with a contented grin. Elastic cord held him in one corner of the room, restricting his freedom.

Enabling his father to turn his back.

John Lawton tidied frantically, trying to make the house presentable. It wasn't often they had visitors, and he hadn't learned to cope with both raising a child and keeping his life in order.

John had aged more in a year than time could be blamed for. The stress of being a single parent kept him from handling the grief for Hope's death, and it had taken a steep toll.

Some days, he could barely even look at the child for resentment, but he managed to push it deep inside and carry on. *After all, the boy was all that remained of his wife.*

There was a knock at the door – the third in as many minutes. John bundled laundry into the corner. Anyone would have noticed the dirty carpets – *the stale smell* – but at least the surfaces were clear.

He left Daniel and rushed into the hallway. The child was used to his own company, spending more time in the rocker chair than in his father's arms, more time in silence than interacting.

Having visitors was especially unusual. When John returned, he was with an elderly couple. "Do you remember these people?" he said. "These are your grandparents."

Hope's mother approached the child tentatively, wrinkled hands clasped together. She and her husband had been shut out of Daniel's life while John couldn't cope, and her excitement showed just how little they saw of their grandson.

"Hello, Daniel," she said. "Look at how you're growing."

The woman looked very much like an older version of her daughter – the same kind eyes, the same frailty. Daniel was unsure at first, but soon warmed to her attention.

"I'm glad you keep sending him clothes," said John. "It seems like every time I buy new ones, he outgrows them."

She leaned down and put her face close to the boy's. "Well, we've brought all sorts of nice things this time," she said, "and we have a big day planned. We're all going out for a drive."

Hope's father knelt down and patted the boy's hair, and John found himself backing through the doorway. He always felt the need to distance himself from tenderness, to somehow preserve the hole in his life. *To suffer alone.*

Daniel's grandmother started to undo the child's straps. "Would you like to come up for a cuddle?" she cooed. "You must be due a feed about now."

"I've got a better idea," said John. "I've got his carrier upstairs. Shall we just put him in and get going?"

Her smile waned, but the woman had patience. "Okay, John. You know what's best."

"I could use your help with it," he said. "Follow me. He'll be fine on his own for a second."

The couple exchanged glances of concern, but they allowed John Lawton to lead them out of the room.

Neither wanted to spoil their welcome, to risk never being invited back.

Daniel was left to fend for himself in the corner of the room. No one else saw the door drift shut, creaking closed of its own accord. No one but Daniel saw who stood behind it.

His mother.

She stood in the green gown she had worn on the day she died, the hem still crusted with blood. She was shivering – not cold, but fighting constantly against the festering agony in her stomach.

Something had spared her from oblivion, sheer willpower to remain. *The irrepressible strength of a mother's love.* Daniel was too young to realise that she only appeared when no one else was around, when his father was asleep or in the bathroom.

And whenever she was there, it was cold.

Tethered to the corner of the room, the baby felt trapped. Hope smiled, trying to comfort the boy, but the pain on her face was too severe to mask. Every moment was excruciating, and the baby could tell.

His expression only worsened her suffering.

"It's okay, Daniel," she said, pushing back tears. Her voice was pale, distant, as though she were fifty feet away. "There's no need to be scared of me."

The child looked at her with wide, cautious eyes. She took a step towards him, but it was too close. Daniel's face screwed up, making ready to scream, and Hope did the only thing she could think of to calm him down.

She backed away.

Once she was in the doorway, the child settled. She sighed with sadness, knowing he was just too young to understand. Her one wish was to never see him suffer, but her very presence made him uncomfortable.

There was no other option. Hope would diligently keep watch over him, keeping him free from harm, but at least until Daniel was older, she couldn't get close.

She would have to give him distance.

***

Once again, Isabel paced up and down the hospital corridor. She felt useless, utterly helpless. The only two men she had ever loved were fighting for their lives and there was nothing she could do about it, just scuff her shoes on the floor and swallow the responsibility she felt for everything.

The hopelessness.

A light rain began to streak down the window pane, and old feelings came flooding back – the dull ache in her gut when she had first heard Daniel was dead, and the heartache on the day they put him to rest.

The more she thought about it, the worse she felt, but it reminded her of a person who could at least be sympathetic, someone who knew her well. *And Daniel, and Ryan...*

He was the only other person who could appreciate her distress. Isabel looked through the window at a bleak horizon as she dialled her mobile phone, a number she would forever associate with death and woe.

"Hello?" came the shaky voice on the other end.

John Lawton, Daniel's father.

"It's Isabel," she said. He knew right away that something was wrong.

"Are you alright?" he said.

Rain pattered against the glass, inches from her face. "There's something I think I need to tell you," she said.

His breath crackled down the line. "About Ryan? That was why you took my car, wasn't it?"

"Yes, but that's not it." She cradled the handset against the side of her face, glancing down the corridor as she lowered her voice. "Ryan's in hospital, and so is Andrew."

"My God," said John. "What happened to them?"

"It was..." She stumbled over her words, having to force them out. "It was Daniel, John. He hurt them both."

The breathing stopped, leaving silence on the end of the line. Isabel stared at the rain, wishing she could be anywhere else.

"Andrew tried to tell me that once before," said John.

"You should have listened to him," said Isabel. "Daniel's still alive."

Her words cut deep. John Lawton took a sharp lungful of air and let it out slowly, before his laboured reply took her totally off guard.

"If anyone else had told me that, I wouldn't have believed them," he said. "But I know you're not a liar, Isabel, and really... I'm not surprised to hear you say it."

She lost control of her voice. "What does that mean?" she said. "Your son is still alive. *How can that possibly not come as a shock?*"

"Perhaps you should come over when you can," he said. "We'll talk it over."

She hung up the phone and marched down the corridor. She couldn't think of a better time than right that second.

32|EGACY

On his eighteenth birthday, Daniel got exactly what he wanted – to lie in bed until three in the afternoon. Even on a normal day, he rarely left the house, content with his own company.

Afraid to love since Maggie's accident.

His father was complicit in his isolation, almost like a stranger in the same household. Daniel came downstairs to find him at the kitchen table, taking his computer apart with a screwdriver.

Afternoon light poured into the tiny room, and through French doors, he had an unspoilt view of rolling hills and forests.

"You'll do yourself no favours if all you ever do is sleep." John Lawton was in his fifties, with a receding hairline and grey eyebrows. Years of self-neglect were catching up to him.

"Good morning, Dad."

Daniel took a seat, avoiding eye contact. Both men had grown comfortable with their distance, rarely paying more than a polite degree of attention to one another.

"Dare I ask what you're planning for today?" said John.

"I kind of assumed we'd spend it together," said Daniel. "I mean, we should, right? I'm old enough for us to go drinking now..."

The screwdriver slipped out of John's hand and it made him swear. "Just because you can drink doesn't mean you have to," he said. "Besides, I can't put this thing away now it's in bits. We'll have to see how it goes."

Silence fell quickly, one that had reigned for years in that house. Beneath the apparent order and cleanliness, there was no sense of a home – pictures on the walls, but not of any people they knew.

"Should I leave you to it, then?" said Daniel. His father responded by sliding his hand under the table and producing a tiny envelope, which he put in front of the young man.

A birthday card, conservative and factual.

'Now you're Eighteen.'

As Daniel opened it, a tiny picture fell onto the table, no larger than a passport photograph. It landed face down, but he knew what it would be straight away – something he had been asking about for years.

"You found one," said Daniel. He looked to his father, who nodded.

"Let me know if you want to talk about it later. I may need that drink after all."

It had been a big thing for John Lawton to part with that picture, more than he would ever admit. Every other one like it had been destroyed years ago, and not just to help him cope with his grief.

Daniel took a deep breath before peeling over the edge. He could make out dark hair, a pale face...

His mother.

The resemblance made her instantly familiar, with full lips and round, gentle eyes. Daniel had never been shown what she looked like before, but now he realised he had seen her in person. *Hundreds of times, always in the distance.*

He couldn't believe it. Daniel ran from the table, bursting through the French doors into the garden. He vaulted the stone wall at the bottom and pelted down the hillside, away from the house, refusing to stop until he was alone in the fields.

With no one else around, he searched for her, shielding his eyes from the beaming sunlight.

"Are you there?" he called to the woman who had haunted him since birth – not a figment of his imagination, but someone real. There was nowhere for her to hide, no sound to drown her out.

"Come out and show yourself," he yelled.

Daniel didn't see so much of her these days, not like he used to. She was always too distant, too fleeting. That figure he had taken as a mirage, that lost and tortured soul.

It was more than he could stomach.

She couldn't possibly be his own flesh and blood.

***

Torrential rain hammered against the pavement, a violent percussion to approaching thunder. It flooded drains and spilled over guttering, bringing a decisive end to weeks of dry weather.

Even in the short dash from her car to John Lawton's house, Isabel was drenched from head to foot. She banged her fists on the front door, shoulders hunched, waiting impatiently to hear a key turn in the latch.

As soon as she could, she barged her way inside, almost pushing the old man over. John looked dishevelled, still in the same clothes she had seen on their last encounter, almost three days ago.

The night Andrew had broken in to steal his car.

Before he could speak a word, Isabel marched to the living room, water dribbling from her flattened hair. He found her pacing up and down by the window.

"Andrew took hours to convince me that Daniel was still alive," she said, leaving a trail of damp on the carpet. "I still can hardly believe it, but you didn't even bat an eyelid when I told you. Why not?"

John shuffled to his seat by the window, shaken by her tone. "There's no need to be so aggressive," he said. "There's a simple reason why I didn't react – it wasn't the first time I've heard of something like this. *It's happened before.*"

"To whom?" she said. "Who else is back?"

"It wasn't someone you know," said John, "and to this day, I can't tell you what happened. That's the honest truth. If I only understood, then I could try to help my boy."

"Help him?" She never once took her eyes off the old man, not even to blink. "Just so you know, Ryan is in hospital fighting for his life, *and that's because Daniel put him there.*"

"It won't be his fault," said John. "It never is. People around him always come to harm, but never by his hand. I've seen it with my own eyes."

"What makes you sure he's so innocent?"

"Because it's true," he said. "Daniel has a protector, ever since he was a child. He used to stare at empty corners of the room, like it was more engrossing than the television. It took me years to figure out what he was looking at."

Isabel stumbled in her pacing. "The woman in green."

"You know about her?"

She shook her head. "I didn't even know she existed until a few days ago."

"Daniel first described her to me when he was too young to realise what it meant," said John. "He called her '*The Lady in The Corner.*' I knew who it had to be almost immediately, just from the colour."

"Oh, God." The hairs on the back of her neck stood up. "She's your wife, isn't she?"

He cleared his throat and nodded. "I'm afraid I don't remember her very well these days, but I remember how much she wanted that baby. There was nothing she wouldn't have done for him, and so there she was, keeping watch."

"All the time?" said Isabel.

"A disturbing thought, isn't it?" he said. "The only woman I ever loved, right there in my house, and I couldn't even see her. Daniel used to talk about her constantly, but as he grew older, that stopped. I thought she must have gone, but I suppose he just accepted her being there."

A shiver ran down Isabel's spine. "Is that why you moved house?"

"No," said John. "We stayed. I never could have denied her contact with her child. Daniel was the one that moved away, when he was older. I supposed she went with him, so after a while, I followed."

"You're wrong about her," said Isabel. "Your wife has tried to kill him. I was there when it happened."

John Lawton shook his head. "She's spent a lifetime keeping him safe, so I doubt that. But she's more than capable of harming others – Ryan or Andrew, if they posed a threat."

"They couldn't help being in his way," said Isabel.

"And neither could my son," he said.

She shifted her balance, growing restless again. "He still has to take responsibly for his actions. Daniel's changed, John. He isn't the same person we both knew."

"If he's hurt, then he needs us."

"The only thing he needs is for you to let him go."

John closed his eyes. "You can't ask me to do that."

She could tell how dearly he wanted to rationalise his family's fate. *How he clung to the past.* But just beneath the surface, he was even more lost than Daniel and his mother.

The one they had left behind.

Seeing his loneliness made Isabel keen to return to the ones she cared about – to stay active, lest she descend into a similar state. She straightened herself up and made ready to leave.

In doing so, John Lawton revealed his true colours.

"Don't go," He gripped the arms of his chair and pulled himself to his feet, pleading with his eyes. "Did you see him?" he said. "How did he look?"

Isabel almost hated him for asking. "We spoke."

"And?"

"Your wife never should have tried to save him."

She took two steps towards the door and John followed. "What are you going to do now?" he said. "She's just looking after her child."

"But at what cost?"

Visibly trembling, he had to lean against the furniture for support. "That's my family out there. I won't let you harm them."

Isabel turned to face him – *a shadow of the man he used to be.* John Lawton's eyes were drained from suffering.

"They died long ago," she said. "I'm sorry if you can't accept that."

"Without them, I've got nothing." He grew increasingly anxious. "Please don't leave me."

Rainwater trickled down Isabel's cheek, an echo of a tear she wasn't prepared to cry.

"Goodbye, John," she said. "For what it's worth, I don't blame you for your part in this. In another life, I may even have done the same."

***

By the time Isabel made it back to the hospital, a lot had changed. She approached the double doors through deep puddles, hesitant, afraid to step inside.

Afraid everyone she cared about was dead.

In the end, chance was on her side. Before she got to the door, it was opened by the nurse who had pulled her out of the emergency theatre that morning.

"Are you alright?" The woman reacted at once, seeing the anxiety on Isabel's face.

Isabel felt like crying. "I'm scared."

"Here, let me help you."

She was taken upstairs to the waiting room, returning to the bank of plastic chairs by the coffee machine. Isabel's eyes were drawn straight to Ryan's ward, but the blinds were closed.

"Sit down for a second," said the nurse. "I'll get one of the doctors."

Isabel did as she was told, feeling imprisoned by that room. There was something about the smell of the hospital that would haunt her for the rest of her life, the clinical stench of disinfectant.

John Lawton had told her so much that life could never be the same again. Daniel's mother – *a ghost* – went everywhere with her son, keeping a watchful vigil, even now.

In the hotel room on Daniel's birthday, and in the little house when Isabel had broken his heart.

Would she hate Isabel for that?

The waiting room was suddenly a cold and distressing place. Isabel understood how it must have felt for Daniel when he was too young to understand, staring at every corner, scared of who could be looking back.

A door slammed. Before she knew it, Isabel was on her feet, poised to run from forces she couldn't possibly fight.

Something appeared – a figure, through one of the doorways. Her heart skipped three beats, then she saw it was a doctor, clean shaven, handsome, and fatherly.

"Are you with Andrew Goodwin?" he asked.

She nodded, awash with a different kind of tension. "I should probably sit down," she said.

"Yes, perhaps you should." Isabel put herself on a plastic chair, and he sat next to her. "Andrew's out of surgery," he said, "but we're keeping him unconscious for the time being. He's broken a lot of bones, and although he doesn't look it outwardly, he's lucky to be alive."

"Is he going to be alright?" asked Isabel.

"Nothing vital seems to be damaged," said the doctor. "We've managed to stop the bleeding, and at this stage, it all looks encouraging."

Despite herself, Isabel gasped with relief. "Thank God," she said. "That's incredible. Do you have any idea why he fell?"

"Actually, we might." Whereas his tone was warm, the doctor's face was deathly serious. "Has Andrew been acting strange lately, perhaps confused, or not quite himself?"

"Yes," said Isabel. "Definitely all of those."

"While we were scanning his head for signs of trauma, we found evidence of a swelling on the front of his brain."

Her face dropped. "Like a tumour?"

"Yes," he said, "and I'm afraid quite a large one. A heavy jolt like that could have been the end of him."

"Can you help him?"

"We're going to keep a close eye on it, but if I'm honest" – she shifted weight awkwardly as he paused – "we might not need to."

Isabel ran short of breath. "What do you mean? Is Andrew dying?"

The doctor shook his head. "I'm not sure how to explain it, but the tumour might be in remission by itself. It was nearly five centimetres when we found it, but now it's down to three. If I hadn't seen the images with my own eyes, I never would have believed it."

"Does that mean he's going to be alright?" she asked.

"The impact must have done something for him, cleared the blockage. We're all a touch confounded, but it would appear so, yes."

She leapt up and hugged him, unable to help herself. "Thank you," she said. "Thank you so much."

Tears started to flow down her cheeks. Isabel stole a moment, closing her eyes, and when they opened again, she was staring at the ward.

The doctor caught her doing it. "You were already in the hospital when Andrew was admitted, weren't you?"

"That's my fiancé in there," she said. "He's been there for days."

"Wait here for a moment." The doctor stood. "I'll see what I can find out for you."

For an agonising minute, he left her alone. Isabel picked at her nails, buckling under the weight she could feel on her shoulders. It was the worst day of her life, and she felt sick to her stomach as he reappeared.

"Is Ryan alright?" she asked.

"This one, you should see for yourself."

Her legs could barely take her weight, but she managed to stand. Numbly, stiffly, she walked down a corridor that felt infinitely long.

It was dim inside the ward, thin blinds drawn across every window. She could feel her arms trembling as she saw Ryan in bed. The machine beside him pipped softly, but he wasn't moving.

Dear God, she thought. *He still isn't moving.*

The doctor stayed in the doorway as she crept across the room, nothing to steady her balance against. It was like crossing a desert, for how hard it felt.

Two days, and he still wasn't moving.

Isabel stared blankly at the wall, afraid to glance at the bedside. She felt the metal railing press into her stomach and took a firm grip, locking her fingers around it, flexing and renewing her hold.

As she looked down.

Ryan lay across the bed, unchanged since she had seen him last. His pale face was covered in bruises and his chest rose with shallow breaths. Her heart froze up.

His eyes were open.

The two lovers looked at one another for the first time in days and she saw recognition, a spark of intelligence.

Isabel held his hand. It wasn't warm, but at least it wasn't cold. The colour was slowly returning, a pulse thumping through his wrist. The expression on his face showed faint wrinkles around his mouth.

A smile.

And for both of them, for sorrow and for happiness, she cried.

EPILOGUE

Andrew Goodwin slept for nineteen hours without a break. There were no strange nightmares, no floating on an endless sea of black.

No memories that just weren't his.

When he finally came around, it was to hauntingly familiar sounds – *scratching, clattering* – but as he peeled open his eyes, he realised it was the bustle of a hospital ward. He saw movement with blurred vision, people crowding around beds.

And he loved it.

The room was a flood of smiling faces – parents visiting children, wives greeting husbands. He lay still and listened to the drone, grateful he was still alive to hear it, and that for once, the voices weren't in his head.

His inner voice was completely silent. After two years of sharing his life with Daniel, he could feel the change right away. *The clarity of a single mindset.*

Andrew felt safe to be surrounded by so many people, until he realised one of them was watching him.

A lone body stood at the end of the bed, golden hair and full, red lips. A familiar sight.

Cheryl.

"You look better than I expected," she said, voice low and soothing. Ever since their first meeting, Andrew had felt a compulsion towards her, an obsession he couldn't explain.

He smiled and felt tightness down the side of his face. It gave him a brief recollection of railway tracks, the sensation of falling.

"It's good to see you." His voice was distorted by his broken jaw, almost like it wasn't his.

"I talked to the doctor," she said. "He's optimistic you'll be fine. Why did you do this to yourself?"

Andrew had been there before – strung up in a hospital bed with a loved one asking questions. He decided not to make the same mistakes. "I'll tell you everything," he said. "You won't believe me, but I'll tell you, all the same."

Without contact lenses, he couldn't see further than his feet. One arm was in a cast and his chest felt tight, numbed by drugs and locked in position.

"I've been so worried about you lately," said Cheryl. It was written in her gaze. There was a time that such a look would make his toes curl – *so warm and familiar, as though he'd known her for his entire life*.

Looking at her now, however, it felt different, as though the connection had been severed. Maybe it was the way he associated her with the woman in green, the woman who had tried to murder him twice.

Maybe it was linked to the emptiness in his head.

"How long have you been here?" he asked.

"I don't know," said Cheryl. "Half an hour, maybe. Long enough to get lost in the corridors."

"Didn't Isabel show you around?"

Her face sank, confusion thinly masked. "Who's Isabel?"

Andrew tried to sit up, secured by binds across his chest. "If you don't know who Isabel is, then how did you know I was in hospital?"

"I had a message on my phone this morning," she said. "I assumed it was from a doctor, but now I come to think about it, they never said who they were."

Andrew felt a dark cloud descend over him, as though the walls were closing in. Not even Isabel would have known to call her, and no one else knew that he was there.

"Did they give you any clue?" he said. "Was it a man or a woman? This is important."

"Don't get worked up," said Cheryl. "It could have been anybody."

He could feel his heart accelerate as his eyes darted around the room, moving from one blurry face to the next, trying to work out if anyone was looking back.

Cheryl's number was stored in his broken phone, smashed to pieces days ago. For someone to contact her would have required more knowledge of his life than he ever dared to share.

No one would have known to do it.

No one.

The bed was suddenly a confining, debilitating place. Andrew wanted to get up, to run and hide from the strangers in the ward, from everyone he didn't trust. In spite of the medication, a familiar feeling rose up inside him, and nothing could convince him it was just imagination.

The slightest pain behind his temples.

END

Also available by the author...

SUBCULTURE

They have an entire city on its knees.

On a hot summer's night, terrorists take over the small English city of Chester. After months of planning, and with carefully chosen targets, they kill hundreds in a string of coordinated attacks, sending the rest into blind panic. Before anyone knows what hit them, the city's Roman walls are cut off from the rest of the world, its population trapped at the mercy of hooded killers.

While everyone else flees from bomb blasts and gunfire, a lone police officer runs towards them. George Ellison finds himself drawn into the terrorist's scheme, desperate to find out who they are, and why they want to wage war on innocent people.

Amongst a hundred thousand men and women under siege, only he and the help he enlists can possibly stand against them.

Subculture is a fast-paced, inventive, visceral thriller where only the strongest have a chance of survival.

Available now on Amazon, in eBook and in print

Find out more at:
http://www.chrishollis-author.com

Printed in Great Britain
by Amazon.co.uk, Ltd.,
Marston Gate.